the accidental diva

tia williams

NEW AMERICAN LIBRARY

New American Library
Published by New American Library, a division of
Penguin Group (USA) Inc., 375 Hudson Street,
New York, New York 10014, USA
Penguin Group (Canada), 10 Alcorn Avenue, Toronto,
Ontario M4V 3B2, Canada (a division of Pearson Penguin Canada Inc.)
Penguin Books Ltd., 80 Strand, London WC2R 0RL, England
Penguin Ireland, 25 St. Stephen's Green, Dublin 2,
Ireland (a division of Penguin Books Ltd.)
Penguin Group (Australia), 250 Camberwell Road, Camberwell, Victoria 3124,
Australia (a division of Pearson Australia Group Pty. Ltd.)
Penguin Books India Pvt. Ltd., 11 Community Centre, Panchsheel Park,
New Delhi - 110 017, India
Penguin Group (NZ), cnr Airborne and Rosedale Roads, Albany,
Auckland 1310, New Zealand (a division of Pearson New Zealand Ltd.)
Penguin Books (South Africa) (Pty.) Ltd., 24 Sturdee Avenue,
Rosebank, Johannesburg 2196, South Africa

Penguin Books Ltd., Registered Offices: 80 Strand, London WC2R 0RL, England

Published by New American Library, a division of Penguin Group (USA) Inc.
Previously published in a G. P. Putnam's Sons edition.

First New American Library Printing, May 2005
10 9 8 7 6 5 4 3 2 1

NEW AMERICAN LIBRARY and logo are trademarks of Penguin Group (USA) Inc.

New American Library Trade Paperback ISBN: 0-451-21507-9

The Library of Congress has cataloged the hardcover edition of this title as follows:

Williams, Tia.
    The accidental diva / Tia Williams.
        p. cm.
    1. African American women—Fiction.   2. Periodicals—Publishing—Fiction.
3. Performance Artists—Fiction.   4. New York (N.Y.)—Fiction.   5. Women
editors—Fiction.   I. Title.
PS3623.I566A64   2004   2003068913
813'.6—dc22

Printed in the United States of America

For Adam, la luz de mi vida

1.

so media-genic

here's *nothing* new to say about mascara," announced Billie Burke to the adjoining cubicles that made up the beauty department of *Du Jour* magazine. She needed a headline for her mascara caption and was utterly tapped out.

"Read it out loud," suggested Sandy Fuller, *Du Jour*'s associate beauty writer. She was one of those pink-skinned strawberry blondes who always looked on the verge of tears.

" 'The newest must-have mascaras plumpen, elongate, and sexify lackluster lashes. The result? Sinfully sultry bedroom eyes fit to make Ava Gardner wail with envy.' "

"Cute!" said Mary DeCosta, the plucky beauty assistant.

"But I'm not sure 'plumpen' is a word," Billie said, unconvinced.

"Plump up?" offered Sandy.

"Hmmm. That's so good," Billie said, quickly typing in the change. She could barely suppress a grin. She knew there was more to life than lashes, but honestly, she *lived* for this stuff. Billie had almost forgotten how not to speak in hyperbolic, insanely descriptive beauty editor rhetoric. When her friends asked her for makeup and hair advice for parties or first dates, she'd wax on about "burnished blush, copper-kissed lids, dewy, sunlit skin — think Iman on safari," or "disheveled, devil-may-care hair, and lips drenched in diva-red, Heart of Glass gloss . . . you know, a red so deeply divine you'll want to *bathe* in it." Billie was as moved by James Baldwin, nineteenth-century Gothic lit, and "Ode on a Grecian Urn" as much as the next English major, but something in her just delighted in the whole beauty thing. It was so entertaining and campy and intrinsically girly. Like Regis Philbin.

"Okay, now I need a headline," continued Billie, on the cusp of panic. "The Azucena lunch starts in two seconds, and it's way downtown. I can't think, I can't think!" Azucena del Sol, like all major beauty companies, launched new products with lavish events that it was Billie's job to attend.

The events were always themed. Recently, for example, a line of wine-colored lipsticks had been launched with a wine-tasting. The same week, a more ill-received event had been a breakfast introducing a line of punky-bright hair dyes. It involved fluorescent dry ice and Day-Glo ribbon dancers who, at the climax of their performance, pelted the bleary-eyed editors with multicolored Styrofoam popcorn. It was 8:30 in the morning.

"How about 'Lash-Out'?" asked Mary. "No, that's the name of a L'Oréal mascara, shit. Hmm, 'Bat Your Lashes' . . . 'Batter Up'?" Mary, who was from Staten Island, said *batcha lashes* and *batta up*.

" 'Batter Up' is a little abstract, but not uncute," said Billie.

" 'Lashes to Lashes'?" suggested Sandy.

"Morbid." Billie stood up and yelled over the partition in the direction of the clothes-strewn fashion cubicles. "Somebody help me! I need a headline for a mascara caption, quick."

"Ummm . . . 'Lash Gordon'?" a lanky fashion editor offered.

"How about 'Lash in the Pan'?" Mary suggested, giggling.

"Why don't you kiss my lash?" Billie said saucily. "Oh, wait, no, I got it, I got it. 'Lash of the Titans.' 'Lash of the Titans'? Is that stupid or cute?"

"That's so cute," said Mary.

"Yeah, and it just *screams* major lashes," said Sandy.

Billie crowned her caption "Lash of the Titans," printed it out and dropped it in the in box of the oft-absent executive fashion and beauty director. Paige "Beige" Merchant was heavily tanned and heavily peroxided in a way that made her skin and hair color look indistinguishable, hence the nickname. Despite her eerie coloring, Paige was a ravishing beauty whose face and supermodel figure were frequently splashed all over society pages. She was old money, as a result of the chain of office supply stores her great-grandfather had started 150 years ago.

After fifteen years in the industry, Paige was over the whole "working" thing, so she was always on vacation—at the moment, in Capri. She trusted Billie, the senior beauty editor and her number two, to unofficially run the department; they'd worked together for five years, since Billie was a twenty-one-year-old assistant. Billie pretended to resent picking up the slack for her lady-of-leisure boss but secretly relished it.

"Okay, I'm gone. See you guys later," Billie said, grabbing her bag and heading for the elevator bank.

"Take the train, you'll never get a cab," Sandy called after her.

"The Azucena people sent a car to pick me up, thank God. Bye!" Billie said over her shoulder before stopping abruptly and running back to her cubicle to retrieve her forgotten cell phone. She managed to make the elevator just as the doors closed. It wasn't until she reached the forty-fourth floor that she realized she was heading up rather than down. "Jesus Christ," she muttered, rubbing her temples.

She had a migraine that could've killed a horse.

. . .

The second Billie located the Lincoln Town Car with a card reading "Burke" in the window, her cell phone started to ring. It was Renee.

"*Girl.*"

"Hey," said Billie. "Lemme call you right back, I'm on my way to this thing—"

"No. I'm so excited. You have to listen to me."

"Wha-at?" Billie said, climbing into the car while balancing the phone between her ear and shoulder. "This better be so important."

"It is, it is! I found my next writer, and he's so perfect I could scream!"

And her history was full of hunches that had turned into gold, which was why, at such a tender age, she was a full-blown book editor at Crawford & Collier Books. Starting as an editorial assistant, a college grad usually filed, typed, and read appallingly bad manuscripts from authors who weren't even good enough to get agents. If an assistant actually found something publishable, she turned it over to her senior editor boss, who then immediately took credit. Even once you got an entertainment budget with which to wine and dine agents—who had the good manuscripts—you'd discover that they'd rather sip an arsenic spritzer than submit something readable to a junior editor. Success in book publishing was all about instinct, luck, and a boss who likes you. Renee Byrd had all three.

At twenty-four, she'd had her first success with *The Women*, a book of new essays on female identity in different decades by great women writers. It included chapters like "Is Love Ever Really Free?" and "Carol Brady Has Left the Building." Sue Snyderman had fairly drooled at the idea. She was one of those civil rights–era Jewish women who considered black women special sisters in arms, and found tough-talking, brilliant Renee delicious. She knew everyone, and was able to convince Toni Morrison and Gloria Steinem to add essays to the project, then handed it back to Renee and allowed her to edit it, herself.

Renee became the darling of C&C Books. She followed up this success by discovering the "Black Jackie Colllins"—best-selling Amy Parsons—and publishing *Sun, Moon, Water, You*, a well-reviewed collection of short stories by a Rastafarian named Columbus that were serialized in *The New Yorker*. Just Columbus (his first name was Just, pronounced *Yoos*).

"Anyway," continued Renee, "have you read *New York* magazine and the *Village Voice* yet?"

"Please, I'm still carrying around last week's that I never got to."

"Well, you saw *The Times*'s Sunday Styles section last weekend, right?"

Billie was embarrassed. "Fashion Week started last weekend! On Sunday, I was too busy memorizing the smoky eye at Marc Jacobs to be literate."

Renee huffed impatiently. "Anyway, there's this guy, Jay Lane. He has a one-man show called *Nutz & Boltz*, where he acts out these brilliant monologues based on five characters."

"Uh-huh," Billie said encouragingly.

". . . and they're being compared to Whoopi Goldberg's early character sketches, and he's getting major, major buzz. But in the *Voice*, he says what he loves most is *writing* the parts, not the performing! He's *fascinating*. We're talking about a twenty-seven-year-old orphan from the projects in Brooklyn, a former hustler—"

"Hustling what?"

"He doesn't say. Crack? I mean, what else, really? Dave Mathews tickets?"

"True," Billie said, with a chuckle.

"Anyway, he has all this shit against him, and he ends up at *Columbia's* creative writing program? And now he's getting fabulous reviews. And he's so hot. He's got this, like, dangerous smile and a scar and dimples and perfect cornrows. Oh Billie! He's so mediagenic!" She paused for effect. "I must own him."

"Then own him you will, goddammit." Billie loved it when Renee got in "taking over the world" mode.

"I'm seeing the book as a series of stream-of-consciousness vignettes based on his show, and unseen material." Billie realized Renee was not really talking to her, she was plotting her next steps out loud. "I have to see *Nutz & Boltz* right away."

"You should, definitely."

"Let's go tonight. Come with me!"

"What? I can't—I have to go to the Sam C. show tonight, and Vida's going, too." Vida was the third in their trio of friends. "What's your boyfriend doing?"

"Moses?" It was as if Billie had suggested sprinting into oncoming traffic. Renee rarely gave him much credit. "No, *you* have to come. I need a trustworthy second opinion. What time's Sam C.? Can't you come after? And bring Vida, too, though God knows that girl has zero attention span." Renee was the type of person who would relentlessly stalk a "no" until it converted to a "yes." Billie agreed to meet her at the East Village playhouse at ten and hung up, pissed.

* * *

She let her head roll to the side and looked out the window. They were stuck on Fortieth and Broadway, with no sign of movement. Billie groaned, rubbed her temples, and closed her eyes again. She loathed not having control over her current situation.

Her entire life, she'd been on the go. Working, working, working. She'd blazed through her Washington, D.C., private school in a flurry of A+ essays, academic awards, and 4.0's. From the time she was in kindergarten, she'd assign herself rigid, near-impossible demands to live up to, and accidentally coloring outside the lines was enough to set off a crying jag. She skipped the third grade, but was still at a higher reading and writing level than most of the other kids. While her fifth-grade classmates were reading Nancy Drew mysteries and *Choose Your Own Adventures*, she was knee-deep into *Roots*. She would stay up all night, trembling and torturing herself with visions of sadistic overseers and slave ships. In eighth grade she made herself sick to her stomach studying for the SATs, which she wouldn't have to take for another three years. She insisted that she go to school anyway, and threw up every five minutes.

Billie's parents thought she was an alien.

She was the *antithesis* of them. Billie's mother, Marie-Therese LeSeur, was a Creole girl from Louisiana. When Billie was a child, the word "Creole" meant humid summer vacations on the bayou in terrycloth shorts sets. Mosquitoes and gumbo. Creoles were black people who looked Latin, but had French names like Jacques and Amelie, and enjoyed zydeco music and marinating things.

Marie was obscenely beautiful, a true Southern belle. She had mounds of black wavy hair that fell to her shoulders, huge dark eyes, and skin the color of crème brûlée. She smelled like lavender, and had a cleavage that would smother an infant. And she oozed Southern charm. Every morning she plucked a white carnation from her well-tended garden to wear in her hair. She called everybody "bey" (a diminutive of the French *bébé*). Billie's mother never giggled or tittered, she laughed big and loud, with her head thrown back. She always sat with one leg tucked beneath her, absentmindedly twirling a curl. When Billie's father was in the room, she looked at him like he was the last man on earth.

James Burke was a happy man with a mustache who grew up in Northwest Washington, D.C. The neighborhood was referred to as "the Gold Coast," as it was filled with upper-middle-class black professionals. The story of how they'd met in 1967, when they were juniors in high school, had been told to Billie a million times. Marie and her boyfriend, Charles Chevalier, had traveled two hours by bus to Shreveport to compete in a cha-cha contest. They came in first place, and won a round-trip train ticket to appear on "Bop-a-Lu-La," Washington, D.C.'s local teenage dance show. As it happened, young James and his girlfriend Paula were regulars on the show. When Marie and James saw each other from across the crowded dance floor, Charles and Paula became invisible. Doing the pony, they danced toward each other as if in a dream. The song playing was "I Say a Little Prayer" by Dionne Warwick.

They fell madly in love. After the taping of the show, James asked Marie to marry him. She said she "wouldn't have it any uthuh way," but she'd have to go back to Louisiana and finish high school. They promised to write each other every day until they saw each other again. They did, and when Marie was accepted into

Washington, D.C.'s Howard University in 1968, the couple was beside themselves. At Howard, Marie let her hair grow down to her waist, and James sported an enormous Afro. They smoked anything they could lay hands on, threw up Black Power fists and peace signs, and practiced free love. Marie studied painting while James majored in creative writing (he specialized in poetry about having sex with Marie). The two got married the day after graduation in a ceremony in Rock Creek Park. Neither wore shoes, and the wedding party consisted of Charles, Paula, and the naked Native American woman who married them. The union was not, by any stretch of the imagination, legal, but the blissful couple was unconcerned.

Marie and James decided that, instead of capitalizing on their creative talents for their own gain, they would open a community center for D.C.'s many underprivileged children. The kids were taught to express themselves through art, poetry, and interpretive dance. In 1973, their own little girl was born, and they loved her to distraction. They didn't name her until she was eight months old, choosing "Billie" because the flower Marie wore in her hair reminded James of Billie Holiday, and Marie thought James looked like Billy Dee Williams.

Billie had grown up in a love bubble, with parents who talked a lot about self-esteem and smoked weed in the basement. They had sex all the time—loud, vocal sex. Marie frequently made breakfast topless.

No one was immune to Marie and James's aura of glamour— the couple had scores and scores of friends and were tireless entertainers. They knew white people who said things like "indigenous" and "ethnic." Between James's expert storytelling and Marie's infamously potent mint juleps, the two were liberal D.C.'s favorite hosts. And when the couple danced together, it was positively cine-matic. The only thing in the world that frightened Marie was dull-ness.

Billie felt desperately uncool in her own home. It was so trau-matic—going through the social hell of junior high and high school is hard enough without thinking your parents are hipper than you. At the same time, Billie was embarrassed by her parents' porno-graphic love for each other. And she just couldn't get down with be-ing naked all the time—other people's parents didn't get high and fuck in the garden. She loved them, but they had it backwards: Kids were supposed to be crazy, and adults were supposed to be . . . organized.

Her parents were constantly trying to get her to chill out, relax, "live in the moment," but she just *couldn't*. Billie possessed some quality that made her push herself, harder and harder. When she was nine, the migraines started. Marie and James tried every nat-ural remedy they could find, everything from acupuncture to aro-matherapy rubs, but nothing worked. Finally, they buckled and took her to a neurologist. The neurologist told her she had to chill out, relax, "live in the moment."

When Billie was thirteen, she became privately fascinated by the way her features were coming together. While her parents were out, Billie would sit at her mother's vanity and make herself up. She got really good at it. With makeup on, she looked so much like her mother it was frightening. Billie would pretend to be her. She'd say things like "Have anuthuh sherry, bey" to the mirror, and bat her eyes. Twirling a curl, she'd try to look sensuous and earthy. Then she'd cry, mascara running down her cheeks. She looked like her mother (she had even inherited her petite, busty figure), but she wasn't her. She couldn't do it right; she didn't have that "thing."

She was stiff where her mother was liquid. This realization made young Billie feel awful—and even worse, *dull*. She knew she was pretty, but felt it was a waste because she didn't have a pretty-girl personality. She had the personality of Alex P. Keaton.

At school, almost all the boys had crushes on her, but they terrified her. She didn't know how to flirt, so she developed a sort of cool, aloof look to scare them away. In high school, Billie was finally asked out by a well-dressed, smart boy named Grant. Marie and James were thrilled their Billie was emerging from her shell, and when Grant arrived to pick her up, James presented him with a condom. Grant took her to dinner at Red Lobster, where he began to cry all over his popcorn shrimp, as he confessed to her that he was gay. He'd asked her out because he wanted to prove to his father that he was a real man. Billie was mortified, but agreed to stop by his house to meet his parents. After that, she came to terms with being an unlovable virgin forever. At least she had brains.

"You *thanks*," she said, taking the glass and a mug. She reached for the milk to make tea. He looked at her blankly. "I don't make the tea, miss," he said, moving on. Billie put in her own tea and ignored the flavor.

* * *

The Azucena del Sol event was being held to launch its new holistic skincare line, developed by Chinese herbologists. The magic ingredient in the cleansers and creams was crushed green tea leaves, the next beauty cure-all. In keeping with the Chinese theme, the event was being held at Double Happiness, a trendy, microscopic lounge down in the farthest reaches of Chinatown. Despite the Chinese association, it was a curious choice—a speakeasy for Williamsburg-bound artsy types, known for its after-hours seaminess.

Billie rushed through the unmarked door and down to the

underground entrance, ten minutes late, head pounding. Thankfully, the luncheon hadn't started yet. At the double-doored entrance, a junior public relations girl gave Billie a spirited air kiss and a name tag. *Billie Burke, Du Jour.* After five years of countless name tags, Billie still got a private thrill at seeing her name next to that of the most prestigious fashion magazine in the world.

Squeezed into the tight space were fifteen or so editors mingling with Azucena bigwigs amid tiny cocktail tables covered in green velvet. Each table was adorned with a basket crammed with green tea bags and the new products. Perched in front of each place setting were seating assignment cards, the names painted in careful emerald green calligraphy. Eastern music was whining softly in the background. Two Asian men in sparkly green cummerbunds wove through the small crowd, offering glasses of a clear green liquid.

Billie entered the room and was immediately targeted by one of the sparkly men. "Iced green tea?" he offered.

"Yes, thanks," she said, taking the glass and a small sip. "Mmm!" She nodded for the man's benefit. He looked at her blankly, as if to say, "I didn't make the tea," then smiled and moved on. Billie put on her party face and entered the throng.

Billie had known most of these "girls" (as women in the beauty and fashion industries were called) for what felt like an eternity. Since there were only a fixed number of beauty editorial positions, and the only way to increase your salary was to hop from one magazine to another, most of them had worked together at some point. The ones who hadn't saw each other often enough at events. Boyfriends, secrets, and clothes were exchanged freely. It was a sorority.

For many of them, no one else in the world, besides each other, even really understood what they did for a living. Really, how could some honest-working doctor or teacher put a finger on the importance of dictating beauty trends? A typical day in the life of a beauty editor: Open more than a dozen packages from beauty companies, filled with their newest products. Put everything on a shelf in the "beauty closet" and survey the goods. Decide what's worth writing about. Look for a common theme, like purple eyeshadows or perfumes that smell like food. Label these as trends. Throw extraneous products, or ones too ugly to photograph, in the "giveaway bin," much to the excitement of the perk-less members of the features department. Simultaneously, edit articles for the current issue (three months in advance), write articles for the next issue, and generate ideas for the next-next issue. Disrupt the days with at least one event, assigning the less important events to the girls lower on the masthead.

In the world of beauty editors, so many free products are tossed around, most of their bathrooms resemble Sephora. They're groomed for free—manicures, pedicures, haircuts, facials, massages, the beauty gamut—eyebrows are pefectly arched, skin is flawless, laugh lines are BOTOXed. It's impossible to tell what anyone's real hair texture or color is, as everyone has a perfect blowout and golden highlights. Their uniforms are skintight Seven jeans, Jimmy Choo or Manolo stilettos, a flowy blouse by Chloé or Marc Jacobs, and a major bag—either by Gucci, Prada, or Fendi. They've all seen each other's G-stringed asses at designer sample sales (invite only).

None of them wear makeup.

And only four are black. Besides Billie, there is Trina Stark, the veteran beauty director of *Radiance* (the pioneering magazine for black women that was launched in the seventies), her associate, Zoe Smith, and her assistant, Mimi Hamm. All of them stick out very unlike a sore thumb. They are fabulous, *fabulous*, every time they are seen, just in case anyone might think for a second that they can't hang with this crowd. It is a subconscious relief to the others, who are happy to be spared the uncomfortable feeling of mingling with a girl who is not only black but all wrong.

"Hiiii! Oh my God, where have you been?" said *Vogue*'s Kim Woods, who gave Billie an air kiss and a broad smile. She was a gorgeous redhead with a slight lisp. Kim had worked as the associate beauty writer at *Du Jour* back when Billie was the assistant. Paige had hated her speech impediment and made life hell for her. Once, in a department meeting, Kim was explaining to Paige why she thought the "new metallic nail polith thould be covered in Dethember." Paige made a big show of wiping Kim's spit off her Chanel cable-knit, and Kim disappeared the next day. She went on to have a solid career at *Vogue*, and was the beauty correspondent on cable's Fashion Network (where her soft lisp went over big in a Melanie Griffith, baby-sexy kind of way).

"I've been chained to my desk," said Billie. This was her stock cocktail chatter line. "*You* know how insane it is over there."

"Oh my God, I *know*. How'th Beige?"

"Seldom seen," Billie said lightly.

"Oh, honey, I know that bitch's got you working your ath off."

Billie rolled her eyes in agreement but said nothing. She knew how easily gossip got back to people. Paige really *could* be a bitch, but she was a powerful, smart bitch, and over the years Billie had won her over. Paige either loved you or hated you, and if she loved you, the world was yours. If she hated you, she threw bagels at you and told industry execs you were a whore.

Billie changed the subject. "Okay, so tell me you've picked a date, Kim. It's been six months, already!" Kim loved to talk about her long engagement, and Billie knew this would open the flood-gates. Now she could just nod and look interested without having to talk. Her head was killing her.

"Oh my God, I *know*. But his mother'th an equethtrian and we have to plan around her riding thchedule, and you know I couldn't care leth about her goddamn hortheth . . ." Billie clucked and shook her head, surreptitiously surveying the crowd. She caught the eye of Trina from *Radiance*, who saw that Billie was being talked to death and shot her a sympathetic look. Trina was chatting with socialite Pilar del Sol, creative director of Azucena del Sol.

"A *Du Jour* and *Vogue* sandwich!" Billie and Kim were inter-cepted by *Cosmopolitan*'s Monica Van Arsdale, who'd just arrived. "My fucking wet dream. How are you, sweetie?" Monica gave Bil-lie an air kiss, and then Kim. She was an aristocratic-looking brunette who liked to shock herself with her filthy mouth.

"It looks like a leprechaun shat all over this room," she said.

"I *know*. It'th like, we get the whole green thing, already. And who dethided to do thith all the way down here when we all work in midtown?"

"And Fashion Week, no less! We're hardly in the office as it is."

"Thank God they sent a car," said bored Billie for the second time that day.

"The gift bag better fucking rock," said Monica. It was standard to complain about the tackiness and inconvenience of these events. "Speaking of bags, I adore yours, Billie! I fucking hate you; you're always so well accessorized."

"Oh, well, we do what we can," she replied, mock-haughtily. Kim giggled.

"How's the tea?" asked Monica.

"Nontoxic. Here comes the waiter."

"No, I can't have tea or coffee for one week. I just had my teeth whitened."

"Really? Thmile," demanded Kim. Monica smiled, and her teeth were indeed white. Blue-white.

"It's for a story on how to primp for your wedding. What do you think? I don't look like Denise Richards, do I?"

"No," promised Billie. Fearless, freebie-loving Monica was always the first to try the new treatments. "You look incredible. Kim, you should do it. Not that your teeth aren't white, but it'd be nice for your wedding. . . ." The conversation was exhausting. Billie had tons of writing to do at the office, and this was a spectacular waste of time. And her *head*. To her relief, Pilar caught her eye and enthusiastically motioned for her to come over. Billie told the girls she'd be right back and inched her way over to the bigwig.

"Billie!" cried Pilar.

"Pilar!" cried Billie. Air kiss.

"You look fabulous as usual. I swear, you just get prettier and prettier every time I see you. I could kill you! Couldn't you just kill her, Trina?"

"Never resort to violence, dear. How are you, doll?" The always classy forty-five-year-old gave Billie a kiss on the cheek, the first sincere gesture of the day. She always wore her auburn-streaked hair slicked behind her ears, showing a pair of formidable cheekbones. She glided, rather than walked. When Billie first had started out, Trina had taken her under her wing. She'd invited Billie to her palatial Westchester home, given her advice, and generally become a kind of mentor. Billie adored her.

"Good, good. You know, busy as ever!" Billie tucked her hair behind her ear and tried to look fetchingly flustered.

"I'm sure. You wrote almost all the beauty features last month. You little superstar," gushed Pilar. "And how's my Paige?" They'd known each other at Brearley, the tony private school on the Upper East Side.

"Oh, you know, Paige is always good. She told me to give you a great big *mwah*, by the way."

"We must all have drinks sometime," said Pilar. She paused and clasped her hands under her chin. "Oh, Billie, I can't tell you how happy it makes me to see your name crawling up the masthead. And thank you for placing our All Day Long All Day Strong lipsticks in the July issue. That was huge. A really, really key placement for us."

Everyone wanted their products featured on the pages of *Du Jour*. "Please!" said Billie. "Don't thank me, Pilar. The lipstick speaks for itself."

"No, Billie. *You* speak for the lipstick." Pilar had her hand over her heart and spoke most emphatically. Earnest tears were in her eyes. Billie restrained an urge to yell, "Cut!"

"How did you find the shows this week?" asked Trina, who clearly had to speak to keep from guffawing. "I've been kind of underwhelmed so far. But we've got Sam C. tonight, who almost never disappoints."

"The New York shows are really becoming pedestrian, what with all the junior lines launching," said Pilar. "It's really all about the London fashion week now, I think. That's where the real creativity is, what with Galliano and that adorable Stella McCartney."

Just then, Alma Levy, the publicist for Azucena, asked everyone to take their seats. Billie was at a table with editors from *Mademoiselle*, *Glamour*, *Elle*, and *Seventeen*. As the sparkly men served the wonton soup, Alma introduced to the editors Dr. Wei Hung, the herbologist, who explained why green tea was the quintessential skincare ingredient. He then asked the editors to sample the products on their tables, while he discussed the technology that made each one so special. His accent was opaque. The editors spread cream and sprayed toner on their hands. They oohed and ahhed in ecstasy. They were all slightly embarrassed and overacting because they couldn't understand a thing the doctor was saying.

Then it was all over. No one had touched the spring rolls but Billie.

They were each given a gift bag topped with a green satin ribbon, then said their goodbyes and filed out into the unseasonably warm September air to their waiting cars, which had been circling the teeming Chinatown block for the past hour. The beauty bunch had lots of package opening and article writing to do.

Within the safe haven of the Lincoln Town Car, Billie let out a huge sigh. She looked at her watch. It was 1:30. It would take forever to go forty blocks uptown in the hideous lunchtime traffic.

She dug around in her handbag for her migraine pain medication. Once she located the bottle of Percocet, she dry-swallowed a capsule and settled back into the noisy leather seat. She closed her eyes, breathed slowly, and waited for the familiar fuzzy-numbness to fill her head. She tried to relax, but couldn't help reviewing her mental to-do list.

She had to finish writing the profile on celebrity stylist John Barrett's new salon for December. Then she had to look at Sandy's Q and A with Bobbi Brown. Fuck, that would need lots of editing— Sandy was a competent writer, but she wouldn't know a good interview if it exploded in her face. Most important, she had to remember to bring home the bag of fragrances for her January perfume roundup. The piece had to be perfect, because this year she wanted to win a FiFi, the Fragrance Foundation's award for excellence. So she'd work on it at home, where she could really concentrate, instead of in the raucous office.

Billie was very, very dedicated to her work.

Billie also hadn't had sex in five years. She was wound tighter than 400-thread-count sheets.

She'd lost her virginity at Duke University. The second she stepped on campus, her life as she knew it in high school changed abruptly. Athletes! Football and basketball players were a world apart from high school boys. They were self-confident, smug, even. They had cars, muscles, and frat-boy attitudes. They were gorgeous and sexy and couldn't care less about Billie's whole aloof thing. These boys weren't scared of Billie because they could get any pretty girl they wanted. Eventually, Billie fell in love with a tall football player with deep brown skin so smooth it appeared to have been mixed in a bowl. His name was Shawn and he didn't care if she could flirt or not. He didn't care, period. Quarterbacks were supposed to have a pretty girl on their arm. Shawn introduced her to things like tongues and orgasms, which distracted her from the fact that he could never remember her last name.

When they'd been dating a year and he didn't know she worked for the newspaper, she started to get worried. When a local preteen delivered his child their junior year, she was horrified. Back to the books. She hadn't had a boyfriend since then. Every now and then she went on a date, but nothing serious. The problem was, she wasn't confident enough in her own appeal to approach a man. So she had to wait for them to approach her. And the men who did were the super-obnoxious ones that wanted a showpiece. She was used to being alone, so she stayed that way. And worked her ass off.

Billie yawned. Her headache was ebbing away, and she was

beginning to feel floaty-good. She realized she hadn't opened her gift bag. She untied the ribbon and sifted through layers of green (Jesus!) tissue paper, and found a forest-green suede Fendi baguette. She was used to extravagant gifts, but this was ridiculous. A Fendi baguette handbag was, like, $750. Inside the handbag was a new Azucena cleanser, a fussily wrapped bag of loose green tea leaves, green laminated chopsticks, and a mah-jongg set. Incredible. Who thought of this stuff? She wondered if she could exchange the baguette for one in a different color, but that seemed tacky. The giveaway bin, maybe?

Her fingers instinctively floated up to her throbbing temples. She yawned again, and returned to her mental to-do list. When could she sleep? Not until at least ten. She had to wrap everything up in the office by eight, and then walk the two short blocks to the Bryant Park tents. Here, the top designers were showing their spring 2000 collections (spring was always shown in September of the previous year, so editors had time to place the fashions in their magazines). She would skip the Sam C. afterparty and go to sleep. Vida would be very persuasive, but she'd have to be stern with her friend of almost ten years.

Vida was a hotshot publicist at Manhattan's trendiest PR firm, Below 14. Her accounts ran the gamut from celebrity-owned restaurants, hipster clubs, and socialites to rappers, cell phones, accessory lines. At the moment she was persuading Sam C. to host the launch party for his new perfume at Heaven, the uber-trendy club/lounge she represented. Vida always knew what was sexy and "right now." And everyone took her word for it. She was out every night until 4 A.M. Vida didn't believe in sleeping. She also didn't believe in sleeping alone. An ornery rapper named Git TaSteppin was currently sharing her bed.

Billie had met her two best friends, Vida Brannigan and Renee Byrd, on the first day of freshman year. They were the only three black girls in the "B" line at registration. Renee was a no-bullshit spitfire from North Carolina, with a boyfriend named Moses, who'd followed her from high school to Duke. She thought he was irritating and precious. She didn't know how to shake him, though, so she supposed she loved him. He waited on her hand and foot, and gave marathon head (she called him "Go Down Moses" behind his back). Renee wore her hair in a sexy Halle Berry shag, and never needed makeup on her even walnut skin and soft brown eyes. When she wanted something, she'd tilt her head down, then look up at you through her eyelashes. Then she opened her mouth and became Dee from *What's Happening*.

Renee was most comfortable when people were afraid of her. She was not afraid to fight, either. Man, child, 7-Eleven clerk, whatever. The only time she was docile was when a book was in front of her. She could take a book, disappear for hours, and return smiling and rosy-cheeked. In this, she and Billie were soul mates. Their junior and senior years, they would sit up all night reading the same book together. Periodically, they'd stop to ask each other where they were in the story, and then launch into a passionate discussion about the plot. Moses tried to sit in on one of their unofficial book club meetings, but Renee had no patience for lip-reading (Moses was a math major), so he was ousted.

Vida found books both boring and annoying. She was a six-foot-tall sexpot from Bermuda—all tits and ass and thick, wild ringlets, the ends of which she dyed purple (for Prince). The daughter of some West Indian real estate honcho, she was really, *really* rich. She hated being rich; it embarrassed her. She harbored a bit of liberal guilt upon coming to the U.S. (she'd gone to British private schools her whole life), when she became aware of the underprivileged state of many black Americans. Vida made it her mission to "rescue the black man from the clutches of disenfranchisement." She dated only local boys, because the middle- to upper-middle-class black boys at Duke made her nauseous, especially when "they tried to act all gangsta, knowing Renee could take two of 'em out at the same time." Her father could buy and sell Duke, but that was no matter to her. She became completely obsessed with hip-hop culture, and flirted with the idea of becoming a rapper. For a time, she tried to get people to call her V-8. She even cut her own demo tape, but everyone agreed that her West Indian Princess Di accent was distracting. Next, she begged her father to fund a summer in New York taking DJ lessons. It was an eventful summer—not only did she begin shadowing New York's famous DJ, Funkmaster Flex, she also landed a gig as the unapproachable hottie in a few LL Cool J videos. DJ Tri (short for Bermuda Triangle) returned triumphant her sophomore year and proceeded to become the premier house party DJ at Duke.

The three of them were inseparable. For the first time, Billie felt totally comfortable, like she was in her element. The day they met, the girls decided to take over the world. And that was that. By the end of the four years, Billie had become the executive editor and lifestyle editor at the university newspaper. Along with her duties as DJ Tri, Vida was the president of the Black Student Association. Renee founded the university's award-winning literary magazine, *Railroads*. By graduation, they'd decided to move to New York together to make it big. Never once did they consider being black a hurdle they'd have to overcome. Their whole lives, they'd been the only (or maybe one of a couple) black faces in the "smart" classes. This didn't make them feel inferior. It made them feel invincible.

They had much practice proving they were not in the room because of a handout. (One of Billie's high school classmates sniffed "affirmative action" when Billie was accepted early decision into Duke. Billie offered that maybe if she'd gotten straight A's and been class president instead of spending her time letting the Latin Society fuck her in the ass, she too would've been accepted.) They'd never come across something they couldn't do, and no one ever told them no. They didn't doubt for a second that they'd be successful.

* * *

At two o'clock, Billie finally returned to the behemoth building in Times Square. The first twenty floors housed some of the country's leading magazines, and the top thirty belonged to a fancy technology outfit. The lobby was intense. To gain admittance, employees had to prove their identity beyond a shadow of a doubt. Once the security guards decided that you were who you claimed, you had to insert a magnetic card into a machine that unlocked a turnstile. Only then did you have access to the elevator banks.

Approaching her cubicle on the eighteenth floor, Billie heard her phone ringing and rushed to her desk. She missed it. Exhausted, she plopped down in her chair and let her bag slide to the floor.

"Anyone need a green Fendi baguette?" she asked no one in particular, and got to work.

getting her culture on

The Sam C. show started an hour late. The tent was bristling with anticipation, as the last show often determined the success of the season. At the far end of the catwalk, a huge cluster of photographers struggled to get the best possible view. Movie stars, rappers, and fashionistas were air-kissing as if they hadn't seen each other three times a day for the past week. In a carefully boxed-off DJ booth, Boy George was spinning eighties dance music. Nu Shooz's "I Can't Wait" gave way to Culture Club's "Do You Really Want to Hurt Me," and he grinned naughtily at the crowd's collective scream of delight.

A-list actresses were graciously explaining their outfits to CNN Style's Elsa Klensch and Fashion TV's Jeanne Becker. The air was thick with Sam C.'s new unisex perfume, Thrust (the party favor placed under each chair). A slutty teenaged It-Girl/heiress was spraying it at cameras and grabbing her crotch, praying for Page Six. Near the entrance, a crowd of sound bite–hungry gossip columnists swarmed until the crowd eventually parted, revealing all four of the *Sex and the City* ladies, plus their fuchsia-haired stylist, Patricia Fields. Personalities were on full-blast.

Finally, at 8:50, the Bryant Park staff (pompadoured fashion boys wearing baby tees and headsets) started tearing the industrial-strength protective paper off the catwalk. People began moving to their seats, which was a show in itself. The front row seated the likes of Sean Puffy Combs, Madonna, Courtney Love, and Gwyneth Paltrow. Also awarded VIP seating were several middle-aged celebrities with their model daughters, including Donald and Ivanka Trump, Mick and Elizabeth Jagger, and Steven and Liv Tyler. Interspersed between the stars were "the Fashion Mafia," the high-ranking editors from *Du Jour*, *Vogue*, *Harper's Bazaar*, *Elle*, and *WWD*. They had the programs in their laps and their pencils poised.

Billie and the rest of the beauty editors were three rows back, or standing room, depending on the status of the magazine. They were the stepchildren of Fashion Week—invited to observe the trends in hair and makeup, which were obviously secondary to the fashion. Billie had been seated in a row that included Kim, Monica, and some of the other girls from that morning's event. Billie scanned the rows for Vida, but she couldn't spot her in the crowded tent.

The lights went down and a hush fell over the audience. Billie's heart was racing. She would never get over the thrill of fashion shows. She loved everything about them. The rampaging bitchery, the costumes, the supermodels. It was campy and glamorous and burlesque, like a movie.

The lights and Chaka Khan's "I Feel for You" came on at the same time. Out strutted uber-model Kate Moss in complicated cornrows, stilettos, and what looked like a Phat Farm jersey transformed into a minidress. The audience's head turned slowly from right to left as she walked. A delighted murmur bristled through the crowd. (She's out of the clinic? Oh, she looks *ravishing*!) Next came Naomi, Shalom, Amber, and Gisele, all cornrowed and sporting variations of Kate's dress. The next set of models stormed the catwalk in frayed denim miniskirts, fishnets, work boots, and rhinestone "SC" pasties over their teeny nipples. Their intricate braids were gathered into ponytails. The rest of the show followed the same street sexpot motif. More than one member of the Fashion Mafia scribbled "ghettofabulous!" on her program. For the finale, two little boys emerged from nowhere and stood on either side of the start of the runway. As the models stepped out from backstage in flesh-colored bikinis and enormous sunglasses, the boys defaced their bodies with fuchsia and orange spray paint. The graffitied models stopped at their marks and posed in various stages of studied funkiness. Then Sam C. came bounding down the runway. "It's all over! Everyone go home!" he shouted, blowing kisses and accepting a large bouquet. The self-described "faerie queen" then pirouetted, curtseyed, and stuck his tongue down Kate's throat. Everyone screamed in ecstasy and a million flashbulbs went off. It was a Fashion Moment. The giggling Kate grabbed his ass, and all the models began dancing around him to the strains of Prince's "1999." Thus ended the last New York Fashion Week of the twentieth century.

* * *

Backstage was bedlam. Naked models flitted about trying to find their clothes while dressers gingerly rescued Sam C.'s ensembles from the floor. Hollow-chested Model Boyfriends chain-smoked and cursed in French on cell phones. International fashion journalists jostled to get a quote from Sam C. Behind a clothes rack, a very young model was believing everything Mick Jagger said. Q-Tip's "Vivrant Thing" was on repeat. Boy George delivered a salacious punch line and tore his corner of the room down.

It was 9:45, the time she'd meant to be heading home for bed when she'd run through her schedule in the car on her way to the office from the Azucena event. But she'd blanked out on the promise she'd made to Renee to see *Nutz & Boltz*. Now she was going to be late meeting Renee.

She'd just interviewed the makeup artist but couldn't leave till she found the hairstylist. Billie was prepared to be annoyed when whoever this Madison Ave. stylist was informed her that cornrows were "coming back," despite black girls having worn them for a million years.

Instead, she spotted Gisele's hair being unbraided by a *very* fly black woman. Billie grinned and felt all warm inside. Notepad in hand, she stepped over a hairdryer extension cord, squeezed past Lil' Kim, and approached the stylist.

"Hi, excuse me. I'm Billie Burke from *Du Jour*? I'm the senior beauty editor. Did you style the hair for the show?"

"Mm-hmm, yeah. Nice to meet you," she said, smiling brightly at Billie. She gave her a proud look like "Do your thing, girl," which Billie returned. It was a sort of unspoken code among black women who found themselves one of the "onlys." The woman was cute in a pixie way, with a short, spiky haircut. It was dyed orange with streaks of red woven through it and made her head appear to be on fire. Billie thought it looked incredible. The stylist untangled her fingers from Gisele's masses of hair and shook Billie's hand. "My name's Pandora."

"Good to meet you," said Billie. "Great work. Honestly, I know how arduous a good cornrow job is. I can't imagine doing fifteen girls at once."

"*Seriously*, girl. Look at my fingers, they're still shaking." She held out her hands.

"It was certainly well worth it! Pandora, do you mind if I ask you a few questions?"

"No, no, no. I'm just gonna finish unbraiding her hair, but go ahead."

Billie realized there wasn't much to talk about. She asked her standard "what was your inspiration" question, but the answer was obvious. She stuck to questions about technique and styling products. Starving Gisele ignored them both, chomping on a turkey sandwich and reading the Portuguese translation of *Interview with the Vampire*. Her always-in-tow Yorkshire terrier was mesmerized by the cherries painted on Billie's pedicure.

"So, what salon are you with? Or are you with an agency?"

"I'm not with an agency. I have my own salon, Fresh Hair."

"Really?" Billie was interested. Most runway stylists were plucked from top salons or A-list agencies.

"Yeah, it's just a small salon, but I got a following." Pandora looked humble but proud. "Christina Aguilera's manicurist is one of my regulars. When she got called to do her 'Make It Hurt' video, she referred me to do the hair. They wanted a really street look on that one. Next thing I know, I'm on the phone with Sam's creative director. It's crazy!"

"You know? But that's how it happens," said Billie. "Listen, congratulations, you did an amazing job. I can't *believe* this was your first show. Do you mind if I contact you later if I need more quotes?" Pandora told her she could call whenever she wanted. She jotted down the number to her salon, then fingered Billie's long, glassily straightened hair.

"You get your hair blown out at those Dominican salons up in Spanish Harlem, don't you?"

"How'd you know?" Billie asked, self-consciously tucking her hair behind her ears. She went every Friday, the day she took a lunch break.

"They make everybody's hair look like cellophane."

Billie didn't know how to take this.

"You should wear your hair natural sometime. I bet it's mad cute."

"Well, that's the problem. It makes me look twelve." Billie was sort of insulted but played it off. Pandora finished unbraiding Gisele's hair and moved on to the next head. Wrapping it up, she told Billie she could come in to Fresh Hair for free, anytime. Billie thanked her for the interview and the invitation and said goodbye. On her way out, she grabbed a clip off the makeup counter and pulled her cellophane hair into a ponytail.

Billie ran into Vida at the craft-services table. She was chatting up a cute blonde with a Reese Witherspoon chin. Vida's rapper boyfriend, Git TaSteppin, was molesting the picked-over vegetable tray. He looked like he needed a nap. Vida looked stunning. She was wearing a low-cut denim mini and a paisley sari she'd converted into a halter top. Slung around her hips was a belt whose buckle spelled out "Vida Loca" in rhinestones.

"Vida Brannigan!" called Billie.

" 'Sup, baby!" They kissed each other on the cheek. Since Vida had met Git a month before, they'd seen a lot less of each other, mostly just on their Sunday brunch dates with Renee.

"What's up, Git?" said Billie.

"Just tryin' to live, man, just tryin' to live." He always acted as if invisible forces were blocking him from his general rights as a human being.

"Billie, this is Diana Golden, Sam C.'s publicist. Diana, this is Billie Burke from *Du Jour* beauty. She's my best friend—basically my sister."

Air kisses were exchanged. Diana was delighted at the chance to plug Thrust to an influential beauty editor. "Oh, *hi*! I just sent Thrust to your office last week. What did you think? Am I going to see it on your pages?"

"Oh, please! It's already on the lineup for a January fragrance roundup. How could we not cover it? I want to pour it on everything I own; it's so delicious." Not to mention that Sam C. pays thousands for advertising space in *Du Jour*, she thought.

Diana looked euphoric. Vida was grinning proudly—she loved to watch her friend work it.

"I'm trying to convince Diana to have the Thrust launch party at Heaven," said Vida.

"Fabulous!" said Billie.

"I just have to check with Sam, but it sounds perfect to me," gushed the publicist. "You'll come, yes?"

Billie smiled. "Wild horses couldn't stop me."

"Great, great! Well, I have to go rescue Sam from the French press. He's so fey they eat him alive. See you ladies later! *So* cute you two know each other!" She gave them air kisses and disappeared.

"Jesus," said Vida.

"I'm saying! Subtlety is *so* not her strong suit. What did you think of the show?"

"I haven't formed an opinion yet. 'Cultural rape' is the phrase that pops to mind, but I don't know. I need time to build on it. Kate Moss looked fucking fly, though."

"You know?" Billie agreed. She checked her watch; it was 9:57. "Oh shit, I'm so late meeting Renee downtown. Are you coming with me?" Billie quickly explained *Nutz & Boltz* and its importance to Renee.

"Ooh, I'm there. Git." Git's head was bobbing to a beat in his head. Vida punched him in the shoulder. "Git!" Disrupted, he jerked his head in Vida's direction.

"What?"

"You trying to get your culture on?"

"I'm down for whatever, ma."

This meant yes, so Vida, Billie, and Git rushed outside to get a cab.

• • •

Renee was angry. She'd been waiting outside the Public Theater for twenty minutes. Impatiently, she whisked through the entrance to see if any seats were left. By now, it was standing room only. The suspicious ticket guy, certain that she'd been trying to sneak in without paying all night, tapped her on the shoulder and pointed outside with his thumb. Renee shot him a withering glance and exited. Billie was *so* lucky it was a warm night.

At 10:08, she saw her diminutive friend, her Amazonian friend, and a swaggering boyfriend exit a cab a block away. Tottering on mile-high stilettos and lugging a huge shopping bag, Billie scurried down Astor Place in the wrong direction. Vida and Git blindly followed her. Despite her annoyance, Renee burst out laughing.

"Billie!" she yelled, throwing her hands in the air. "Vida! Where are you going?"

All three whipped around and rushed over to Renee.

"I'm sorry, I'm sorry," said Billie. "You hate me!" She gave Renee a hug. She was breathless. "I've been all over this city today. I've lost all sense of direction."

"It's okay. But I've been standing out here forever, and me and this ticket guy are about to go at it." The ticket guy made a face at her, and Renee sucked her teeth at him.

"Oh, girl, calm down," Vida said, giving her a kiss. Everyone was accustomed to Renee's difficulties with self-important bouncers.

"What's up, Git?"

"Just tryin' to be me."

Renee rolled her eyes; she had little patience for Git TaSteppin. "All right, let's go in." They each handed the grumbling guy $20 and entered the theater.

Inside the tightly packed space was a small stage with large speakers on either side, blaring DMX. On the stage was a wooden stool. Rising diagonally from the stage were pewlike rows, which seated a cross section of twenty-something Manhattanites. There were black bohemians from Brooklyn, white bohemians from the West Village, hip-hop music industry players, and poetry café heads. A handful of square-looking newspaper reporters from various Metro sections pretended to jot notes on their steno pads. Billie and Renee stood behind the last row next to a group of carefully thugged-out Asian-American NYU students (raised on Eric B. and Rakim, Wu-Tang, and Jay-Z, they went to great lengths to prove their street credibility, from wearing the hottest kicks to saying things like "word life, that shit's *fresh*, yo!"). In unison, they nodded their heads to the pounding bass. One of the guys watched Billie struggling with her shopping bag and said, "I'm sayin', shorty, you need some help?" He smiled, revealing expensive gold fronts. Billie assured him she could manage.

"For real though, Billie, what's in that bag?" said Vida. It was clinking and clanking.

"Perfume. A million bottles of perfume for an article I have to write this weekend. And a gift from an event. Either of you want a green Fendi baguette?"

Vida wrinkled her nose.

"What am I going to do with that?" Renee never wore colors. "Actually, Moses's mother's birthday is next month. She loves loud things. Like one of those birds that are drawn to anything that sparkles."

"This is perfect, then."

"How was your day, girls?"

"Crazy busy," said Vida.

"Plastic but productive," said Billie.

"Your eyes are glazed over," noticed Vida.

"I'm postmigraine." Vida made a concerned face, and Billie waved it away. "How was your day, Renee?"

"I'll let you know in an hour and a half!" she said excitedly, as the lights went down.

The music changed to Nice & Smooth's old school classic "Sometimes I Rhyme Slow." Jay Lane walked out onto the stage to cheers and applause. He was wearing a faded red T-shirt over a long-sleeved T-shirt and jeans. He was tall, lanky, and brown. A dreadlocked girl in the front exclaimed, "Mm-mm-*mmm*!" He grinned and called out, "What's up, y'all?" Somebody yelled, "Chillin', playa! How you livin'?" Jay scratched the back of his neck and replied, "Shit don't look too bad from here, nahmean?"

One of the Asian boys nodded and muttered, "True, true." The clapping eventually died down, and the music faded out. Jay shot the shit with the audience and looked generally bashful for a couple of minutes. Then he turned into someone else.

He took a loooong drag from an imaginary spliff and leaned back. Slowly, he exhaled. He slumped on the stool, silent, balefully shaking his head. The audience could almost hear a blues guitar wailing in the background. He took another drag and gazed scornfully at the audience. In a grave, smoked-out voice he announced, "Biggie stole my rhymes." The crowd burst into laughter. He launched into a rant and rave about how everyone he'd ever known capitalized off of some enormous talent he had. The local pimp recruited all his ex-girlfriends because they were so dope he knew they'd make a fortune. The boy he used to play basketball with on West Fourth got recruited to Georgetown only because he copied his killer crossover. He went with Jennifer Lopez when she was chunky. He griped on and on and on until midsentence, Jay paused and turned back into Jay. Exasperated, he yelled (along with most of the audience, who chanted the line by heart), "Man, coulda, woulda, shoulda. NIGGA, GETCHA *OWN* HUSTLE!"

Before the hour-and-a-half show was over, Jay had inhabited five more characters. He turned into a teenaged girl who locked herself in a room for days, quitting crack cold turkey. He became a ninety-year-old man on a Bed Stuy stoop, watching a group of boys about to fight ("knives in hand, shackles in place"). He was Flexuality, a frighteningly untalented writer of erotic poetry, and a self-described "Adontis." Most amazingly, he became a little boy who was so ignored that he'd convinced himself he was invisible.

And, clearly as a reaction to the *Village Voice* article, he was an eager reporter trying to "Angry Black Man" him. At the end of the interview, Jay collapsed to the ground, having been fatally "soundbitten." The Metro journalists in the audience looked uncomfortable.

Jay Lane seemed to *be* these people. It was as if he was jumping into their skin. He had boundless manic energy—he was up and down, on his feet, animated, then withdrawn. It was an eerily perceptive, insightful, dead-on performance. Yet somehow, it never felt preachy or maudlin. Even at the show's most harrowing moments, he would insert a pop-culture reference or a tongue-in-cheek tone. The audience never got that self-conscious "this is the serious part" feeling. And it was obvious Jay Lane was a writer. The way he strung words together was abstract but almost technical. The show was amazing. When *Nutz & Boltz* ended, Renee, Vida, and Billie were all knee-deep in epiphanies.

Renee decided he was going to be the next literary sensation.

Billie decided he was going to be her husband.

* * *

Most of the crowd was filing out, but the reporters and a small group of admirers lingered, hovering around Jay. A cameraman was taking a picture every five seconds.

"That was so hot! Oh my God," exclaimed Vida.

"I know. All right, listen," Renee, Miss Bottom Line, said to Vida. "What's my approach? Everyone's bumrushing him, and I don't want to look desperate."

"Please! Like you've ever looked desperate," encouraged Vida. "Go up to that man, give him your card, and it's a wrap."

"Okay." Renee took a deep breath. "I'll be right back." She coolly walked down the stairs, very Strictly Business with her sexily mussed shag and Diane von Furstenberg wrap dress. She split the crowd and approached him.

Vida was giggling at Renee, who had gently shoved a reporter aside and was shaking Jay's hand. "Look at this girl. Who's gonna say no to her?"

Billie said nothing. She hadn't spoken in ten minutes. She was outrageously embarrassed. She felt as if it was all over her face. Her chest was hot and her heart was racing. She didn't know what to do with her hands. This feeling was completely foreign to her.

Vida looked at Billie and raised her eyebrows. "What's wrong? Are you okay? Headache, huh?"

Billie found her voice and lied. "Yeah, I've been fighting this migraine all day. I don't know . . ." She trailed off and shrugged. She wanted to leave.

"All right, just breathe." Vida fanned her hand in front of Billie's hot face.

Then something terrible happened—Renee and Jay came up the aisle toward them. Billie tried to look busy. She assigned herself the task of fiddling with her earring.

Renee was radiant. "Everybody, meet Jay Lane, who's having lunch with me on Monday." Vida told Jay how much she had enjoyed the show, and awarded him a congratulatory air kiss. Git said, "Sup, son?" dapped him up, and resumed his head bobbing.

Jay turned to say hi to Billie and paused. They caught each other's eye for a split second (did she imagine it?). Billie's stomach hit the floor. He shook her hand, and she said, "I'm Billie, you were great," and felt like an asshole.

"Your name's Billie? What's it short for?"

"Nothing, just Billie. Billie Burke. It's so bubblegum. Like I should be on TRL," she said in a stupid, laughy voice.

"Billie Burke? You know that's the actress who played Glinda the Good Witch in *The Wizard of Oz*, right?"

Vida started laughing, and Renee exclaimed, "He's good!" Billie could tell they suspected Jay was flirting with their innocent Billie, which they found delicious. Neither one of them realized the state she was in. Save disastrous Shawn, they'd never known her to catch feelings for anybody. And they'd learned not to bring up the subject with her.

"I know. Very few people catch the whole *Wizard of Oz* connection." She was aware this sounded haughty and didn't know how to fix it. His eyes met hers again and lingered a beat too long.

Meanwhile, Git was looking at him suspiciously.

"Where I know you from, man?" he asked.

"I don't know," said Jay. "You from here?"

"Naw, Illadelph." Philadelphia.

"I don't know, I never been to Philly."

They looked hard at each other. Slowly, a look of recognition crossed Jay's face.

"Wait, wait, you ain't Bone's cousin? TyJuan?"

To the girls' surprise, Git burst out laughing. "J-Nut? From Myrtle Ave.? Naaw!"

"What the *deal*, baby!" They gave each other an enthusiastic hug and pounded each other on the back. Billie, Vida, and Renee shot each other amused looks. *Taiwan?*

"Wait, how do you know each other?" Vida was kind of annoyed. She'd never inspired this much emotion in Git.

"I grew up in the same building as his cousin Bone," said Jay.

"And I'd come out there every summer till I was, like, what, thirteen? Fourteen?"

"Yeah, yeah. Shit, it's been that long?"

"Yeah, somethin' like that," said Git. "Man, you was a crazy motherfucker! How'd you end up here? Look at you, on fuckin' Broadway and shit!"

"It's a long story, man, a long story," Jay said, changing the subject. "How long you been here?"

"For a minute," said Git. "You know, I got some rhymes and shit. Tryin' to get that demo tape, cut a few tracks, whisper in some ears. Get this thing started."

"Word? Your shit's hot?"

"I mean, I got a little flow."

"Lemme hear it." Jay looked like he wanted to laugh.

"Aww, come on, man. Don't blow up my shit."

"Naw, for real. Freestyle. Look, if you're really tryin' to do this, you gotta be impromptu about your shit."

Git thought about this. He looked at Vida.

"Man, I ain't got no beats."

"Come on! Do it! Look, I'll beatbox." Vida was excited. She channeled DJ Tri and expertly began spitting a mid-tempo beat into her hand. They all nodded their heads, hyping him up. Git started feeling it and launched into his rhyme.

"Fuck watcha heard it's Git TaSteppin
Only shoot words ain't got no weapon
Believe that nigga you a fucking fool
Your flow is bull
Don't hate me cuz I'm beautiful

It's my intention to squash your bitchin
I'll pluck your chickens
I'm Richie Richin'
Your pimp is slippin'
You get no tip and
I'm blazin, amazin, stop hatin — you're shallow
While you were beatin meat I fucked Meadow Soprano"

"Oh shit!" they all cried out simultaneously, and burst into laughter. Hysterical, Jay pounded Git on the back and said, "Your shit's all right, man, your shit's all right. And you got the Human Beatbox over here."

"Stick with me, baby. I'll take you places. Show you things." Vida's personality was now busting at the seams.

"Git, you just blew my mind," said Renee. "I didn't know you spoke."

"Go 'head," muttered Git shyly. He was embarrassed.

Billie was still giggling, grateful for the comic relief. Now she wanted to go before Jay looked at her again. She gave Renee a subtle "it's been a long day" look.

"All right, Jay, we're not going to keep you," Renee said smoothly. "Think about what I said, and I'll see you on Monday, okay?"

"No doubt, no doubt." He said his goodbyes, took Git's cell phone number, and headed back down to the dozen or so people waiting for him. As Billie headed toward the safe haven of the exit, she mustered up the nerve to sneak one last glance at him. When she turned her head she saw that he was staring at her. *Staring.* She froze and left.

Once outside, the group left in separate cabs. Billie, Renee, and Vida all lived in Fort Greene, but Billie was the only one going home. Vida and Git went across town to the suddenly trendy meatpacking district for the Sam C. party. Renee, bound by duty, took a cab to Moses' cavernous apartment near the Twin Towers. Billie sat in the cab, stiff as a board. She was mortified. Why was she so awkward? Someone like Vida would've left with his phone number. Or bound him with her belt and dragged him into a cab.

Billie was halfway across the Manhattan Bridge before she realized she'd left the bag of perfume in the theater.

"Noooo!" she wailed out loud. Of course, now it would look like she left it on purpose. Billie groaned and asked the driver to turn around. She prayed that Jay was gone.

The door to the theater was locked. She knocked on the door several times. There was no answer. Again, she pounded and pounded, but no one came. It was a warm Friday night in the East Village. Lafayette Street was alive with pierced people and foreign hipsters smoking clove cigarettes. She waited for a couple of seconds, raised her hand to knock again, and the door opened. It was Jay. It looked like he'd still been talking with some friends who'd been at the show. They said goodbye and left.

"I figured it was you," he said to her. "You forgot your bag."

"Yeah. I . . . it's really important. I don't know what I was thinking! It's been a really long day." This involved a lot of gesturing. "How'd you know I forgot my bag?"

He looked at her like she was crazy. "Cuz I was watching you."

"Oh."

They stood there for a minute, Jay in the doorway, Billie

outside. People were looking at them. She didn't know what to do. Was he going to bring it to her, or did she have to walk past him to get it? This was so hard.

"Do you wanna come in?"

"Yeah, yeah."

He backed out of the doorway, and she passed him, holding her breath. She heard voices backstage, but the front of the tiny theater was empty. There it was, her troublesome fucking bag, leaning against the wall behind the last row. She picked it up and sighed with relief. Jay sat in front of her on the bench.

"This is really important," she repeated. The gaping shopping bag was filled to the brim with perfumes, so she realized how flighty that sounded.

"Are you a Mary Kay lady?"

"No! I'm a beauty editor."

"I don't know what that means."

"I write about makeup and hair and skincare. For a magazine."

"Which magazine?"

"*Du Jour.*"

"Fancy."

"Well, I don't know."

He nodded approvingly. "That's hot, Billie Burke."

Billie kind of half-smiled, half-shrugged. She noticed the scar on his cheek and thought it made him look like, like, a *man*. More men should have them.

"How come you ain't wearing any makeup?"

"Do I look awful?"

"I mean, you write about makeup, but you ain't wearing any."

"Most beauty writers don't wear makeup. I don't know why. Maybe it's because we get sent so much of it, we're immune."

"Does that really happen?"

"What?"

"I mean, can you really get so much of something you love that you become immune?"

"I . . . yeah. Of course." Billie was nervous. He was looking at her like he knew her.

"That's never happened to me."

"What's your favorite food?"

"Nathan's hot dogs."

"Okay, you love Nathan's hot dogs. Could you eat them every day for two weeks?"

"I try to eat one every day," he said.

Billie cocked her head and wondered if he was lying.

"I can't cook for shit. And I can't get enough of Nathan's hot dogs. Have you ever had one? They're the right kinda salty, and they got that burned strip running down the middle? Oh my God. Why complicate matters when you got a sure thing?"

"Isn't that boring?" she asked.

"I don't get bored." He stood up. Without thinking, she backed up against the wall.

"I'm frequently bored," she said.

"I believe it."

Billie looked insulted. Jay grinned at her, his eyes sparkling like the ones in Japanese animation. He had lashes longer than a man has any right to have. Billie wondered when she could tell him she loved him.

"Do you like tea?" she asked him, wondering what the hell she was saying.

"Do I like tea?"

"Yeah. I have this bag of green tea that someone gave me today. I'll never drink it, so . . ." She trailed off and offered him the fussily wrapped bag of tea leaves. It was bound in a frilly pink and green ribbon. "Do you want it?"

"You're serious."

"Take it, it's a gift."

"I'll take it. But only because you put so much thought into it." He smiled and slung the bag under his arm. She saw a muscle bulge under his T-shirt. She flushed and bit her bottom lip nervously. Jay stared at her mouth, transfixed, as if he'd never seen one before. And then their little conversation turned into something else entirely.

He was riveted. It seemed he couldn't take his eyes off her. Helplessly, Billie returned his gaze. He leaned toward her as if he was going to kiss her. She prayed he wouldn't touch her, but if he didn't she'd die. It felt like hours were passing. Totally out of her element and feeling like an adolescent, she chewed her lip again.

"What's your favorite place?" he asked.

"What?"

"Here, in the city."

She was shaking like a toy poodle. His mouth was inches from hers. "The Biography Bookshop, I guess. On Bleecker. Why?"

"Meet me there tomorrow at twelve." It was not a question.

"Okay." She would do anything he asked if he would just kiss her.

"I'm not kissing you," he said.

"Why not?"

Lightly, he ran his fingers up the side of her neck and behind her ear. When he reached her ponytail, he unfastened her clip. It fell to the floor. He slid his hand from the back of her neck up into her hair. Gently grabbing a handful, he tilted her head back and kissed her throat. He let the tip of his tongue graze her skin. She let out a tiny moan. He brought her face in front of his.

"If I kiss you, I won't stop," he said.

"What?" She was dizzy.

"I won't stop. You have to go." He grabbed her bag and walked toward the door. She stood there in utter disbelief. This man had just given her the most boldly erotic moment of her life and was now throwing her out.

"Glinda!" he said.

Billie whipped her head around in surprise. Did he just call her that?

"You ain't gotta go home, but you gotta get the hell outta here." He opened the door, and she snatched her bag and walked out.

"You're crazy."

"I'm not challenging that. Meet me at twelve."

"What if I don't?"

"You will."

3.
clout, cash, and ass

Portrait of an intelligent hoodlum: In 1973, Jerome Lane, Jr., was born at home, in Fort Greene, Brooklyn. This was two decades before Fort Greene became a mecca for young, black, urban professionals, long before anyone had heard of Moshood's upscale Africana-chic ensembles, or Carol's Daughter's all-natural beauty products, or Brooklyn Moon Café's poetry night, or Chez Oskar's Sunday brunches (attended by the who's who of black media). If anyone had suggested that one day a studio in Fort Greene would rent for $2,000, they would've been laughed right back across the East River. In the early 1970s, the only people in Fort Greene were the people who'd always lived there. The storefronts that would one day be fancy restaurants serving steak frites and mussels were bodegas and liquor stores. Crime was high, rent was low, and gentrification was forever away.

Jay lived with his mother, Linda, on the twelfth floor of a Walt Whitman project building, off of bustling Myrtle Avenue. She was a part-time cleaning woman and full-time heroin addict. She only spoke to Jay to yell at him for existing. The yelling was usually punctuated by a mighty punch. She was a heavy-handed, resentful teenager.

Linda wasn't married to Jay's father, Jerome Lane, Sr., and they didn't live together. But unlike many of the boys in his neighborhood, he saw his father all the time. He came over every night for "dinner." Dinner went like this: Jerome would walk in the apartment screaming at Linda, then Linda would start screaming at him. She'd throw something at him, he'd hit her, she'd hit him back, and they'd end up in a tangle on the floor. Then, before dinner was even contemplated, they'd shoot heroin together and pass out. This was the only time they were quiet. They were black and blue and battered, but they'd nod out holding hands and smiling.

Jay wanted no part of this craziness, so every night at dinnertime, he escaped to his best friend Khalil's apartment two floors down. Khalil's family was the exact opposite of Jay's. Whereas Linda always spoke in a near-shriek, no one in Khalil's family seemed to speak at all. They seemed totally uninvolved with one another. His mother, Janet, and his stepfather, Frank, never spoke to each other. Khalil never spoke to them. In fact, Khalil loathed them, especially Frank, which mystified Jay, who loved their silence. To him, it was a blessed relief from the turbulence upstairs. After dinner, Jay and Khalil would play Space Invaders until Frank came in, oddly averting his eyes, and announced that it was time for him to check Khalil's homework. Jay would then return upstairs. He'd step over his parents, take a bath, and put himself to bed.

One night when Jay was seven, he was having dinner at Khalil's, as usual. At their dinner table, his chair faced the window, which looked out over the dilapidated playground. During Janet's pound cake, he saw his parents free-falling through the sky.

Everyone ran to the window and saw Linda and Jerome lying faceup on the cement, holding hands and smiling. Janet began screaming, but Jay was used to seeing them like this. He knew something terrible had happened, but it felt very far away from him, like the starving Ethiopians on TV. From then on, he lived with Khalil.

The two of them were inseparable, though they were almost polar opposites. K, as everyone called him, was the tough boy in the neighborhood. He took absolutely no shit, none. He was short and chubby, but remarkably fast. K always had an answer for everything and was quick to fight. It was as if he had two personalities— at home he was tight-lipped and subservient. Outside, he was explosive. Big on action, he wasn't a talker. Jay, on the other hand, talked everyone to death. He was a tall, skinny, animated kid who was adept at slipping out of near-fatal situations. No one ever messed with him. First of all, K would kill anyone who tried, and second, because he always had such good ideas.

When Jay and K where nine, they became lookout boys for the local gang of crack dealers, led by a frighteningly gaunt eighteen-year-old named Bone. While Bone negotiated deals, Jay and K rode their bikes up and down the block, looking out for police, or strangers who looked suspiciously unsuspicious. After the two boys spotted a middle-aged white man in hip-hop clothes (and knocked him out with Jay's boom box), they were each given a .38-caliber pistol and a promotion.

The boys were assigned to count the sale receipts in the "stash" apartment, which was conveniently located three floors down from K's. After school, the boys would count the thousands of dollars with their state-of-the-art Commodore calculator. They'd rap their favorite songs (anything by DJ Kool Herc, Grandmaster Flash, or Afrika Bambaataa) and force whoever forgot the words to say "uncle."

One day, the boys heard sirens and a furious pounding at the door. Thinking quickly, they stuffed all the bills into their backpacks and ran for the back window. Below was a pile of trash bags. They looked at each other, figured seven stories wasn't exactly *fatal*, and jumped out onto the trash bags. Jay's cheek was sliced open from a broken wine bottle, and K broke his arm, but they escaped with all the cash. It was a star-making feat.

Jay and K's ability to pull this off earned them much-coveted respect from Bone's crew, and they were deemed mascots. Bone began calling the two boys "Nuts." Because they always hung together. But mostly because they were crazy.

The next couple of years were a flurry of successful errands, schemes, and heists. Life was lovely. School was easy, making money was easy, and because of his "Nuts" status, Jay held the privilege of partying with the older crowd. In the summer, DJ Kaptin Krunch would plug his turntables into a streetlight, spin records like "Top Billin'" and "The Real Roxanne," and madness would ensue. These parties lasted till dawn and passed in a blur of shell-topped Adidas, velour tracksuits, and mushroom hairdos.

Due to the Nuts' mascot status, their best friends, Yellow Andre, Black Andre, and Darryl, were deemed cool, too. Less clever than Jay and K, they weren't in the game, but they were master shit-talkers and could hold their liquor. During the summers, the boys included Bone's surly little cousin TyJuan in the group, though he was far less entertaining.

In the winter, Kaptin Krunch moved his parties into his apartment on Cumberland Street, where sometimes the high voltage of his equipment would cause a power shortage. No one cared. Boys took turns freestyling while Krunch beatboxed. Some brave soul would inevitably move the furniture, produce a cardboard box, and break dance — risking being dissed if the crowd sniffed a poseur. At one of these wintertime parties the Nuts lost their virginity. Bone got them high on all sorts of things, and thrust them in a room with everybody's favorite hood rat, Sonata. Jay-Nut and K-Nut were both forever changed. K decided never to touch another girl with a Jheri curl, and Jay became a Lover. He fell hopelessly in love with Sonata, and she him. They decided to go together. Sonata was sixteen and Jay was twelve.

This was as good as it gets. Clout, cash, and ass.

The summer after eighth grade, everything changed. First of all, Bone's crew got busted, and they all went to jail. This was terrifying, and everyone went underground. After this, it became clear to Jay that shit flows downhill.

The Nuts slept in bunkbeds, Jay on the bottom and K on top. Since Jay's parents' death, he hadn't been able to sleep through the night. Without fail, he'd wake up at 3 A.M., with no hope of going back to sleep for hours. During this time, he would write in a steno notebook he entitled "My History." He wrote short stories about his day, his friends, and Irene Cara. Then he read until he fell asleep. (His favorite authors were Donald Goines, infamous writer of junkie/pimp fiction, Edgar Allan Poe, and Robert Ludlum. He checked these out from the library on Hall Place — this was far enough away from his building that he wouldn't be caught in this rep-shattering act.)

Sometimes during his insomnia bouts, Jay would notice that K wasn't in bed. He couldn't see up there, but he could just feel it. He never asked K where he went. He reasoned that at night, everyone has their own agenda. You don't have to answer to anyone, and you don't have to deal with daytime rules. Jay read and wrote in secret, so he respected whatever K was getting into.

One night, Jay got up to get a drink of water. In the dark, he padded toward the kitchen and stopped abruptly in his tracks. He heard Frank ordering K to do things to him, in a raspy whisper. Jay's blood froze, and he stopped breathing. Later, when K crawled up the ladder to the top bunk, he pretended to be asleep. He pretended not to hear K say, "Got to, or he'll kill her." Jay said nothing, and never did. Most middle-of-the-night happenings are remembered like fragmented dream scenes, but K's calmly resigned "everybody has their cross to bear" voice would reverberate in his mind forever.

The next day was a Saturday, and K woke up wanting to fight. After Masters of the Universe and He-Man, they knocked on doors and rounded up their friends. It was a blazing day in August, a month before school would start. Everyone was restless, over-heated, and end-of-summer bored. Jay, K, the two Andres, Darryl, and TyJuan stood on the corner, chain-smoking, waiting for an opportunity to present itself. It came in the swaggering form of Paco, a Puerto Rican thug from Spanish Harlem. What the fuck was he doing there? Paco used to go with Darryl's older sister, Margie, but disappeared soon after she gave birth to a pink, curly-haired boy. Also, Darryl suspected he was responsible for Margie's messy suicide attempt. (Who really believed her bloodied wrists were the result of a nail file accident?) Given these factors, no one could figure out what Paco was doing on their block by himself.

Jay proclaimed it divine intervention. His friends bought this, and jumped Paco. After the other boys were through, K continued to pummel Paco unmercifully (much to the consternation of Darryl, who felt K was stealing his moment). Jay finally had to drag him off, wildly punching the air. They fled the scene, leaving Paco a complete mess and mumbling revenge epithets in Spanglish.

Two days later, word got around to Nuts and company that a group of Puerto Rican boys were rumored to be somewhere on Fulton Ave. They hid out at Black Andre's apartment to assess the situation (save for TyJuan, who, after the Paco thing, decided now was as good a time as any to catch the train back to Philly). K was furious, and refused to hide like a pussy in his own neighborhood. His warlike bravado got everyone excited for battle. They grabbed their pistols and flew down the eleven flights of stairs (the elevator hadn't worked in fifteen years). They burst through the double doors and were met with a hail of eardrum-shattering bullets. Paco and his friends were speeding away in a stolen car, firing ill-aimed shots out of the windows. The two Andres and Darryl jumped back behind the steel door at the last second. But a bullet passed through Jay's left shoulder and struck K in the heart. He was killed instantly. It all happened in a matter of seconds, in broad daylight.

Everything stopped for Jay. The shot to his shoulder knocked him to the ground. His body wanted to lose consciousness, but he fought it and managed to stand up. The two Andres and Darryl were shouting for help and frantically shaking K's limp body, but Jay stumbled away. He couldn't look at his friend like that. Darryl kept shouting after him that Paco and them were long gone, but Jay wasn't going after Paco. Why get into a war that wouldn't end until everybody was dead? K was already gone.

Instead, Jay's feet took him to the nearby Brooklyn Academy of Music, where Frank was a janitor. He wandered through the echoing corridors and eventually found him, mopping the men's room. He could tell Frank was surprised to see him. Jay told him that Khalil was dead, but Frank said nothing. In a blind rage, Jay grabbed his face and slammed it against the tiled wall, knocking him to the floor. Frank didn't put up much of a fight. Jay pistol-whipped him until he could no longer raise his arm and Frank was semiconscious. Wordlessly, he held the mouth of the bloody pistol to Frank's temple. He kept it there for a while, lost in thought. Finally, he pocketed the pistol and pulled out his house key. Steadying his hand, he carved a huge, unmistakable "K" on Frank's forehead. He took all the money in Frank's wallet ($17) and stumbled off. He never saw Frank or Janet again.

4.
accidentally sexy

I
t was one on Saturday, and a bright, gorgeous day in the West Village. Billie hurried down rainbow-flagged Christopher Street toward Bleecker. All morning, she'd been hovering near hysteria. She'd revisited and revisited the previous night until it became surreal. She prepared herself for being stood up.

Billie dressed hot, though, just in case. After serious deliberation, she'd decided on a look she termed "Accidentally Sexy." She wore skinny gold hoop earrings, a short, yellow Betsey Johnson slipdress, a little jean jacket, and tan knee-high stiletto boots. Pocahontas meets Chiquita Banana.

Nonchalantly, Billie strode into the Biography Bookshop. Most of New York was still asleep, so the store was empty. Except for Jay, who was knee-deep in the true-crime section. He'd shown! She snuck up behind him and tapped him on the shoulder.

"Hi."

"Hey! What's up, ma?" He hugged her, careful not to touch anything important.

"How are you?"

"All right." He not-so-subtly looked her up and down, eyes widening. "Yellow is a good color."

"Thanks." Billie smiled fetchingly. "What are you reading?" She peered at the open book in his hands. It was a biography of Lizzie Borden.

"Yikes. Didn't she slaughter her parents with a hatchet in the eighteen hundreds?"

"An axe. But I only picked it up because I used to love the TV movie about her."

"There was a TV movie about Lizzie Borden?"

"Way, way back in the day. Elizabeth Montgomery played her. After *Bewitched*. You know how Lizzie takes off her bloody clothes and throws them in the fireplace?"

Billie nodded. "To destroy the evidence."

"Right," he said. "In the movie, they showed Elizabeth Montgomery naked from the back. This was a key moment in my sexual awakening."

"Really? Elizabeth Montgomery?"

"I mean, look. I'm eight. I'm looking at a woman who, to me, is a virginal, suburban housewife with flipped-up hair. All of a sudden she's naked and bloody. That mad titillating."

"Ohh-kay." Billie searched for something cute to say. "Maybe you just have a thing for witches."

He raised an eyebrow at her. "Maybe you're right. So, tell me why we're here."

"What?" She panicked—this had been his idea!

He smiled. "Why is this your favorite place?"

"Oh. Well, I love old bookstores. And I'm obsessed with biographies, especially ones about really fabulous women. Divas, really."

"What do you consider a diva?"

"Hmmm. A woman with a lust for living, who has epic love affairs, a glittery career. A woman with, um, balls."

"Okay. So, what's your favorite biography?"

"Well, hmmm. I'll read anything about Zora Neale Hurston. Her life was so fascinating. I mean, this is a woman who wrote *Their Eyes Were Watching God*, the most perfect novel ever" — Jay nodded in agreement — "in *seven weeks*. She totally revolutionized Southern fiction, and died a broke waitress. It's a very romantic, tragic story." She paused. "And I have another favorite, but you have to promise not to laugh or think I'm wack."

"I promise."

"Elizabeth Taylor."

"No."

"Look, if Elizabeth Montgomery ushered you into manhood, I can have a Liz Taylor fetish."

"Okay, you got that. Why, though?"

"Her life is *cinematic*. She was beautiful, beautiful, beautiful. She had great loves, broke up marriages, won Oscars. All her husbands went broke buying her the world's most expensive jewelry. How do you get eight men in a row to do that?" Billie shook her head in awe. "She never second-guesses herself. She's gutsy, and glamorous, and a broad — "

"And a drunk, and a slovenly mess . . ."

Billie grabbed one of her biographies from the entertainment section. "Look at this woman, she's flawless." The cover illustrated the icon in full mid-sixties mode, huge bouffant, major cleavage, the whole nine.

"Her hair looks like a Peppermint Pattie."

"You were supposed to not be laughing at me."

"I ain't laughing, just bewildered." He looked at Billie standing there with her hands on her hips. "You know something?"

"What?"

"I find it hard to believe that you don't know how to make a man do whatever you want. Buying jewelry, or otherwise."

"I didn't go to that school," she said.

"Hah."

"Clearly *you* did."

"What do you mean?"

"You didn't ask me to meet you here, you told me. And I'm here."

"Somebody had to do something. You were being molested."

"If you want something you just take it, huh?"

"Me and Elizabeth Taylor."

"So why didn't you kiss me?"

"I told you why."

"But you *wanted* to," Billie said. She was feeling saucy and completely out of character. "So what if you didn't stop?"

"I knew you couldn't handle it."

"Excuse me?!"

Jay laughed. "You couldn't. You're, like, delicate."

"I'm not that delicate." She stepped toward him and tried to look brazen.

"Why are you blushing, then?"

"Honestly?"

"Honestly."

She took a deep breath and went for it. "You smell so good I want to bite you?"

"Do it, then," he dared.

She grabbed his arm and bit his bicep.

"God*damn*!" Jay said, rubbing his arm. The hipster salesgirl looked at them curiously from behind the register. "I think I'm delirious."

"Oh, I didn't hurt you." Billie's heart was racing. She was not delicate. She was a wanton animal.

Jay shook his head and grabbed her shoulders. "Okay, listen. We're gonna make some rules. If you want to bite me, bite me. If you want to tell me something, say it. Life's too short to waste time blushing and shoving tea in my face and being all nervous and shit. You're driving me crazy."

The salesgirl nodded to herself. Right on.

"Okay. I think . . ."

Before she figured out what she thought, he put his hands on either side of her face and kissed her. His kiss was slow and deliberate. He sucked her mouth, sucked her tongue, relishing her. Softly, he bit her bottom lip and her knees buckled.

Billie was drowning. She grabbed the back of his shirt in her fists and held on for dear life. Hungrily, he kissed her deeper. Shamelessly, she wrapped her leg around him. He pushed his leg in between her thighs, ran his hands over her ass, and pulled her to him. She moaned, instinctively grinding her hips against his.

The salesgirl's mouth dropped open.

Billie's head fell back, and Jay seared her neck with soft kisses and love bites. When he reached her ear he whispered, "I will fuck you right here in front of this girl if we don't leave," and ran his tongue over her earlobe. Billie managed to nod in agreement before melting into another of his devastating, all-consuming kisses. Without breaking it, they somehow stumbled out of the store and into a cab.

Billie and Jay couldn't keep their hands off each other. Ripping off her jean jacket, she straddled his lap and kissed him anxiously. He pulled the spaghetti straps down over her shoulders and her flimsy dress fell to her waist. When he unfastened her strapless bra, he stopped breathing. He'd never seen breasts that full on a girl that small. With a muffled "Oh my God" he pushed them together and ran his tongue over her taut nipples, kissing and softly sucking them. The scandalized cabdriver almost ran through an intersection (atop his dashboard sat a photo of his adolescent daughters left back in Calcutta, which he quickly flipped facedown).

Billie trembled, her whole body aflame. It was broad daylight, and she couldn't have cared less—she wanted him. She pushed up his shirt and ran her hands over his obscenely well-sculpted chest. Unzipping his jeans, she found his cock, rock-hard and huge. Following the new rules, she climbed off him and knelt on the floor of the cab. She took him in her mouth. He groaned and commanded her to stop. She ignored him. He felt the situation called for a power shift. Jay pulled her up onto the seat. Sliding her dress up to her waist, he found a see-through thong with "Saturday" embroidered across the front. Awww. He grinned and bent down, hooking his arms under her thighs.

Through the flimsy material, he lightly flicked her with his tongue. She let out a broken little moan. He thought this was cute, so he teased her with another chaste lick. Pleasure tore through Billie. Boldly, she grabbed his face and pushed him into her. Then he pulled her thong to the side and ate her so deliciously and thoroughly that Billie became religious. Her moans got louder as he sucked and licked and sucked and she was so wet and she arched her back and he told her to come in his mouth as if she had a choice and then she exploded with a fearsome shudder.

They were in front of her brownstone building. Billie was half-naked and in a languid stupor. She thought to herself, "I am a whore," and smiled. Jay paid the sweating driver and half dragged, half carried Billie to her first-floor walk-up. She fumbled with the keys for what seemed like hours, because his mouth was on the back of her neck and his fingers were deep inside her and she felt that in seconds she would come again. Instead, he grabbed the keys from her and they finally burst through the door. Lips locked, they fell on the couch together. Somehow, everyone's clothes came off and Jay was on top of her, covering her with his strong, lean body. He slid just the tip of his cock inside her. She gasped. His lips softly touched hers. Trembling, they breathed each other's breath. He sank in slightly deeper. Softly, she cried out. Holding himself back, not wanting it to end, he pulled out almost completely.

"How much do you want?" he asked her.

"Everything, all of it," she breathed, out of her mind.

"You sure?"

"Yes, yes . . ."

He held her hands on either side of her head, kissed her deeply, and plunged into her as far as he could go. She arched into his thrust and came, her senses shattered. He kept going, fucking her and fucking her until she came again, brighter than before, and so did he.

* * *

Jay didn't say, "You're mine, you've always been mine," and Billie didn't say, "I've been waiting for you my whole life." They didn't say these things to each other because it wouldn't ring true after knowing each other less than twenty-four hours. Instead, they lay naked on her rose-embroidered couch, in her shabby chic studio (which had never seen a man, naked or otherwise), and talked circles around "I need you I want you I love you."

Billie and Jay were thrilled at what they discovered, which was that much of the same *stuff* floated around in their heads. They became obsessed with traversing each other's brains. They reminisced over "The Bloodhound Gang," and *Right On* magazine, and *The Last Dragon* (Jay had been "Sho Nuff" one Halloween, and Billie knew all the words to Vanity's "Seventh Heaven" song). They argued over whether the best Seinfeld episode was "Junior Mints Surgery" or "Mulva," and realized they were the same episode. The following were the hardest motherfuckers, ever: Miles Davis, Geronimo Pratt, and Sonny Corleone. They wondered whether, in real life, Rocky would ever have beaten Apollo Creed. Billie loved Anaïs Nin, Jay loved Henry Miller—and the memoirists had loved each other, too, which was a nice thing. Both missed Jodeci and Jell-O Pudding Pops. They were intrigued by the Doors and anything starring Robert Mitchum. They hated the phrase "the black experience" because it suggested only one. They agreed that Old Dirty Bastard taking a limo to pick up his welfare check, on MTV, was trifling. They both got Evelyn "Champagne" King and Cheryl "Pepsi" Riley confused, but were aware of the vast differences between Jeffrey Osborne and James Ingram. Sometimes, at night, Jack Torrance stormed the hotel hallways in their minds. *On the Road* made them both want to, oh, just get away from it all. They traded dialogue from *The Mack*. They didn't trust religious fanatics, or anyone who didn't recognize that *The Golden Girls* was hilarious. They both figured that the voice of God probably sounded a lot like Nas. They didn't say what they didn't know, which was how incredibly lonely they'd been until today.

"Quiz!" announced bruised-lipped Billie, who was draped around Jay like a sari.

"Okay."

"Mel Gibson or Mel Brooks."

"What? Mel Gibson is garbage." He paused. "Actually, *Braveheart* was kinda all right. But Mel Brooks wins, without question. Madeline Kahn singing 'Sweet Mystery of Life' in *Young Frankenstein? Blazing Saddles?* Even though Richard Pryor wrote half of it, the man's a genius."

"I support that."

"Tony Montana, Tony Manero, or Toni Morrison?"

"Hah! Well, Tony Montana has the whole 'Say hello to my li'l friend' thing, which is an important moment for everyone. The American Dream, soured. Tony Manero overcame his Italian-American inner-city rage in a Bensonhurst disco, which is sort of fascinating if you think about it. And the Bee Gees, forget it." She paused, lost in thought. "I have to say that *Scarface* and *Saturday Night Fever* are iconic — but really dated. Toni Morrison is timeless. *Beloved* blows your mind every time you read it."

"No doubt, no doubt. Nicely executed, good delivery."

"NCAA or NBA?"

"NCAA. There's more heart in the game without the dollars."

"Good answer. Who's the bigger playa, JFK or Bill Clinton?"

"JFK, easily. They're both playas. But you always know a true playa by the company he keeps. Bill married Hillary, who's mad intelligent but homely. JFK married Jackie, a fly debutante in pimped-out sunglasses. Bill runs around with women like Gennifer Flowers and Monica Lewinsky. JFK ran around with Marilyn Monroe and Angie Dickinson. If you're gonna get caught out there, make it *count*. This is a *gangsta* we're talking about."

"Angie Dickinson was a gangsta, too. She slept with the entire Rat Pack."

"True." He kissed the top of her head. "Billie?"

"Hmm?"

"Your hair smells like peppermint."

"Aveda Rosemary Mint shampoo."

"Billie?" He enjoyed saying her name, like when you learn a really good word.

"Hmm?"

"What's the worst thing that ever happened to you?"

"Last year I had to write an article about getting a Brazilian bikini wax. Do you know what that is?"

"Um, no."

"It's when you get everything waxed off. All your pubes. It's very trendy among, you know, raised-pinkie-finger types. So I go to get this thing done, right? Everybody at work says it's no big thing, you hardly feel it. So I'm not worried. I go to the salon and wait in this tiny room. In comes a mean, mean old Brazilian woman. I'm instructed to take off everything from the waist down, lay on this table, and hold my knees to my chest. She lays down a layer of boiling hot wax and rips it off. Jay, I'm telling you, I can't even relate this pain to anything you'd understand. I begged her to stop. She ignored me and did it anyway. I'm sobbing."

"Stop playin'."

"Then she orders me to get on all fours."

"Stop playin'!"

"I'm serious. It was the most mortifying experience of my life. And the whole time I'm thinking to myself, this costs a hundred dollars. Women *pay* for this. This is a choice. If someone chased you down a dark alley and poured hot wax in your ass, you'd have them arrested."

Jay appeared disturbed. "I'm speechless."

"It's okay."

They lay together in comfortable silence for a while.

"What's the worst thing that ever happened to you?"

Jay thought about this. He didn't know how to rank the things that had happened to him. To him, his story was just his story. Everybody has one. Either you learn how to live with it, or it eats you up. But Billie was totally unlike anyone he knew. The girls he grew up with were wily and thick-skinned. They'd lived five life-times by the time they were sixteen. Billie's worst experience had occurred at a spa. Jay wanted to protect her. He didn't want to fuck her up. He didn't know what she could take, and he didn't want her to go. Ever.

"I don't know."

"What's the best thing that ever happened to you?"

Jay looked at Billie. He tilted her chin up and kissed her sweetly. She wouldn't believe him if he told her.

* * *

After he had left K's father, Jay wandered in circles until it was dark. He was losing a lot of blood from the gunshot wound. People he knew called out to him and offered help, but he just kept walking. Around 1 A.M., he found himself sitting on a crate in front of a bodega in Clinton Hill, the next neighborhood over. He was reeling. He was surrounded by groups of teenagers smoking weed and generally fucking around. Eric B. and Rakim's

"Paid In Full" was blaring out of a huge, silver boom box. Across the street, a cluster of old men sat on folding chairs wiping their sweaty faces with handkerchiefs and drinking Schlitz malt liquor. Four little girls were playing a heated game of double Dutch on the corner. This wasn't his territory, but no one bothered him. In the dark, no one could tell he was covered in blood, but the look on his face was not sporting.

Eventually, a tiny, rail-thin girl approached him. She was wearing cut-off denim shorts and a striped tube top. Her face was pockmarked, and she had deep bags under her eyes. She looked no older than twelve. She asked him if he wanted his dick sucked. He said he didn't. She asked him if he wanted to fuck. He said he didn't. She asked him what he wanted, then. He said, "A bed." She said, "Come on," and he followed her up the block.

They stopped at a dilapidated Victorian apartment building. The girl fumbled with her key for what seemed like hours. Finally, she managed to unlock the door, and Jay followed her up three trash-strewn flights of stairs to a graffitied door. Inside, it was totally dark. Judging from the lively grunts and groans, there seemed to be people fucking all over the apartment. Stumbling over a writhing couple on the floor, she led Jay into a closet-sized bedroom in the back. She turned on the light and there were two men and a girl in a sweaty knot on a mattress on the floor. The girl screamed at them to get out, and didn't they know the rules, that this was *her* room. She slapped the naked girl across the face, who slinked out of the room, followed by the irritated men. With disgust, the tiny girl snatched the outdated, psychedelic-printed sheet off the mattress and threw it in the hallway. Wearily, she looked at Jay and saw the state he was in.

"Jesus Fucking Christ! Get in here! Somebody followin' you?"

He shook his head, shutting the door behind him. He collapsed on the mattress and put his good arm over his eyes. The room was 100 degrees, at least. The girl took the pillowcase off the pillow and tied it around his arm, like a tourniquet. She scurried out of the room and came back with a wet towel and a blunt. Gingerly, she began mopping off the dried blood on his arm. She lit the blunt and popped it in his mouth.

"Can you hit the lights?" Jay muttered, inhaling deeply. He didn't want to look at anything. She hopped up, flicked the switch, and resumed her position. They sat there in silence, the sounds of fucking all around them. Slowly, the weed eased some of his pain. The girl felt his forehead. His skin was ablaze with fever. Again, she disappeared. She returned with a washcloth soaked in cold water and placed it over his eyes. He lay there, floating in and out of consciousness, while she sat cross-legged next to him. The tiny girl watched him, curiously. After a time, she spoke up.

"Are you runnin' from something or somebody?"

"I ain't runnin'."

"Why you here, then?"

Jay didn't know.

"What happened?" Her question was met with silence. "Listen, I don't know nobody. I ain't from here," she said. "I won't say anything."

He didn't know why he told her. Maybe it was because he was in shock. Or maybe he responded somehow to her soothing voice, or felt safe because she was a complete stranger. But he told her what had happened. The girl held him in her skinny arms, and he trusted her.

In return, she told him her story. Her name was Tammy. She was seventeen and from Newark, New Jersey. Her teenaged mother ran away when she was an infant, and she was raised by her grandfather. He was a fanatically religious alcoholic, and beat her up on Sundays for sins he imagined she'd committed. When she became pregnant at fifteen, he almost killed her. She suffered a violent miscarriage and moved in with her boyfriend, a twenty-seven-year-old hustler. Two months later, her boyfriend woke up on Rikers, and she was stuck with a $600 rent. Tammy began bagging groceries at Safeway and baby-sitting. Struggling. She started drinking heavily and hanging out with her boyfriend's brother, a charming junkie named Damon. Eventually she moved in with him. And stayed drunk. Often, during Damon's parties, he would pass her around to his friends in exchange for drugs. Tammy was rarely coherent.

One night, she slept with Damon's cousin Cap (short for Capricorn). He was an up-and-coming pimp from Bed Stuy, and managed to lure her away from Damon with the promise of cash and a rent-free apartment. She was thrilled to find out he wasn't lying. All things considered, Cap was a good guy. He never hit her, or any of the girls she lived with, and wouldn't let the johns mistreat her, either. Unfortunately, his crack habit proved to be contagious, and she was now a full-blown addict.

Tammy began to cry. Her life sounded horrible out loud. Then for the first time that nightmare day, Jay cried. For hours they cried for each other. The windowless, boiling, pitch-black room became a kind of confessional. They gave up their secrets, copped to their fears, and made promises. At dawn, they had sorrowful, necessary sex. She did everything. It wasn't love sex; it was blood-brother sex. Without saying it, the two knew they were now inextricably joined for life.

The next afternoon, Tammy presented Jay to Cap as her long-lost, distant cousin, and asked if he could stay. The chubby man jumped at the sight of the obviously ill boy.

Cap looked long and hard at Jay and said, "You Jerome Lane's son?" Jay looked miserable enough to prove that this was true. "I knew your pops. S'shame. He was a funny motherfucker." Jay was kind of intrigued. He didn't know a thing about his father, and an utter stranger—a pimp—was telling him he was funny. His mood lightened a bit. A bit.

Cap decided that Jay could stay in Tammy's room, under three conditions: He had to disappear when she was working; he couldn't fuck her unless he paid; and he had to be Cap's crack gopher. This meant nothing more than taking his money, buying drugs for him, and bringing them back. Jay happily accepted the rules. Cap then escorted him to the emergency room, and Jay began a new life. The first thing he did after leaving the hospital was buy a notebook. He began writing a new history.

Jay's position as a crack gopher turned out to be a profitable career opportunity. Turning on his infectious personality, he convinced the local crack baron to let him start selling some, here and there. In a matter of weeks, Jay had regulars. Hundreds of dollars turned into thousands. Jay didn't care, he just wanted to make enough money to take care of himself and Tammy, his new sister. He wanted a better life for her, but she had to want it, first. Jay figured out how to trick her into quitting crack. At the Nathan's on Thirty-fourth Street, Jay announced to Tammy that he wasn't going back to school.

"*What?*" Jay was the smartest person she'd ever met, and this was almost sinful to her. "You got too much brains not to go to school."

"Baby, I got too much *paper* to go to school. I ain't gotta do shit."

"If you don't go to school, I'm kicking you out."

"You ain't kickin' nobody out."

"Watch."

Jay considered this.

"Okay. If I go to school, you gotta quit smoking."

"How you gonna ask me to do that, when you out sellin' the shit?"

"Sellin' and smokin' is two vastly different things. Smokers are puppets, and sellers pull the strings. If you ain't playin' the game, the game's playin' you. How long you wanna be played?"

"It ain't that easy and you know it."

"Okay, look. We'll buy some hot dogs and some Skittles. I'll get you some tapes"—in three weeks' time, Jay had made enough money to buy Tammy a TV, VCR, and stereo—"and we'll lock ourselves in that room till you over it."

Tammy looked terrified. "I don't know, I can't . . ." But she trusted Jay more than anyone else in the world. If he said she could do it, then she could.

"What do you wanna do when you grow up, Tammy?"

"What kinda question is that?"

"What you wanna be?"

Tammy looked dreamy. "I always wanted to do hair and have my own salon. Back home, not here. I'm good at it."

"Ain't nobody gonna pay no jittery crackhead to do they hair."

"Fuck you."

"Think I'm playing? Look, you gotta get outta Cap's. That ain't no kinda life, what you doing. I know you ain't had a choice, but you do now. I got enough money for us to get our own place. You gotta quit. Both. And I'll promise to go to fucking ridiculous ninth grade." He took the last bite of his second hot dog and looked at her expectantly.

"Fine but I hate Skittles," she said, her enormous doorknocker earrings bobbing.

That night, Tammy told Cap she was sick and couldn't work. Then she and Jay locked themselves in her room. The first night was agony. The second night she prayed to die. On the third night, she finally slept. The next morning, August 30, 1987, she woke up and smiled at Jay. It was his fourteenth birthday.

He got Tammy and himself a huge apartment in his old neighborhood, and started his freshman year. In a high school full of hustlers, he became almost a cult figure. He rose through the ranks from street dealer to street manager. A kind of middleman between the dealers and the suppliers, he handled distribution. This was an underage orphan who, somehow, had managed to become a crack executive and rent his own crib (shady landlords were abundant in the drug-controlled neighborhood). He made everything look effortless, and mysterious. Who was that quiet, older girl he lived with? Where'd he disappeared to after K got shot? Even more curiously, he wasn't flashy about the fact that he was so incredibly *paid*. He pushed a very used Beamer. He barely had any furniture in his apartment. He didn't spend all his cash on jewelry. It was like he was too cool to profile. People treated him like he was Superfly. It was a favorite pastime for classmates to sneak into BAM to see if they could spot Khalil's father, who had a gnarly "K" emblazoned on his forehead. Rumor had it that he had something to do with K's death, and his guilty brand had to be Jay's doing. Who else was crazy enough to do some gangster-revenge shit like that? He was a legend. Boys wanted to be him, girls wanted to be next to him. Everybody was in awe.

Jay was oblivious to his reputation, and if you told him that he was the mayor of Fort Greene at fourteen, he'd deny it. He moved through life in a kind of fog. Everything was mechanical. Still, he had that quality that made people want to know him. He had so many selves occupying his body—drug dealer, intellectual, thug, orphan, caregiver—that everyone could relate to one. But Jay couldn't relate to anyone—not even to Tammy, on some levels. She was older than him, but he took care of her. He wasn't her peer.

Of course, being a teenager, he obviously wasn't immune to girls. He took them out sometimes, fucked them, whatever, he wasn't really there. Jay lived inside his head. He always had to keep his mind occupied. Whenever he could, he threw himself into books and movies (he had no discretion, he'd go to anything that was playing—he saw *Mannequin* three times). He filled up his mind with made-up stories. It was the only way he could drown out the memory of Khalil's horrible, middle-of-the-night voice.

He was failing everything at school. He knew he really didn't even have to be there—but he had to keep busy, he had to outrun his thoughts. He was like a machine. Totally preoccupied, he wrote through all his classes. One day, his furious English teacher, Miss McCargo, asked him what was more important than her lesson on *Catcher in the Rye*.

"Many things, seeing as how I read it when I was nine," Jay replied.

She snatched the notebook off his desk and was astonished to find a beautifully written short story. Miss McCargo submitted his story to a writing contest at the tony Eardale Academy on the Upper East Side. He won a full scholarship.

He spent the next three years profiting from some of Manhattan's richest, youngest crackheads. They thought he was "rad!" Fancy Education Boy was added to his list of personalities.

Meanwhile, Jay put Tammy through cosmetology school. Jay and Cap (who gracefully accepted her career change) were there at her graduation, beaming like proud parents. Jay's present to Tammy was not only her own salon, but also the apartment above it—in her hometown, Newark.

Their separation was teary and sad, but Tammy was finally living her dream. His work done, he retired. He passed the torch to Black Andre, who had been shadowing him for years. He had cash for the rest of his life.

Jay graduated from Eardale in 1991 with a creative writing scholarship to the University of Virginia. He lasted there for two weeks. He loathed the South. It took people too long to talk.

He came home and embarked on what he would later call his "Blue Period." Jay was aimless. None of his old crew was around. Yellow Andre, Darryl, and Bone were in jail. Black Andre, who wasn't blessed with Jay's wiles, was shot and killed in '92.

Jay rented a huge, impersonal, industrial loft in Williamsburg, Brooklyn, miles away from Fort Greene. The neighborhood was virtually empty save for some abandoned warehouses. Jay spent the next couple of years drunk, high, and wide awake. Sometimes, nerves completely shot with insomnia, he'd catch the NJ Transit and seek refuge at Tammy's. They'd have their therapeutic, nonsexual sex. Despite the vaguely incestuous undertones—or because of them—he'd temporarily feel reconnected.

Eventually, he ran out of cash and started hustling again. Low-level. After some research, he found out that the real money was in heroin. Grunge was in full swing, and the East Village was full of white slackers scouring the streets for a hit. Jay claimed the corner of Second Street and Ave. D. This was two blocks from the famous Nuyorican Poets Café, where the early nineties' spoken word/slam poetry revolution originated. On slow nights, he'd stop by the café and listen to poets like Saul Williams, Paul Beatty, and Jessica Care Moore. They were becoming Names, publishing books, and reading in places like London and Amsterdam. Inspired, he began to rise out of his funk. He started writing short stories again. One of his café clients, a scatterbrained, purple-haired Columbia student named Adam Wunderman, owed Jay money. Adam never went to his creative writing class (at 10 A.M., it was too early for him) and knew Jay was a writer, so he offered to let Jay attend it, free of charge. All he had to do was use his name. Jay became Jewish for art.

The class ("Yeah, my name's Adam but my friends call me Jay") was a workshop format, where you read your work out loud and the students critiqued you. When he read what would become the "old man on the stoop" monologue, a cute girl named LaLa began hyperventilating. She wore a dyed-orange Afro and a dashiki, and hosted an open-mike night at Brooklyn Moon Café. Immediately, she asked him to be a guest. He agreed, and was an immediate scene-stealer.

And then it happened the way things happen. His name was on everyone's lips. A woman in the audience invited him to a showcase downtown at School of Collective Thought. Jay became a regular there, and the owner of the East Village's Performance Space 122 asked him to write a one-man show. He started making money and dropped hustling for good. One thing led to another, and he ended up at Public Theater, causing all kinds of stirs.

This is how a boy from the projects becomes a sensation in NY.

Speaking of success, Tammy's salon hit the ground running. So she wouldn't confuse herself with the messy girl she once was, she went by her middle name, Pandora.

Billie, Vida, and Renee were having Sunday brunch at Chez Oskar. This ritual began two years before, when the trio moved out of their shared apartment and into ones of their own. Their careers had begun to hit their stride, and they were in danger of never seeing each other. So, every Sunday they took their place at the trendy bistro among the writers, musicians, engineers, artists, designers, and publishing folk who made up the turn-of-the-century Fort Greene scene.

Billie was deliriously, blissfully happy. Her entire body felt bruised and wonderful, and she was in love, love, love. Jay Lane was delicious, in every way imaginable. She was all atingle and couldn't calm down. Yet she was waiting for the right time to divulge her secret to Vida and Renee. This would blow their minds. Billie was used to hearing the details of Vida's torrid affairs and Renee's Go Down Moses, but she'd never had anything to tell.

The girls were discussing their week over omelettes and French toast.

"... and so, basically, I told Diana that she wanted to launch Sam C.'s perfume at a location that really says 'Thrust.' Somewhere that screams sex. And what venue is sexier than Heaven? On a *slow* night you have supermodels giving brain in the VIP lounge."

"So what did she say?" asked Renee.

"She said yes!"

They whisper-screamed, as it was a public place.

"Oh, Vida, that's so huge!" exclaimed Billie.

"I know, I know! I'm sure I can get at least two party photos into *New York* magazine."

"Of course," said Renee. "Without trying, even."

"You know I had a feeling about Heaven, from the very beginning." Vida sipped her mimosa. "I've never thrown a beauty event, though. Who should I put on the list? Besides my standard photogenica."

"Make sure you invite all the beauty editors from all the magazines. Even the teen ones. Sam C. is high-end, but you never know what they'll cover. Also, when a beauty event is so closely tied with fashion, the crowd is more intense. Especially since it's a night event and at Heaven *and* it's Sam C. The whole city'll be there."

Vida opened her mouth in a silent scream. "Okay, I can't talk about this anymore—I'm so excited I'm gonna earl." She changed the subject. "So, what are you gonna write about Fashion Week, Billie?"

Fashion Week was the furthest thing from Billie's mind, but she scanned her memory and recalled what she'd thought of the shows. "The whole week was an orgy of ethnic borrowing," she pronounced.

"Okay?" agreed Vida.

"How? Explain, explain," ordered Renee.

"Don't get me wrong, the shows were beautiful, they really were. But, look. Dale Bane's show was basically a parade of Chinese pajamas. The models were made up like China dolls. And I'm not even gonna talk about the Azucena event on Friday. It was Chinese everything—they even put a mah-jongg set in the gift bag."

"Is that racist?" Vida wondered aloud.

Billie continued. "The Kotillian show was a suede-and-fringe homage to Native Americans. Pocahontas braids, bronzer, the whole nine. Gaston Arnold was trying out, like, some kind of agresso-chic, Black Panther aesthetic."

"What?" Renee didn't do fashion speak.

"There were Black Power fists, Afros, and camouflage Nehru jackets. I don't know what he was thinking. And the Sam C. show was all ghetto, all the time. I mean, fully. Little minidresses that looked like they were made from FUBU jerseys. The models wore Timberlands and straight-outta-the-Bronx dark lip liner around frosted lipstick."

"You're kidding."

"I kid you not. But the models had these really beautiful corn-rows, and I found out backstage that a black girl—with her own sa-lon, mind you—did the hair. At least Sam C. was authentic about it. I was ready to be so mad at some Fifth Ave. stylist trying to tell me how to cornrow hair."

"Oh, don't get me started," said Vida. "That's so Bo Derek."

"Thank you. So I want to do an article on the inspiration for the ethnic beauty at the shows. Give a little credit where credit is due. Anyway, that's what I'm throwing around."

"That sounds hot, baby," Vida said, as she picked at Billie's un-eaten omelette. "It's so crazy. Black culture is *the* culture now. Every-body wants to be on some black shit. Look at Sarah Jessica Parker on *Sex and the City*. This girl is rocking Kangols, gold bamboo ear-rings, name plates. What is that? Rocking it like it's new. And now it's all the rage and high fashion cuz a white woman's wearing it."

"Girl, that ain't nothing new," said Renee. "That's America, always wanting to jock what we're doing. And claiming it, too.

Debbie Harry invented rap, Gwyneth Paltrow invented weaves, Elvis invented rock and roll . . ."

"As if Little Richard didn't even exist," added Vida.

"And the first rock star to wear eyeliner was Alice Cooper," said Billie.

"Yeah, when it all started with Little Richard!"

"Damn, Vida, are you related to Little Richard?"

"I just saw his Behind the Music," she replied sheepishly.

"Are the tables turning?" asked Billie. "We've spent the last four hundred years trying to define ourselves by white standards of beauty, trying to keep up with them. Ten years ago you had Spike Lee hating on Whoopi for her fake eyes. Now you have a former *Footloose* costar spending millions to look like Lil' Kim."

"Okay, ya'll are hating on Sarah Jessica Parker," Renee said, laughing. "Please admit the bitch is fly."

"Oh, without a doubt," said Vida. "Doorknocker earrings are mad cute. But I knew that when Salt-N-Pepa wore them in *nineteen eighty-six*."

"Everything comes back, and there's an inspiration for everything," said Billie. "But at least flip it on some new shit. Be creative."

"Like Madonna," said Vida. "She's a shameless cultural rapist, but she makes it interesting."

"What?" Renee was shocked. "How does Madonna flip it?"

"Don't mess with my girl," warned Vida.

"No, I love Madonna. But really. She had her black moment with 'Lucky Star.' Then she was Spanish for 'La Isla Bonita.' Recently, she was Hindu. Then she read *Memoirs of a Geisha* and became Japanese. We all read that book and loved it, but we didn't *become* Japanese. Now she's British."

"The Scone Age," said Billie.

The model/waitress came by to clear the table. Vida and Renee ordered café au laits, and Billie asked for a double espresso. She hadn't slept a wink the night before—there was too much to do.

"Renee," enthused Vida. "Good call with Jay Lane. He was incredible. That's a talented man—and *fine*. Oh my God."

Billie needed smelling salts.

"I know, I know!" said Renee. "In that article in the *Voice* he was so vague. But he has, I don't know, that thing. And he already has a manuscript written. It's a compilation of his monologues from *Nutz & Boltz*, plus tons of other ones. All I have to do is edit it."

"No!" exclaimed Vida.

"It's crazy. An easy A." Renee was hyper-animated. "Crawford & Collier's gonna sign him, I know it. There's nothing like an intelligent brother with street cred. It's like he was sent from heaven. We need his voice out there, girls."

"I know, right? And he has such a crush on you," Vida said to Billie. "Did you see the way he was looking at you? With those eyes?"

Billie felt faint. "No, I know. I know. Ladies, I have something to show you." Discreetly, she raised her knee-length denim skirt. On the upper reaches of her thigh was a trail of hickeys.

Vida and Billie screamed in the middle of Chez Oskar.

"Where did that come from?"

"Not Jay. Not Jay!"

Billie beamed, turned bright red, and hid behind her hands.

"Yes, yes, yes!" She was bursting at the seams. "Oh my God . . . you don't understand . . ."

"Honey, breathe," coached Vida. "When, where, and how did this debauchery begin?"

Billie told them about the theater, and the bookstore, and the cab, and her apartment. She told them about his hands and his brain and how they were with each other. When she was finished, Vida and Renee were gazing at her all dreamy-eyed.

"This is a beautiful thing," breathed Renee, as mushy as she gets.

"Look at our baby all grown up," Vida said proudly.

Billie hugged herself with glee. Then she got serious all of a sudden. "I don't know what to do with myself. It's like, he left this morning and I was devastated. I don't want to be without him. I'm completely out of my mind."

"Good!" exclaimed Vida. "It's about time you're outta your mind."

"But, and . . ." Billie struggled to find the words. "I feel so relieved. I know I've only known him for five minutes. But I feel like I've been waiting for him forever and now he's here and I'm just so *grateful*." She was aware she was gushing and felt ridiculous. "What, did I just win an Oscar? And I'd like to thank the Academy . . ."

"Girl, but that's how it feels when it's good," said Vida.

Renee looked sad. "I don't think I've ever felt *grateful* to know Moses."

"Oh, stop," said Vida. "Moses is your man. You've just been together too long for you to remember this part. Ya'll are like the Ropers."

"Thanks," said Renee.

Billie took a deep breath. "I think I love him."

Her friends looked at each other, eyebrows raised.

Vida gently placed her hand over Billie's. "Honey, try not to let him know."

* * *

hen Billie got back to her apartment, the first thing she did was check her messages. She pressed the red button, and her mother's moonlight-and-magnolias voice swept through the room.

"Bey! It's Mama. Your handsome daddy and me are throwin' a soiree this evenin' for ya aunt Colette. She just came in from Nwahlins for a visit, and she don't know that I invited her out so she could meet your daddy's friend, that handsome, um, what kinda doctor is he, bey?" Billie heard her father's muffled voice in the background. "Billie darlin', are you there? Your daddy says he practices mid*wif*ery, which is what you do when you're a midwife. Ain't that a clevah word? Mid*wif*ery. It sounds like perfume. Anyway, he's got salt-and-peppa hair? Colette wanted to say hi to ya, darlin', but look like ya ain't home. I'ma go, bey, cuz your daddy's got a thousand hands on me . . ."

Billie smiled. Her mother was crazy. There was another message. It was him.

"Billie? It's Jay. Uh, Jay Lane? I think I forgot my bag of perfume at your crib. Can I come get it?"

She burst out laughing and called her man.

5.

i'm your pusher

Jay was on his way to Tammy's. He'd just finished having lunch with Renee at Michael's, the time-honored publishing haunt in the East Fifties. Actually, he'd eaten while Renee went on about how over the moon she was about his work. He also thought she did a fine job of pretending not to know about him and Billie. After calling Billie to tell her the news (and to play off how excited he was), he took the N crosstown to Port Authority and caught the NJ Transit. Fresh Hair was closed on Mondays, and that's when Tammy did his cornrows.

He stood in his best friend's doorway, grinning like an idiot.

"What are you all happy about?"

"Many things. Sup, baby?" He came in, kissed her on the cheek, and sprawled out on her love seat. She looked at him like he'd lost his mind. He remembered the rules, and took off his boots. Over the years, Tammy had dealt with her issues by adapting a very Zen way of life. She'd read about feng shui and immediately hired a professional to reorganize each of her rooms in the healthiest way possible. She was familiar with the state of her chakras at every given moment. She did yoga and daily meditations. She was extremely spiritual, and treated Susan Taylor's "In the Spirit" column in *Essence* magazine as gospel. Twice a month, she visited a color therapist. And her apartment was filled with tiny, tinkering things like wind chimes and those dripping Japanese waterfall jobs. Jay found these things profoundly irritating, but hey. Whatever works.

Plus, he knew that despite her "centered" persona, she'd cuss you out in a second.

"You want some tea?" She headed for the kitchen.

"You ever known me to drink tea?" Why was everyone offering him tea?

Tammy returned to the living room with a steaming cup of chamomile/lemongrass blend. She set it on the marble coffee table in the dead center of the room (very balancing) and inhaled the aroma for a couple of seconds. Then, she gently edged him off the love seat and onto the floor, where he sat between her legs. Tammy began unbraiding his perfect cornrows.

"So, what are these many things you so happy about?"

"I met a book editor at the show last week."

"For real?"

"For real. I just had lunch with her, and she's tryin' to publish my shit."

"Word? For real?"

"She's got a meeting tomorrow. I mean, you never know what's gonna happen. But she got a mothafucker's back. I don't know."

"Jay! That's so beautiful!" Tammy wrapped her tiny arms around his neck and almost choked him to death. She was fiercely proud of him—she always had been. "She black?"

"Yeah."

"Even better."

"I mean, I don't know." He was bashful.

"Shutup. You know you don't do anything halfway. If you want it, you always make it happen. Period. You're a Leo."

Jay changed the subject. "How'd your fashion show go? Ow! Fuck!" Tammy didn't know her own strength.

"Sorry. The show was hot, the models looked sexy as shit. And I got a really good reception. I had editors approaching me and, like, celebrities taking my card. It was mad exciting, but it's a blur now. It all happened so fast."

"Look at you!" Jay was happy for her. "About to be famous and shit. Ain't got no choice with a name like Pandora."

"Naw, it ain't even about fame. It's about *the hair*."

"You lyin'."

"I know."

They both laughed and then were quiet for a while. Jay thought about Billie. What was it about her? It felt really . . . urgent. He had to be near her. He had to be inside her. He had to get in her head. Like it wasn't even his choice. It was baffling.

"So I met this really positive chick," Tammy said, making light conversation. "A black magazine editor. At *Du Jour*, no less."

Jay had been sort of zoning out, but then he snapped back to the present. "What?"

"At the show. Hello?"

"Yeah, yeah," he muttered, trying to sound nonchalant. "So, uh, you were talking to her?"

"Uh-huh. She was really inspiring, you know? And she wants to put me in an article. Can you imagine?"

"That's . . . that's some hot shit. Um . . . what'd you say her name was?"

"I didn't. It's Billie. Why?"

"No reason. I thought . . . well, I met a black girl who works for a magazine the other day, a friend of a friend, but that ain't her." His stomach was tied up in knots—why was he lying?

"Oh. So what else happened?"

"Huh?"

"You said you were happy about many things. You got an editor and what else?"

"Oh." He wasn't sure how to approach this. And he certainly wasn't prepared for them to already have met. When—and if—they met, he wanted it to be on his terms. He *so* wasn't ready to explain Tammy to Billie. And now, once he was faced with it, he realized he felt a little sensitive and weird telling Tammy how in love with Billie he was. He'd never had this conversation with her before. He'd never had this conversation with anybody before. And now he'd started with a lie. *Fuck.* "Um. I think I met my baby's mama."

"What?"

"I met a girl. I met a girl."

"Where?"

"After my show." He was short.

"You trippin' off her?"

"Yeah."

"What's she look like?" Tammy was finished, and she massaged her fingers. She was a fast worker.

"She's, um." He exhaled. "Fly, you know? She's beautiful. But she don't act like it. I don't think she knows it."

"So why she got you trippin'? Did you fuck her?" Tammy was blunt. It was the only way she knew how to be with him. Over the years, she'd dealt with all his girls the same way. She always demanded the cold, hard facts. She wanted to hear about them like they were nothing more than a piece of ass. She wanted to know what they looked like, how they fucked, where he took them, everything. To Tammy, as long as she had every detail, she had power over them—they were just sex objects. She was his confidante, in a way that they would never be; no woman could understand him the way she did. Who could last three rounds in a "real" relationship with Jay? He was difficult, moody, self-absorbed, and inconsistent. He had a habit of disappearing for months, then popping back into her life like a day hadn't passed. And she always accepted him. He was irresistible.

Unbeknownst to Jay, Tammy was in love with him. He was everything to her—father, brother, best friend, protector. In her head, try as she might to push the thought away, he was her man. The thing was, Tammy didn't know how she'd react if she ever felt that Jay was really, really serious about one of his girls.

They'd never had a romantic relationship. Sometimes they slept together, but she knew Jay just considered this an extension of their friendship. So she was careful not to stop her life for him. She even had a boyfriend. His name was Pete, and he was a corporate lawyer at a high-post firm downtown. He was a respectful, upstanding, stable man who bored her to tears. He was constantly traveling, so she only saw him about once a week, which was fine with her. He wasn't Jay.

It was simple—Jay had saved her. When he was just a boy. Whenever she'd long for him, or cry for him, she'd tell herself that he was just sowing his oats, and one day he'd realize what he already had. It was worth the wait.

Maybe she was just a masochist.

Whatever Tammy was, she'd never heard Jay this hesitant to divulge details about one of his hoes, and that was definitely not cool.

"Hello? Did you fuck her?"

"Yeah, I fucked her."

"What's she like?"

"She's dope." He didn't want to talk about Billie anymore. He didn't like Tammy's tone. Usually her little interrogations were harmless; it was like locker room talk. Tammy was his nigga. But he couldn't talk about Billie like that.

"How many times did you fuck her?"

Jay didn't say anything.

"You brought this girl up and now you don't wanna talk about her?" She was beginning to panic.

"What do you want me to say? I fucked the shit outta her. I'm 'bout to go fuck her again. Damn. Why don't you go get you some?"

"Mothafucker," said Tammy. "Get the fuck outta my house."

"What?

"I said get. The fuck. Out. Who you talkin' to like that?"

"Like what? What you grillin' me for?"

"Get outta my house!" She was yelling and hurt and didn't want to be found out.

"I'm gone. But let's be clear about whose house this is."

She flinched. The door slammed and he was gone.

* * *

Later, Billie met Jay in the East Village after his show, and they'd had soul food at Mekka. Afterward, they were jonesing for ice cream, so they started walking down to Little Italy for Italian ice. But then, one jones outweighed the other, and they ended up at her place. On the floor, in the kitchen, and finally, in the bed.

Now, they were marinating in a fragrant bath custom-made by the beauty expert. She'd added ginger bath salts, rosemary bath beads, and a splash of lavender bath oil. Initially, the aroma assortment had given Jay a violent sneezing attack, but now he seemed to be doing better.

It was a jarring thing, being so instantly adored. Neither one of them could imagine why the other needed them so much. It was fascinating. They spent a lot of their time poking around inside this, trying to figure it out. All Billie and Jay knew was that they were addicted. They were vital to each other. Who were they before two days ago? Billie and Jay wanted to be experts on each other.

There was one problem, though: Billie thought her life was crushingly bland. She didn't want to break the spell with shout-outs from suburbia. And Jay thought his was a little too spicy. He didn't want to be some ghetto novelty to her, and, even more, he couldn't take pity.

So there they lay, squeezed in the tub, facing each other. They were going to get to the bottom of things. Somebody was going to talk. And Jay had rolled the blunt that would spark the conversation.

"I'm not smoking that."

"Yes, you are."

"Noooo."

"You ever smoked before?"

"Never in my life."

"The fuck outta here."

"My parents smoked weed in the basement the entire time I was growing up."

"Word?"

"I hated it. Parents aren't supposed to smoke weed."

"Maybe in your neighborhood."

"But they'd get high and have sex in my mother's garden. It was unseemly."

"That ain't unseemly. That's some Wordsworth shit, right there. Smoke a tree, fuck in the grass . . ."

"But these are *parents*. Who wants to see their parents having sex when they're eight?"

"I ain't saying it's a pleasant visual. But what's it got to do with us?"

"I'm not smoking."

"Yes, you are. Come here, baby. I'm your pusher."

Billie couldn't resist him. With a lot of splashing and readjusting, she stood up, turned around, and lay against his back. Jay lit the blunt and took a drag. Then he popped it in her mouth and gave her instructions on inhaling. She followed them, and coughed till she retched. She tried it a couple more times, and it got a little easier.

Then it got reeaaallly easy. Billie began to find herself very interesting. In between puffs, she told him every story she could think of. She told him about athlete Shawn and gay Grant. She told him about Vida, Renee, and herself in college. She told him about her dashing parents. What it was like growing up with a beautiful, sexy mother that everybody fell madly in love with.

"Everybody?" asked Jay.

"Everybody. Men, women, toddlers, Chihuahuas . . ."

Jay puffed and passed to Billie. "You ain't your mom, Billie."

"I've been choking on it for years."

"What I mean is, you ain't gotta be nobody but you. You're good, you're all you need."

"But do you think my hair looks like cellophane?"

"Cellophane? No." He fingered her hair. It had gone from straight to a wild mountain of ringlets in the steamy bathroom. "I do think it's gone on home, though."

Billie puffed, passed, and giggled hysterically. And giggled, and giggled.

They were hazy, and blissful, and perfect. Jay's strong arms were around her, and she felt like she'd been born there. She curled into him and gave a contented sigh.

"I feel like I'm in utero."

Jay kissed her ear. "The Amniotic Woman."

"Hey."

"What?"

"Tell me about you. Wanna know everything."

He took the last drag, and exhaled. Well, here it was.

"Like what?"

She rolled her head to the right and traced her finger along the KJ tattoo on his arm. "Is this a girl? Did . . . do you love her?"

"No, it ain't a girl."

"What about the scar on your cheek?"

He paused. "I'll tell you everything. But you gotta know that we ain't from the same place."

"Am I stupid? Don't give me a disclaimer. I won't judge you. Everybody's gotta do what they gotta do." Billie disentangled herself from him, stood up, and slid behind him. She wrapped her legs around him and held him to her breasts. "I want to know," she whispered. "I want to learn your stuff. Tell me. Tell me."

He did. He got up to when he met Tammy without a hitch.

". . . and I, uh, was just, like, fucked up, and all woozy cuz I was bleeding . . . I don't know. I was trippin'. I don't really remember all of it. The gist of it is, I met a girl who helped me. Took me to the emergency room and gave me a place to stay for a minute."

"My God." Billie couldn't imagine the things Jay was telling her. "That girl's like your guardian angel. Do you still know her?"

He paused. Tammy. How could Jay explain to Billie what he and Tammy were to each other, in a way she could understand? Billie was different than them . . . she'd had a different kind of life. He didn't want to scare her away. He didn't want to lose her, it was too good.

And he'd already told Tammy that he didn't know her.

So he left it blank. He told Billie he'd lost track of her, and he continued his story.

After, they were quiet for a long time.

"It's what's mine, that's all," he said, finally.

"I know," she said, refusing to let herself cry. She pretended her heart wasn't breaking for the boy he once was. Billie squeezed her eyes shut and vowed to make his every breath worth it.

⁂

The next morning at *Du Jour*, Paige Merchant held a department meeting in her office. She was just back from Capri; more beige than ever. To showcase her tan, she wore an orange Hermés sarong (which clung desperately to her bony hips) and naked gold stilettos. Her beyond-blond hair was tied back in a fuchsia and orange–swirled Pucci scarf. She wore smoky eyeshadow, pale lipstick, and an assortment of baubly cocktail rings. She looked very South of France, circa 1968. All she needed was a caftan and a cigarette holder.

Billie, Sandy, and Mary sat on the plush, winter-white couch that faced her desk. Sandy nervously fingered the fringe on the leopard-print scarf draped over the seat. At their feet was a bag containing beauty products that would hit stores in the spring. The department was wrapping up its "ideas meeting" for the February issue, which forecasted spring trends. Usually, women's magazines cover spring trends in March, but true fashion addicts looked to *Du Jour*'s coverage in February.

". . . and there's a lavender lip moment," said Sandy, who was very intimidated by Paige. "It's kind of an Easter Egg situation? Very flirty and soft?" "Moment" and "situation" were industry-speak for what was happening at that very second. This could mean anything from a trend to dinner. She pulled out six lipsticks and lined them up on Paige's product-cluttered desk.

Paige considered the lipsticks. "Walk me through how one can wear lavender lipstick without looking very, very cold."

"Ooooh. I see what you mean. I . . ."

"No, no, no, wait a minute. Let's learn something here. I don't care how many companies are making a product. I don't care if Chanel tells us it's the freaking cure for cancer. If it gives me hypothermia, it ain't happening. 'Kay, Pony?"

Billie shook her head. Paige could be very evil.

"I totally see your point," continued Sandy, even redder than normal. "Well, there's another lip moment happening. The major companies all have a red lip stain in their spring collections. This isn't a true Marilyn red, but a sheer *wash* of red. Like you've been licking a lollipop." Sandy replaced the lavender lipsticks with a group of red ones.

"See, now this I like. I'm gelling with the lollipop visual. This could be a very sexy Lolita moment. Sandypants, I need you to do a

closet search. Round up products that have kind of a preschool quality, but that also make you want to roll around in honey and screw."

Sandy looked puzzled. Billie gave her a "don't worry about it"
look. She'd help her. It was scary, but at this point she could read
Paige's mind. The idea approved, Mary grabbed the lipsticks and
quickly jotted down the names of each one for the record.

"Thanks, 'Pants. Next?" Paige had trouble calling people by
their real names. Mary was either Mare Bear or Mary Unbirthday,
depending upon her mood. Billie had started out as Billie Putty, but
over the years had become Putt-Putt. When Paige was preoccupied, everyone was Chicken, Pony, or Flower. Expressing annoyance at these infantile nicknames was out of the question.

"You'll love this, Paige. I think we're finally over glitter. At least,
I sincerely *hope* we're over glitter." Billie arranged about a dozen
Crayola-colored shadows on the desk. "Behold, the rainbow coali-
tion. The new eye for spring is graphic, graphic, graphic. It's not
about the natural look, it's not about shimmer or translucence. It's
just, like, fuck-you color. Straight, no chaser."

Paige surveyed the yellow, blue, red, and green shadows on her
desk, as a slow smile crept across her face. "This is rocking my
world, Putt-Putt. This is rocking my world."

"They're like eighties pop art colors, right?" said Billie. "Don't
you want to just eat them?"

"I love it," declared Paige. "Mare Bear, are you getting all this?
Are you writing these shadow names correctly? Be a maniac about
this—last month we ran a Lancôme blush credit as Pretty I Think,
which obviously should've been Pretty In Pink. Um, that was on
you, Chicken."

Mary nodded and continued taking notes. Billie knew she was
thinking "I fucking didn't go to Radcliffe for this shit."

Paige continued. "I love it! I'm seeing the shadows smashed across a white brick wall. Sort of a graffiti situation."

"Exactly, exactly. Which brings me to Fashion Week." Billie launched into her article idea. She believed in knowing her audience, so she replaced the "can you believe them" tone she and her friends had used at brunch with a distant, sociological one. It worked.

"And the ethnic borrowing is happening everywhere, not just on the runway," continued Billie. "Have you seen Christina Aguilera's 'Make It Hurt' video? Red extensions a mile long. In fact, the same woman who did the hair at Sam C. also did Christina's. Anyway, black girls have been wearing colored weaves for a million years. I think it'll be very, um, *journalistic* of us to shed some light on where these trends originated."

"That's such a cute idea!" said Mary. Paige looked at her sharply, as if to say, When you've mastered spelling, then you may have an opinion.

Sandy said nothing. She was happy to have scored with the lip stains, and was now keeping a low profile.

Paige smiled warmly at Billie. "I'm so obsessed with you today! This will be our opener for February, and it's *sure* to get a coverline. I'd say, four pages? Three thousand words? Pony, I really want you to get Margaret Mead on this one." Paige scanned her Visionaire calendar. "You've got five weeks. That's more than enough time for you to club that story to death and drag it back to the cave. Yes?"

"Of course!" Billie was beaming.

"Okay, chickens. Meeting's adjourned. Mama needs to smoke." Paige dismissed her subjects. "Putt-erama, can we have a moment?"

Mary hurried to her desk to sob on the phone with her boyfriend. Sandy headed for the beauty closet to find makeup that suggested kiddie porn. Billie stayed behind, and Paige closed the door, which she hardly ever did.

"Alone, at last. Sometimes I think those girls have been lobotomized," she said, collapsing into her chair. She lit a cigarette with a Swarovski crystal–studded Versace lighter and grinned saucily at Billie. In a Marlene Dietrich voice she purred, "Ve haff to stop meeting like zis."

"You're making me nervous."

"Whyyy, Flower? I have good news for you."

"You do?" Billie couldn't imagine her world getting any better.

"Indeed. Last night I had drinks with Fannie." Fannie Merrick was the legendary editor in chief. Paige and Fannie loathed each other, so the drinks date came as a shock to Billie.

Paige must have read the surprise on Billie's face. "Not pleasure, dear, business. British *Du Jour*'s current beauty and fashion director is quitting to complete her coffee-table book. It's on British beauty, which God knows is an oxymoron. Anyway, they're looking to us for a replacement." Paige paused and took a dramatic drag from her cigarette holder.

Billie's jaw dropped in shock. "Don't tell me you're going to British *Du Jour*! That's incredible, Paige!"

"Please! I am thirty-eight years old," said Paige, who was forty-six. "I can't bring anything new to this job."

"But you're the best."

"Perhaps, but I'm tapped out. Done. And Mars Bar just finished finalizing the contract on our Tuscan villa." Mars Bar, or Mario Luis Bergamotto, was an international financier/model fucker, and

Paige's fiancé. He would be her fourth husband. "I give this beauty shit two more years, and then I plan to pack it up and become Lee Radziwill."

"Well, who else could possibly do that job?" Me, thought Billie.

"You."

"*What?* Are you kidding? I'm too young . . . and London, that's a whole new thing . . ."

"Oh, save the whole 'who me?' bit. You're amazing. You know it, and so does everyone else. Now you don't have to look over your shoulder when you tell Annie in research to consider you the department head. You can scream it from the hilltops!" Paige giggled naughtily.

Goddamn, thought Billie—this bitch hears everything. "But, Paige, I'm only twenty-six. I mean, did Fannie think this was a good idea?"

"Fannie thought it was a great idea. Since when has any of *Du Jour*'s publications done the traditional thing? It's not official, though. Truth be told, the powers that be are concerned about your age, too. For the next couple of months, you're going to be watched very closely. Think of it as an audition. I would even suggest meeting with the old bag to tell her how honored you are just to be nominated."

"Oh my God."

"Exactly. So this whole ethnic moment that you're doing? It better blow everyone's minds. Knock this story out and get a huge coverline, Chicken."

"Oh my God."

"By the way," said Paige, "is that Pretty I Think blush, or have you finally gotten laid?"

Jay.

* * *

Crosstown at Crawford & Collier, Renee was entering her acquisitions meeting with the air of Scarlett throwing the Yankees off Tara. Renee was all about going into battle. She wore a fitted gray BCBG pantsuit and her shaggy bob sleekly tucked behind her ears. She was Not Fucking Around.

At the meeting were her superiors, the "grown-ups," who decided if a manuscript was worth buying. Presiding over the meeting was the publisher, Jim Davidson, who at forty was both surprisingly young and surprisingly handsome for a man in his position. He was a womanizer who enjoyed embarrassing his female employees with off-color remarks too vague to be reprimanded in court. A brilliant man, he knew not to take even a step in that direction with Renee.

Also in attendance were Sue Snyderman, Lynn Cohen, the executive VP, and Gabbie Cairns-Whyte, the managing editor (she figured out the finances for each book). Gabbie's assistant, Jenny, was dutifully pouring coffee and taking notes.

The night before, Renee had given the grown-ups each a copy of *Nutz & Boltz* as well as photocopies of the *Village Voice* and *New York* magazine articles. Having done their homework, everyone was prepared to assess Renee's newest find.

"Before we discuss the manuscript," started Jim, "I'd just like to thank you ladies for wrapping up the spring catalogue copy in record time. You never fail to impress me with your dedication and perseverance. I'm so proud of my team." The "ladies" nodded their thanks. It was 9 A.M. and everyone was tired.

"So, Renee, talk to us about Jay Lane," said Jim.

Renee cleared her throat. "Simply put, the man is brilliant. As you all know, I saw his show last Friday night and was blown away. I was delighted to see that he was just as impressive—if not more so—on paper. His style is searing and urgent, but unforced. It's vital cultural commentary, but at the same time it's just really enjoyable storytelling."

"You know, I have to agree," said Sue, who always had Renee's back. "I found his words delightful and haunting. Very important voice."

"What's your take, Lynn?" Jim asked, as he undressed the matronly lesbian with his eyes.

"I'm on the same page as Renee and Sue," she said, taking a sip of the cheap coffee and ignoring Jim's lecherous looks. "I really, really enjoyed this. His works are quite appealing in a voyeuristic way."

"Not my cup of tea," said Gabbie. "I don't know, I was just underwhelmed. Did he really say something new about the ghetto, or did I miss something?"

"Well, the ghetto is the ghetto is the ghetto," replied Renee, a tad testily. "It's been the same forever. What's new is in the telling. To me, this recalled some of the great Harlem Renaissance essays: Langston and Hurston and the like. They were talking about jook joints, and gin, and rent parties. And pain and loss. None of those topics are new, but they're slices of culture."

"But right now, when the country's enjoying such prosperity, does anybody want to read about drunks and junkies?" asked Gabbie. "No, seriously. We've got a nation full of twenty-one-year-old dotcom millionaires. That's where it's at right now. Quick money, the fast track, technology. It's my feeling that these stories are very, um, antiquated. Kind of a bummer, even."

"I totally disagree," said Sue.

"They just didn't send me," said Gabbie, shrugging.

"I don't know. I thought it was very refreshing to hear from such an articulate young African-American," countered Lynn. Renee was furious. Articulate? Why was it always so surprising when a black person can speak English? She bit her tongue, but her tongue won.

"Jay Lane's uniqueness doesn't lie in his being articulate. I'm articulate. Jim's articulate. It's not about that. When Frank McCourt wrote *Angela's Ashes*, no one said, 'Wow, this former shanty Irish street urchin is really articulate.'" Renee masked her irritation with a smiley, uncombative tone. "Jay's uniqueness lies in his talent."

"Renee, I didn't mean to imply—"

"No, don't worry about it. I know what you meant." Renee grinned to herself. They hated feeling culturally insensitive. Hated it.

Jim spoke up. He didn't like tension among his ladies. "My feeling is that this guy is going to be a contender. I dig him, I really do. He's a smart, good-looking kid. He already has in-person presence—he's going to be a cinch to market. But obviously, I wouldn't place him top-list. I see him as mid-list."

"Mid-list?" Gabbie was skeptical. "How much do you think it'll sell?"

"A good ten thousand, at least. Figure in the sales at shows and readings. And surely foreign sales will be a force. Cities like London, Berlin, and Amsterdam are eating up urban New York talent. Look at what happened with spoken word."

"I think it's important to continue pursuing literary projects. Our list is so overwhelmingly commercial," said Renee. "There is an audience for this kind of book. Look at how well Just Columbus's book is doing."

"Oh, Jim, I agree," said Sue. She downed her second cup of

coffee, and her silver bangles—a gift to her from Philip Roth—clinked melodically. "It's been my experience over the many, many, *many* years"—everyone chuckled politely at the legend's reference to her tenure—"that it's wise to have smaller writers on your list; you never know where that voice'll go. Anyway, we make the big books so we can afford the teensy ones. I have full faith in Renee's opinion—look at her track record."

"Thanks, Sue," Renee said, with a smile. Then it was business as usual. "Bottom line is, if we don't get Jay, some other house will. And then I'll be impossible to live with."

Jim tapped his fingernails against his perfect teeth. Gabbie looked skeptical. Sue smiled at her star pupil. Lynn swished her coffee around in the paper cup, fuming and embarrassed. Renee held her breath. Jenny pretended to take notes while writing the eighth chapter of her novel.

Jim spoke up. "I'd say it's a go. Good job, Renee." He directed his gaze at Gabbie. "Let's talk about money, honey."

• • •

Jay was at home, outraged. Tammy had been ignoring his calls for two days. He'd just tried her salon, and one of her stylists, a surly bitch named Sabina, said she was too busy to talk. Finished, he left her a message on her home phone.

"Tammy. I'm sorry for what I said to you about your crib. It was fucked up, and I didn't mean it. Period. I didn't mean it. Everything that's mine is yours. Ain't nothing I wouldn't do for you, and you know it. You're my family, and your crib was a gift. What I don't know is what got you so heated. We was just talking. If I disrespected you in any way, you gotta tell me. If not, you know I ain't the nigga to stress. It's on you now, I ain't callin' again. Love you."

Frustrated, he hung up and fell back on his mattress, his one piece of furniture, besides the reams of paper he used as a nightstand. He liked to keep things minimal. What had he done to her? He went over their conversation again. He'd just been telling his best friend about his girl. Tammy couldn't possibly have picked up that he was being shady about who she was. No, it wasn't that . . . she hadn't even asked her name. Why'd she sounded all funny? She acted kind of like a jealous girlfriend, which was insane. They weren't like that, and they'd never been. Besides, Tammy had been going with Punk Ass Pete for two years.

Jay was totally perplexed. Tammy had a volatile temper, but he normally knew where it was coming from. Maybe it wasn't about him. Maybe she had her period. Did she need money? No, Fresh Hair was huge. She was even talking about opening another one in the city.

And a teeny, tiny part of him resented her for preoccupying him with her petty drama when all he wanted to think about was Billie.

The phone rang and eagerly, he picked up.

"Is this Jay?"

"Yeah. Who's this?"

"Your fairy godmother. No, the other one. It's Renee. I hope you're sitting down, baby, cuz I'm about to blow your fucking mind!"

6.

the perfect september

t Fresh Hair, the phone was ringing off the hook. Tammy had just finished the aqua hair extensions of her last client of the day, an up-and-coming female rapper named Silky Sexxx. Silky had worn out her welcome hours before. When Tammy asked her if she'd like something to drink, the rapper requested a Pellegrino, only to become belligerent upon discovering it wasn't champagne. Tammy was totally drained, and feeling miserable about the scene with Jay. For the first time ever, she felt like they were on shaky ground. What if she lost him to this random girl who was apparently too special to discuss? She was jealous, and what made it worse was that she didn't even know who she was jealous of. She'd been driving herself crazy trying to imagine what this girl looked like, what power she had over Jay. What the girl had that she was missing. Was she prettier, sexier, smarter? Fighting back tears that had been threatening to spill all day, she plopped into a styling chair and continued to ignore the persistent ringing.

"Look, you need to answer the phone and talk to that man," Sabina said, swiveling around in the chair next to Tammy's. The

German cleaning lady, Bierget, clucked disapprovingly and resumed sweeping up frayed blue hair with the speed and agility of
an arthritic mule.

"I'm not speaking to him."

"What did he do to you, girl? It ain't even like he's your man.
Not that you speak to your man, anyway."

"Pete and I broke up."

"Get outta here!"

"It's true. I felt like he was stifling my creative process."

"He was so boring."

"That too."

"Anyway, why aren't you answering Jay's calls?"

"Because he disrespected me in my own home, which is a vessel
of serenity and positivity."

"I hate it when you talk like a yoga instructor. Girl, answer the
damn phone." Sabina and Tammy stared at each other archly for a
second, as the phone continued to ring. Then, in a flash, Sabina
lunged for the wall phone above Tammy's head. Tammy tried to
grab her arm, missed, and landed on the floor. Bierget muttered,
"*Gott im Himmel*," without pausing her slow shuffling.

"What, what, *what*?" Sabina growled into the phone, exasperated.

"Um, yeah, this is Daisy Schwartz, Mariah Carey's publicist?"

Sabina grimaced. "Oh my God, I'm so sorry. I thought you were
someone else." Interested, Tammy brushed herself off and perched
on the edge of Sabina's chair.

"No, it's okay. I, um, wanted to talk to you about possibly working with Mariah?"

"You're serious?"

"Very. She's going in a, um, more urban direction on her latest album? And she saw your work on MTV and really fell in love. She'd love you to do her hair for her new video, 'Playa Please.' Should I book you through a publicist, or, um, how does this work?"

"Okay, hold on. You want to talk to Pandora. One sec." Sabina put Daisy on hold and favored her boss with an enormous smile. "Mariah Carey's people want you to work on her next video."

Tammy's mouth dropped open. Working with the honey-haired singer would send her career into the stratosphere. Between this and being covered in a *Du Jour* beauty story, she couldn't imagine life getting better.

Still, when she produced a smile for Sabina, it didn't reach her eyes. The success wasn't worth it without him. That fucker.

* * *

For Billie, it was the one perfect September by which all others would be measured. She tried to memorize every moment, put them all away for safekeeping, in case all the rampaging joy couldn't sustain itself. Billie and Jay had spent the past two weeks doing little else besides basking in the glow of each other. Billie felt she was likely to be crushed underneath her all-consuming need for him, but she didn't care. Billie and Jay flung themselves at each other like pigskin-crazed quarterbacks from opposing teams— unflinching, unmindful of the outcome, and likely to suffer a concussion. They were ravenous love junkies.

She hadn't told Jay yet about her London offer. The only people in the world who knew were Renee and Vida. She was torn between feeling thrilled at the prospect and feeling terrified of losing Jay. The thought of being oceans apart was hideous, so she finally filed it under "to be dealt with later." It was hard enough leaving him for *Du Jour* every day.

For the past two weeks, Jay had basically been living with Billie. They stayed at her tiny studio as opposed to his huge loft because, well, the loft held as much warmth as a coffin. Every night after his show, he'd take the C train to Lafayette and squeeze himself into her apartment. They'd stay up all night watching AMC and eating takeout from Fulton Street restaurants.

On the two nights Jay didn't have his show, they traversed the city looking for new ways to amuse themselves. They spent hours getting all dusty and exploring the rows of used books at the Strand, Jay turning Billie on to Bret Easton Ellis (whom she loved until the nightmares began), and Billie forcing Jay to read Donald Bogle's famous biography of Dorothy Dandridge. They dined at the Algonquin, just to see if they could catch some writerly vibes. Jay took Billie to Bayou, a Creole restaurant in Harlem, which Billie found to be astoundingly authentic. (Billie ordered crawfish, and Jay almost had a stroke watching her happily suck the meat out of the shell and lick butter off her lips.) They went to every art film house in Manhattan. They saw randy Almodóvar imports like *Tie Me Up! Tie Me Down!* at the Screening Room way downtown on Varick Street. At Cinema Village on East Twelfth, they saw *Romance*, a wincingly explicit French film about a young woman looking for sexual fulfillment from random strangers on the streets of Paris. Besides Billie and Jay, the only other patrons were a sprinkling of tweedy professor types. Even though they missed fifteen minutes during their frantic fuck in the ladies' room, they agreed that the movie was fascinating.

Billie was in erotic torment. She was useless at work. All day long her heart ached and her pussy throbbed. She sat at her desk rubbing her thighs together and gazing cross-eyed into her computer. All she thought about was Jay—his mouth, his hands, what he could do to her. Brushing up against his arm could send her over the edge. Jay knew he could have her any way and any time he wanted, which was a dangerous thing. If he asked her to crawl naked across the floor in nipple clamps, singing "Have You Ever Been Mellow," she would.

One evening after his show, they met Vida and Git at Lotus. While Vida danced up a storm to Aaliyah's "Try Again," and Git smoked weed in a blurry corner, Jay and Billie sat at the bar for a drink. Locked in a shameless kiss (they'd become one of those couples), Jay reached underneath Billie's multitiered peasant skirt and stroked her, steadily squeezing and letting go until she came in front of God and Lizzie Grubman and everybody. It was both thrilling and . . . *daunting*. He knew where she lived. Jay could practically make her weep with pleasure. He had taken her over.

For Billie, the sex stuff was not instinctual. She was too self-conscious to go there. She followed his lead, absorbing his energy as they went along. If he was rough, she was rough. If he was slow and deliberate, she was, too. And this dynamic spilled over into the rest of their relationship. Billie willingly and trustingly gave herself over to him. She was a skittish, trembling Question, and he was the Answer. When he experienced her first real "Give my daughter the shot!" migraine, he knew what she needed. He entered Billie's pitch-black studio to find her lying on the futon, stiff as a corpse, with an icepack on her head. She was miserable—floating on a Percocet high, but still in throbbing, insistent, unreasonable pain. Jay knelt beside her and whispered in her ear.

"Baby. Let it go. You're trapped in there and just let it go. Give it away. Give it to me." He gently kneaded her neck, her forehead, and her shoulders until she slowly began to release tension. She unclenched her teeth and hands and unfurrowed her brow. "Let whatever it is out. You're safe, baby. You're safe." Billie began to cry. He did this for an hour, until impossibly, she fell asleep.

When she awoke, the pain hadn't gone away completely, but something was released in her. Jay managed to get to her, to open her up.

Who was this guy?

She didn't know. All she knew was that she had a new purpose—to shower this man with boundless love and affection to make up for the harrowing, broken nonchildhood he'd suffered. All she wanted to do was love him, and take care of him, and make sure he was okay. Of course, wild horses couldn't have dragged this out of her. Billie went to great lengths to pretend that his past didn't affect her that much. The truth was, if her thoughts lingered on the image of his parents jumping to their deaths, she'd burst into tears, but she didn't want him to think she was a cheesy, "un-down" naif who couldn't handle the reality of the mean streets. Even though she was.

But they had more in common than they thought. Both were heartily ambitious and fiercely proud of each other's accomplishments. In the middle of the night, giddy and sticky with love, they'd fantasize about taking the publishing world by storm. They'd be the black Tina Brown and Harry Evans.

Billie was unbearably curious about Jay's book but never pried. She could've chosen to be hurt that Jay wouldn't show her his manuscript until he was finished, but as a journalist she knew how it felt to have people read your stuff before you were ready. And to

Jay, the writing ran deeper than the performing—it was his life force and he was sensitive about it. Billie understood.

Their one dark moment occurred one evening after *Nutz & Boltz*. Billie met him at the Public Theater, and they walked to a nameless hole-in-the-wall sushi spot on Ninth. Seated at the rickety, pale green linoleum café table, the two launched into comfortable conversation about the beauty industry's shameless bribing. As Billie reminisced over last year's Salon Selectives–sponsored press trip to Anguilla, she noticed that she'd lost him. He was right in front of her but not at all present. Too much sake?

"Helloooo," Billie started, sucking the salt off an edamame bean. "You okay?"

"Huh?"

"What's wrong? Did you have a bad experience in Anguilla?"

Jay paused. "I feel guilty."

"For what?"

"For being with you instead of writing."

Billie's stomach hit the floor. He was looking right through her, like she wasn't there. "You mean, you wish you were somewhere else right now? Am I . . . I mean, do I keep you from your work?"

Jay looked at her and slowly realized the gravity of what he'd said. "No, no, no," he started, frowning in frustration. "You know I love being with you. But this book deal is *real*, and I'm so caught up in you that I'm acting like I don't have to work on it. I ain't written a word in, like, a week." He scratched his head and sighed.

Billie was quietly destroyed. "If you think you need some space . . ."

"No, baby. It' s my fault. I'm just stressing." He smiled at her, held her face between his hands, and kissed her. He was back.

"Clearly can't stay away from you, so I just gotta manage my time better and shit. That's all."

Billie managed to smile and nod, but she was hurt. The last thing she thought about when they were together was work. She decided to file this moment away with the London thing.

And so they moved on with their glorious September.

• • •

It was noon on Saturday, and they were lying in a tangled heap on Billie's rumpled bed. Billie was sound asleep, but Jay hadn't slept a wink all night. The night before, the two of them had stopped by Jay's loft to pick up a chapter of his manuscript, so he could work on it at Billie's if he suffered one of his bouts of insomnia. He noticed the red message light flashing on his phone, and he checked his caller ID. It was Tammy. He immediately got sweaty and uncomfortable and wanted to leave. Any suggestion of the two women in the same vicinity gave him a panic attack. Billie could tell there was something wrong.

"Was that the other woman in your life?" she asked, joking.

"No, it was, uh, my boy . . . he's . . . he's locked up." It just came out. He knew she turned to mush at all matters hood-related.

"Oh." Billie immediately looked concerned. "And you're sad you missed his call."

"Yeah. *Damn.*" He pounded his thigh with a fist, for emphasis. To hell with this writing shit, Jay thought, I need to pack it up and move to Hollywood.

"Oh, baby, I'm sorry. Can you call him back? Are you allowed to do that?"

"No, but I ain't gonna stress. He'll get at me later, don't worry. Let's go."

And that was that. But Jay felt horrible about lying to Billie. He hated it. He wished he could just tell both of them the truth, but he didn't know how. And so he'd tossed and turned all night, with a guilty knot in his stomach. He decided taking Billie around his old neighborhood might alleviate some of the guilt. Somehow, keeping such a huge part of his past hidden didn't seem so bad as long as he showed her the rest of it.

This is what he'd told himself.

He kissed Billie gently on the mouth and whispered in her ear to wake up.

"Today I'm gonna be your tour guide."

"What?" Billie was cozy-groggy.

"I'm showing you Fort Greene today."

"Honey, I live in Fort Greene."

"You live in Disney World Fort Greene. Did you know Disney World was built on a swamp? Today we're going to the swamp."

"I'm not sure I'm equipped for the swamp." Billie had a sheltered, suburban girl's fear of the projects. She could see them from the window of her tiny studio, looming beyond her gentrified immediate surroundings. The projects made her nervous, which made her embarrassed. Why was she nervous? What did she think was going to happen? This wasn't New Jack City, for God's sake.

"You gotta get over that Huxtable shit," Jay said dryly.

"I'm kidding!" She cleared her throat. "So, are you going to show me where you grew up and stuff?"

"Yeah . . . if you want. I gotta go holla at Yellow Andre over at Whitman. I want you to meet him." The infamous and curiously named Walt Whitman projects were right off Fort Greene Park, on

Myrtle Avenue. Today, the park hosted peppy Rollerbladers and horn-rimmed lesbian couples overdosing on Evian, but when Jay and Yellow Andre had been kids, it was littered with crack vials, violent drug deals, and hookers.

Jay had been paying visits to Yellow almost every weekend since his early release from Rikers the year before, just to make sure he was surviving. Yellow had come home different, sort of glazed-over and jittery, like a shell-shocked Vietnam vet. He'd been living with his wildly manipulative and charismatic mother in the apartment he grew up in, and working at White Castle. It wasn't a good scene, and he wondered how Billie would react. Jay had never brought anyone from his clean life into his childhood. Mostly because everyone was locked up or dead, but also because he compartmentalized his people into "back in the day" and "now." And never the twain shall meet.

She could hardly mask how flattered she was. Darryl, K, and the two Andres were like mythological figures to her. "Really? I feel like I've known him for *years*. What should I wear?"

Jay grinned, kissed her mouth and each of her nipples, and hopped out of bed. Billie watched him walk across the room to the refrigerator, stark naked and beautiful.

"Will you tell me colorful stories about the old days?" Billie playfully put on a wide-eyed innocent face.

"Uh-huh." Jay opened the fridge and took a hearty swig of red Gatorade. Billie crawled out of bed and slinked over to him.

"Will you introduce me to all the big bad gangstas you used to know?"

"Uh-huh. I'll even tell them you're my bitch."

"You better tell them you're *my* bitch," Billie said, dropping to her knees in front of him.

* * *

ater, Billie and Jay headed out for Walt Whitman. Despite Jay's suggestion that she wear a do-rag and a sneer, she went with low-rider Marc Jacobs jeans, a lacy Chloé T-shirt, and kitten-heeled Jimmy Choo ankle boots. This was Billie's casual, just-kicking-it-on-a-Saturday look. It was a clear, bright, sixty-five-degree day, and they were in no particular hurry. They held hands as they walked, loving the feeling of being a couple, of sprouting a fabulous new appendage. They took the scenic route, strolling happily down the idyllic, brownstone-lined streets.

They perused a couple of stoop sales, had an Italian ice, and stopped by Carol's Daughter, the super-trendy organic beauty boutique off the park. Here, Billie recognized three sleek UPNs (a Renee-coined term signifying Uppity Negresses) who had been a class behind her at Duke. She could tell the Coach-bag-carrying lawyers were utterly shocked and intrigued by Billie's sexy, roughneck boyfriend, who was wearing baggy jeans, Timberland boots, and an XXL T-shirt emblazoned with Che Guevara's image. It was like she was dating an exotic foreigner. Billie bristled with pride at their obvious envy.

As they sauntered away, loudly whispering, "He's so thug-life!" Billie turned to Jay with a triumphant smile. "I have street credibility!"

"I feel so objectified."

"Oh, you like it."

"No amount of you running around with me could give you street credibility."

"What? Are you kidding?" Billie started strutting around, launching into NWA's "Fuck the Police."

Jay burst out laughing.

"What? Okay, so I'm repping the wrong coast, but whatever. I can be hard when I wanna be. I'm tougher than leather."

"You're tougher than pleather."

Billie punched Jay in the arm and giggled. Life was good.

* * *

When they finally reached Walt Whitman, it was about four. The tall, red-bricked buildings that made up the development took up a whole block. Everyone was outside, basking in the Indian summer weather. Old ladies sat gossiping on benches while elementary school–aged girls played complicated hand-clap games. Somebody's mother screamed out the window for Rafiq to leave Ms. Parker's daughter alone before she came down there and stopped him herself. Teenaged boys huddled together, laughing uproariously as they dissed each other for sport. The block was abuzz with the percussion of basketballs bouncing off walls and double-Dutch jump ropes scraping the concrete.

They stood on the sidewalk outside the development, looking up at the tenth floor of the tallest building.

"That's me and K's bedroom window."

"Do his parents still live there?"

Jay shrugged and turned around to face the street. He pointed to a laundromat on the corner. "That used to be a bodega back in the day. I almost got arrested right out front."

"What?"

He nodded in a let's-not-make-a-big-deal-out-of-this way.

"How old were you?"

"Fifteen."

"Oh." Silence. "What happened?"

"I was just being stupid. That was one of the places where I used to sell. The thing is, when you're doing so much dirty shit—and I mean *various* forms of illegal behavior—you can't ever sleep on your surroundings. You absolutely cannot, not even for a second. You got to always be aware, checking for plainclothes cops and shit. Cars you ain't never seen. Unfamiliar-lookin' niggas. After a while, it's just instinct. You immediately know when the block's hot, and then you gotta get the fuck outta there. You're in so much shit, you could get got for anything at any time, you know?

"The thing is, that day I was thrown off my game cuz I was high. It was an accident. I hate being high. I mean, high on some ill shit. You know I'm not a drug-type person."

"No, I know," Billie said.

"My man gave me a cigarette that was laced with PCP."

"PCP?"

"Yeah."

"Huh. I always thought PCP was an urban legend. Like one of those generic 'just say no' drugs that Nancy Reagan would always preach the evils of, but that no one was really doing."

Jay looked at her like she was an alien. "You thought PCP was an urban legend?"

"Well, I don't know . . ." She trailed off, deciding to speak less. "Anyway, so what happened?"

"So, I was all fucked up. It makes your heart beat really fast, and everything's on fast-forward. This white cat came up to me and asked if I had any dope. Shit, I shoulda known right then he was shady. When I reached into my back pocket for my bags, he pulled out a nine and his badge. I don't even remember thinking, I just took off. And the PCP made me fast. I was *out*. I ran and ran and, you know, I finally lost him."

"Jesus, Jay." Billie clutched her heart.

"I hid under a garbage truck for three hours, tweaking and sweating and shit. It was awful."

"Honey."

"And it wasn't that I was particularly scared. It ain't in me to be shook. Besides, I woulda ended up in Juvy, and I knew half the niggas in there. The thing is, you don't stroll out of Juvenile Hall and end up a normal person chillin' on Wall Street with a 401(k). Chances are, you're going right back in. You don't know how else to be." Jay shook his head. "It wasn't for me. I had too much shit to take care of."

Billie was speechless. Her heart broke for him, but at the same time, deep deep down, she found it sort of exciting.

Jay changed the subject. "Okay, enough reminiscing. You look like a deer in headlights. Let's go." He grabbed her hand, kissed it, and led her to Yellow Andre's building.

They stood in the hallway outside Yellow's door. The walls were decorated with amateur, ball-point graffiti, and the elevator smelled like piss. Jay knocked and knocked, but there was no answer. Just as they were turning away, a shapely, middle-aged Latina woman opened the door. She was quite pretty but tired-looking.

"¡Hola, guapo!"

"What's up, Mrs. Jones." Jay gave her a hug and a kiss. She looked happy to see him.

"The livin' could be easier. *Cómo estás*, baby?"

"Good, good. Mrs. Jones, this is—"

"I remember you! Jou still doin' hair, mami?"

Jay's eyes widened. She couldn't possibly think Billie was Tammy. They looked nothing alike, and Tammy hadn't lived in the neighborhood for a good five years. No, no, no.

"No, no, uh, this is my girlfriend, Billie," Jay said quickly. "You're thinking of the girl we all used to run with in high school, what's her name? I know it ain't been that long since I've seen you, Mrs. Jones. Anyway, Billie, this is Yellow's mom."

Billie smiled and gave her a kiss on her powdery-soft cheek. She shot Jay a suspicious, slightly amused expression. Luckily, Billie was secure enough in his devotion to know that if Jay was looking nervous, there had to be an innocent reason.

Mrs. Jones moved closer to Billie and, squinting, looked Billie up and down. "Ooooh, jou not her. My eyes is bad, but I'm so vain I no wear the glasses."

"Don't worry about it," said Billie.

"*¿Eres puertorriqueña?*"

"No, no, I'm black."

Mrs. Jones squinted suspiciously. "*¿Seguro?* I think somebody lied to jou, baby." Mrs. Jones invited them into the small, cozy apartment, and they sat down on her plastic-covered plaid couch. School portraits of Yellow competed with stylized pictures of Jesus for wall space. A rainbow of rosary beads hung over the kitchen door. The apartment smelled like a cross between garlic and Lysol.

"Yellow's daddy was black. He left me for a peep show hoochie in nineteen eighty-two. But I no allow that incident to make me prejudiced." She gave Billie a welcoming smile. "I'm open to all kinds." She turned to Jay. "So whatchoo know good, *guapo*?"

"Nothing much, nothing much. Is Yellow around?"

"No, he outside watching some basketball game. At least, that's what he said. Don't let me find out he's out there all loco."

"He ain't, Mrs. Jones. You know Yellow's on the up and up."

"I don't know shit. Excuse me, Beelie." Billie waved her away. "He ain't like you, *niño*. I wish he'd bring home a nice girl sometime. He gotta settle down, jou know? He ain't getting no jounger."

"True, true. But he's doing all right, considering."

"Consider this. He out there bettin' on games and ain't got a dime and a nickel. If that ain't loco, *no sé*." She fixed her fawnlike eyes on Billie. "Whatchoo do for a living, baby?"

"I write for a magazine. About beauty products . . . makeup, haircare, trends. That sort of thing."

"Really? Thass a job?"

"I know, right? It's fun. I'm lucky — I'm one of the few people I know who actually likes their job."

"Betchoo make money, huh?"

"Well, not really. Magazine writing isn't what you do if you're looking for a big salary."

"At least jou get a salary. My son works at White Castle. I don't know where his dollars go. I don't see any of it, that's for sure. He's loco, my son. Always, always, always broke. Jay, you got to talk to him. He's jour friend."

"I know, Mrs. Jones. He's trying to get himself together. He's trying."

"Hrmph." Mrs. Jones didn't believe it. She leaned in conspiratorially. "Jay?"

"Yes?"

"I'm gonna ask a serious question."

"Of course. What's up?"

"My son's a fruit?"

"What? Naw, Yellow ain't gay. Where'd you get that from?"

"He never be bringin' no girls over, and he's been so *funny* since he came back home. Jay, I tell you he's a *maricón*. I try to ask him, but he say to stay out his biz. I tell him, I say, '*¡Mira!* Andre! If I find out jou running around with little boys I'll right away die, *entiendes?*' And he just say to leave him be."

"Mrs. Jones, I really don't think—"

"Well then, maybe he just no have the proper tools for normal relations. I tell him when he was jung not to mess around with that marijuana and stuff. It kills jour nature." She raised her eyebrows and looked knowingly at Billie. "She knows what I mean."

Billie nodded politely.

"I'm sad, Jay. Sometimes I don't want to live no more. Andre's *mi niño*, but he no good. He stupid and weak. I wish jou were my son. Jou a famous comedian . . ." Comedian? ". . . and jou always in the paper, and my own son is such a mess." Her voice began to shake. She widened her large eyes, blinked, and produced a tiny tear. "I am cursed."

"Mrs. Jones, don't get upset. I told you to ask me if you needed anything."

"I'm too proud to ask. *Boricuas* don't take handouts." She sat up pin-straight.

Looking vaguely embarrassed, Jay took out his wallet, counted out $100, and handed it to her. She shook her head, her brown curls bouncing.

"No, no, no, *guapo*. I can't take jour money. I'd rather starve and also die tragically of a broken heart."

"Take it. Really, it's no problem."

She paused, daintily wiping a tear from her cheek. "Beelie, I'm sorry jou had to see this," she whispered, accepting the cash. "Jou was always a good boy, Jay. Help my son. He's a non-money-earnin' fruit and I know it."

Jay winced and stood up. "Okay, Mrs. Jones. Well, we're gonna go see him now. You take care, though." He kissed her and led Billie to the door.

"Bye, joung lovers," she trilled. "Go with God!"

"Nice to meet you," said Billie.

Outside the door, Jay let out a huge sigh. "She watches too many novellas."

Billie wrapped her arms around his waist and looked up at him. "You're wonderful, you know that?"

"Aw shucks."

"Now, who's the bitch that does hair?"

"Oh that." Jay made a waving motion with his hand. "Mrs. Jones gets mad confused. You know, she's been through a lot. She was talking about this girl from the neighborhood, but I think she moved a while back."

"I only believe you because you're so cute."

"Shit, whatever works," Jay said, grateful for Billie's naïveté. Not that he was doing anything really despicable to her, like cheating, but still. His insides were churning. He'd have to come clean soon . . . nothing felt right while he was keeping her a secret. It wasn't fair to anyone, and he knew it. And he really wanted things to be right with Tammy, dammit.

"Let's go see your friend."

"Okay, but I need an ATM machine. Mrs. Jones cleaned me out." *Jesus Christ*, Jay thought to himself. *Women.*

The basketball court was packed. In the center of things was a handsome boy in Knicks basketball shorts and a wifebeater. Two teenagers in variations of the same outfit were arguing over who was going to play him next. The tall boy was absentmindedly dribbling and gazing at his girlfriend, Sheree, who was reclining on a crowded bench with her friends. She was licking a Blow Pop and suggestively running a pink Timberland-clad foot up and down her shapely leg.

Jay scanned the crowd and spotted Yellow sitting alone on a cracked lawn chair on the far side of the court. Jay raised his fist in the air and Yellow nodded, but before they could head in his direction, Jay was mobbed.

Jay looked sincerely happy to see every single person who rushed up to him. He navigated through the crowd like a politician, shaking hands, kissing babies, kissing babies' mamas (to Billie, he seemed like a cross between Jesse Jackson and Ferris Bueller). They were all beaming with pride at their local boy made good. They always knew he was a star, and it was about time the outside world caught on.

"That nigga Jay, whassup! How you livin'?"

"Shady ass mothafucka, why I gotta pick up *Vibe* to see your face? Where you been at?"

"Yo, son, lemme get at you a minute. You blowin' up and shit, but don't forget the little niggas. I been on some writing shit, too . . . what I gotta do to get put on?"

"Just tell me you still gangsta. That's all. I know you all Broadway now, and you probably got white bitches on your dick, but I'd be disheartened to find out you ain't keeping it gangsta."

" 'Sup, Nut. So, who's your shorty?" The tall boy with the basketball was the only one with the nerve to ask. His name was Air, and he was thirteen. His father was Bone, the dealer who had first noticed Jay's hustling abilities when he was only nine. Ever since Bone died of AIDS in jail, Jay had taken it upon himself to keep an eye on Air, to make sure he didn't surrender to any street insanity. But the truth was, Air was such a brilliant player that none of his boys wanted to involve him in shady activities. They wanted to see him make it out. And between the demands of basketball and Sheree, Air didn't have any time to fuck up.

"This is my girl, Billie. And don't be calling her no shorty."

"Hi, Air." Billie smiled up at him. He was at least six-foot-five.

"Damn, girl. You fine! What you doing with a boy's name?"

Billie laughed and Jay rolled his eyes.

"Fuck you get the nerve to ask somebody about a name? Your girl's name is Sheree-Amor."

"Awww, man, go 'head." Air looked bashful and started bouncing the ball.

"So what's the deal? Who you playin'?"

"Everybody. I been playin' all day. I'm killlin' 'em out there."

"Word?"

"Yeah, man, these niggas can't *see* me, man."

"You tired?"

"Naw, I'm Air. You betta recognize."

"Your mother e-mailed me your *Catcher in the Rye* paper. Not bad."

"Word?" He shrugged, embarrassed. Then he leaned in toward Jay and whispered, "Oh, and, uh, thanks for those notes."

"The Cliffs Notes?"

"Yeah. Them joints was off the hook."

"I loved *Catcher in the Rye*," offered Billie, who immediately felt like an asshole. Air nodded uncomfortably and looked around. He was mortified by this conversation.

"All right then, don't let me get in your way. I'm about to get at Yellow."

"All right, man. Keep it gangsta." Air pounded him on the back. Jay chuckled and moved on, dragging Billie through the crowd. What did Air know about gangsta?

Yellow hadn't moved a muscle since Jay entered the court. He was rail thin and slumped over in the chair. A Dodgers cap was pulled low over his butter-colored face. When he lifted his hand to punch Jay's fist hello, Billie noticed he was shaking. She couldn't believe she and Yellow were practically the same age. He did not look well. Jay introduced Billie, and Yellow nodded.

"Whassup, Yell?"

"Chillin'." He threw back some Red Stripe and took a bite of some Sara Lee pound cake he'd been eating.

"I was just at your crib."

"Word?"

"Your moms thinks you gay."

"I know. She trippin'."

"You ain't getting no pussy?"

"Ain't trying."

"You need to get up off your ass. You look like shit."

"Aww, nigga, fuck you." He glanced sideways at Billie. "Sorry, ma." For the second time that day, Billie waved the comment away. Who was she, Our Miss Brooks?

"How's the job?"

"I flip hamburgers. We can't all be you."

"Don't start that shit."

"Anyway, I quit."

"Tell me you lyin'."

"I wasn't challenged."

"You got something lined up?"

"Naw." He finished off the pound cake and wiped the crumbs on his sweatpants. His eyes darted around, and he seemed uneasy. "The block's hot, nigga. Watch your back."

"What?"

"Streets is watchin'."

Jay looked around. What was he talking about? Everybody was chilling, having a good time. He squinted at Yellow. He was paranoid. Rikers had fucked him up.

Jay said, "I'm hooking you up at the Public Theater. They need someone at the door. Taking tickets and shit."

"Word?"

"It's a job."

Billie tried again. "The Public Theater is very nice. It's a nice space." Dammit, she thought, everything she said landed with a thud.

Yellow sucked down some more Red Stripe and managed a bleak smile. He gave Jay a pound. "My nigga."

"All right? So, I'm gonna get at you later. Handle your business, Yell."

"Peace."

They weren't two steps away before Yellow Andre called Jay back. Billie watched them talk back and forth for a minute—Andre doing a lot of gesturing—and then Jay handed him some cash out of his pocket.

A nd that was Yellow.

"What was that all about?"

"Same old thing. He needed cash so I hit him off."

"But you just got him a job!"

"But he needs it now."

"For what?"

"To get high."

"Why'd you give him money to get high?" Billie was outraged. "He's supposed to be getting back on the right path and everything. 'Weedhead' practically equals shiftless! Hello? Haven't you seen *Friday*?"

"It ain't for weed . . . and stop talking so loud."

Billie stopped walking. "You didn't give him money to buy *for real* drugs."

Jay looked as if he were about to explain Reaganomics to a small child.

"If I didn't give it to him, he would do very bad things to get it."

"Jay . . ."

"Listen, baby, he's a junkie. Ain't nobody gonna stop that man from being a junkie. What I can do is make sure he don't hurt nobody else in the process."

"But . . . but . . . you of all people know what, like, serious drugs can do to you. He's gonna end up killing himself, slowly. I don't understand how you can knowingly contribute to—"

"Billie." Jay cut her off in a way that made it clear the conversation was sort of over. "No, you don't understand. You couldn't. What, you think he don't know how he's gonna end up if he don't stop? There's a place you get where you don't give a fuck. He's there. What, I'm gonna cry and scream like a bitch? He's a grownass man. It don't work. Trust me. You don't know nothing about this. I lived this shit, you didn't."

Billie was taken aback. "Well, you don't have to talk to me like that."

"I'm sorry." He was. "I mean, I know where you're coming from. It's . . . it's frustrating."

Billie was totally aghast. She didn't understand this way of thinking at all. In a thousand years she would never understand what had just happened. How could he contribute to Andre's drug problem? And Jay looked so certain, so sure of what he'd just done. For the first time, she fully grasped how fundamentally different their experiences were. What else would they differ on? What if they got married and had kids? She could see it now: her fourteen-year-old son, coming home with his pregnant girlfriend. *"But, Mommy, Daddy said I could fuck DeeDee without a condom because I'm a grown-ass man!"*

"Stop lookin' so traumatized," Jay said, tipping up her chin. "I'm sorry."

"We're from totally different planets."

"True."

"There are things we'll never understand about each other."

"True. We just gotta accept them." Jay put on a roughneck expression. "The streets made me, ma. Either you with it or you not."

Billie grinned. "I don't think I have a choice." She leaned up and kissed him on the cheek. She was over it.

He took her hand and walked with her. The sun was going down.

"Yellow seemed sweet," Billie managed with difficulty.

Jay chuckled.

"You know, you're like the godfather over there. You take care of everybody."

"You can't choose your family," he said, shrugging.

Billie was amazed at his nonchalance. And then it became all about her: What did she ever do for anybody? Whose mentor was she? Who did she ever bail out? Once, her sophomore year, she was a character witness on a case involving Vida and $200 worth of shoplifted babydoll dresses from Contempo Casuals. But she'd never done anything really, *really* significant. Jay was like a mini-messiah.

She stopped him in his tracks and kissed him. Then she burrowed into his arms and stayed there awhile, rocking back and forth.

* * *

Later that evening, they stopped by Brooklyn Moon Café to catch the weekly poetry reading. Ordinarily, this was something Billie would never attend. It wasn't the café—she loved their fried chicken—it was the whole poetry scene. When they first moved to New York, Vida had gone through a brief but prolific poet-dating phase. Most of them were con artists who talked an awful lot without saying much, like cowrie shell–accessorized used-car salesmen. And they had clearly thought Billie and Co. were slinky, mistrustful sellouts, which enraged her.

Tonight, though, Jay wanted her to meet LaLa, the girl who organized the Saturday night slams and had set him up with his first gig.

When they entered the café, the reading hadn't started yet. There were about fifty people crammed in the tiny café, crushed onto overstuffed velvet love seats and wrought-iron barstools. Most of them were standing. The walls were painted a fiery maroon and decorated with antique-gold-framed paintings by a local West Indian-American artist. Somehow, a DJ had managed to squeeze himself, his turntable, and his records in the back of the room, by the kitchen door. He was spinning the greatest hits of the neo-soul movement. D'Angelo's "Brown Sugar" was fading out, giving way to Maxwell's way out there "Submerge: Till We Become the Sun." Erykah Badu's "Appletree" soon followed. Everyone was bobbing their collective heads to the beats.

The guys were very Salvation Army meets Bob Marley, all done up in camouflage cargo pants, Jesus sandals, and Rasta caps. The girls were a boho blur of Afro-puffs, dreadlocks (in every incarnation— miles-long, short, twisted, hennaed), and head wraps. The scent of Egyptian Musk was overwhelming. Not for the first time that day, Billie stood out like an overly fashion-conscious sore thumb, while Jay was greeted like Norm on *Cheers*.

Just then, a tall, sylphlike woman with a dreadlock ponytail on top of her head caught Billie's eye. She was wearing a carrot-orange dashiki minidress and brandishing a burning stick of incense. She was insanely ravishing, and headed straight for Jay.

"Love, love, *love*," she moaned, engulfing him in an airtight embrace, breasts-first. "What's happening, black man?"

"I'm chilling. Just stopping by to see what y'all conscious motherfuckers are talking about tonight." He grinned playfully, his eyes twinkling.

The woman burst out laughing and hit him on the arm.

"And I wanted to introduce you to my girl, Billie," he said. "She's heard all about you. Billie, this is LaLa."

Billie and LaLa smiled at each other, and polite kisses were exchanged.

"Peace and blessings, sister."

"Hi, it's nice to meet you."

LaLa's gaze fixed on Billie, with her trendy, off-the-shoulder T-shirt and straight hair. She was clearly not impressed. Neither was Billie. She'd had to deal her whole life with earthy types like LaLa thinking she was less "down" because of what she looked or dressed like. She'd gotten over that whole Whitley Gilbert association a long time ago—and besides, what was so wrong with Whitley? The interesting thing, though, was that Jay was all hip-hop slouchy and the furthest thing from neo-soul style, but he was accepted anywhere.

If LaLa touched him again, there would be a problem.

"My brother, are you going to bless us with a reading today?"

"Naw, yo, I just came to watch."

"You can't do that to your people! Sister," she said, turning to Billie, "I don't know if you know, but this man is a phenomenon. The way he embodies the soul of his characters, it's like, it's like . . . he's conjuring up the wisdom of the ancestors. Heralding the most ancient oral traditions, transcending the present . . ." LaLa clutched her chest with one hand and Jay's bicep with the other. She was rapturous.

"Girl, go 'head," he said. "It ain't about all that . . ."

"Sister, have you experienced his performance?"

"Yes, he's amazing. I could never get up there and do what he does." Just then, Jay was swept up into a conversation with a short balding gentleman who looked like a young George Jefferson. He excused himself and shot Billie a "hang in there" look. Billie's heart began to pound. She felt as miscast in this crowd as Diana Ross in *The Wiz*.

She and LaLa were left facing each other.

"So, what do you do, sister?"

"I'm an editor at *Du Jour*. A beauty editor."

"A beauty editor? Whose beauty are you editing?"

"No, I write about trends in makeup, hair, that sort of thing. Do you read *Du Jour*?"

"No, there's nothing in there for me. How could I support the continuing massacre of black self-esteem by funding a magazine that only speaks to a white standard of beauty?" She waved her incense stick pointedly, ashes sifting down onto Billie's boots. "My soul couldn't rest at night."

"Have you ever read it?"

"Like I said, I make it a point not to."

"Oh. Because if you read it, you'd know that our beauty section is incredibly diverse. That's what I'm there for; it's my responsibility." Billie was outraged but graceful. "And hopefully, since *Du Jour* is the world's leading fashion magazine, others will follow suit and things will eventually change."

"I don't need to see my face on the pages of *Du Jour* to feel beautiful, sister. And neither should you."

"That's not what I'm saying."

"Sisters are beautiful, period. The sooner we learn to accept our wide noses, our nappy hair, our big behinds, the better we'll all be. We need to love ourselves, not hate."

"It's interesting that you say that, because I'm a sister and you're hating on me."

LaLa flinched and raised her eyebrows. In a split second she recovered, smiling condescendingly. "Be easy, love. I'm just taking a walk with you."

"Mmm-hm." Billie wondered how LaLa would look choking on that incense stick. She looked around for Jay. Luckily, the DJ got on the mike and announced that the reading was starting.

"Emcee time." LaLa winked at the DJ and faced Billie. "We're all in the struggle together, sister. Go in peace. Oh, and take care with that man. He's a sacred, *sacred* spirit." With a flip of her buoyant ponytail, she edged her way to the DJ table.

Billie stormed up to Jay and dragged him away from George Jefferson. "How could you leave me with that 'I'd Like to Teach the World to Sing' monster?"

"Oh, she ain't all that bad." He nodded back at somebody across the room.

"Not that bad? Not that bad?"

"You can't take her seriously. Besides, you can take care of yourself." Jay put his hands on his hips and delivered a pitch-perfect Billie imitation. "'I'm a sister and you're hating on *me*.'"

"You heard that?" She laughed and hid her face in her hands.

"Guess what?" whispered Jay, as LaLa took the mike. She asked her brothers and sisters to give love to Jay Lane, a griot in the true African tradition.

"What?" asked Billie. The crowd did as it was told, giving props where it was due. Jay grinned and nodded at the crowd. Billie marveled at how comfortable he was with being adored, just like her mother.

LaLa introduced the first poet, someone called Profundity.

"That little guy I was talking to over there . . ."

"George Jefferson?"

"Yeah. He works for Cinemax and shit. They're starting a weekly variety-type show starring spoken-word artists. It's called *Wordstock*."

"Ha!"

"I know, right? And he wants me to headline the first show. He's here scouting out new talent. He was gonna call me on Monday."

Billie grabbed him and squeezed him tight.

"I feel like everything's happening for me at once," he whispered in her ear. "I'm trippin' . . . I can't believe it."

"You deserve it, you really do."

"I'm a lucky motherfucker." He looked down at her. "And guess what else?"

"What?"

"I love you," he whispered in her ear.

7.

come to jesus

nd just like that, Billie was gone. She would later characterize this chapter of her life with a quote from her favorite diva, Elizabeth Taylor, upon falling in love with Richard Burton: "I love not being Elizabeth Taylor, but being Richard's wife. I would be quite content to be his shadow and live through him."

Every ounce of her neurotic, workaholic personality was absorbed into her relationship, which left her job for dead. This was not a good thing.

Billie just couldn't get it up for *Du Jour*. She came in late, left early, and she began blowing off important after-work events, asking Sandy to fill in for her, which irritated certain big-name beauty companies. Sending an editor farther down on the masthead was considered insulting—better to just skip it altogether.

Worst of all, she thought less and less about the London thing, and kept putting off her hard-won "Culture Club" article. Her deadline was two weeks away, and Billie usually liked to spend a good six weeks writing and researching her bigger articles. She knew the piece would help Fannie, her editor in chief, seal the decision on sending Billie to London, and that was the trouble.

Love, and all the yummy side dishes that accompanied it, had eluded Billie her entire life. She'd sat through dozens of Vida's affairs, coached Renee through her trials with Moses, and grew up in a house that was steeped in love and passion. Yet she'd never had it, herself. Now that she did, she felt that she had lost time to make up for. She'd never allowed herself to float away on anything—she was always focused on getting the best grades, being a perfect student, climbing to the top of her career. Billie was tired of being Miss Responsible. For once, she just wanted to feel weightless and frivolous and lovable, dammit. Hadn't she earned it?

Hell yeah, she thought to herself, rolling over and snuggling up to Jay's strong, sculpted chest. It was the Monday morning after their amazing weekend spent roaming around Fort Greene. Billie didn't remember ever feeling this sparkly, this satisfied, this . . . content. Lazily, she opened one eye to check the time, but not really caring. It was 10:15. What?! With a yelp, she bounded out of bed, her hair defying gravity.

"What? What happened?" Jay was torn out of his usual restless, semiconscious slumber.

"Shit, shit, shit. I'm so late. Why didn't I set the alarm?" Billie raced into the bathroom, brushed her teeth in two seconds, and ran back out. She rummaged through her closet, throwing clothes on the floor, freaking out. "I totally forgot about a breakfast event I have to go to. It's so, so important, Jay, oh my God."

"What's the event?"

"It's Clairene, you know, Clairene . . . Glow! Gleam! Hair like a dream?" Billie sang the commercial and wiggled into a pair of black leather Joseph pants at the same time. "They're launching something, I forget, and they have some new celebrity spokesperson that's gonna be there and *fuck*, if Paige finds out I'm so dead."

"What time it started?"

"Nine-thirty!" Billie grabbed a random top from a drawer, threw on some Jimmy Choos, blew Jay a kiss, and sprinted out the door.

Jay was saying, "You forgot to do your hair," but the door had already slammed behind her.

The breakfast was held at Norma's in the famously snooty Parker Meridien on Fifty-seventh Street, a beauty industry favorite. (The restaurant was known for its insanely rich, gourmet breakfast dishes, like almond-stuffed brioche French toast dipped in chocolate. Clearly no one came within a foot of these confections, but, my, they were pretty!) Billie arrived at exactly eleven. She guiltily accepted her name tag from a junior PR girl and flew up the glittery staircase to the restaurant.

Billie's jaw hit the floor. The space, usually decorated in pristine, ladies-who-lunch elegance, had been transformed into what looked like a set from *Breakin' 2: Electric Boogaloo*. Graffiti-splattered canvas screens clung to the walls, shouting out "Rock the house with Clairene's new Street Style Gel-Wax!" and "Funk it up with Clairene's new Street Style Gel-Wax!" Scary-thin models were stationed in various tough-girl poses around the room, each with a different "street-inspired" hairstyle: crimped, spiky, teased out to there. Billie felt like she was walking through Pat Benatar's "Love

Is a Battlefield" video. Accompanying each model was a certified Clairene National Hairstylist, available to explain how to achieve the look with the new Street Style Gel-Wax. In groups of three and four, the beauty editors roamed from station to station, chatting with the National Hairstylists and fingering the models' stiff hair with unbridled fascination.

And, dear God, someone had hired break-dancers to perform in the center of the room. On flattened cardboard boxes. Billie's heart went out to these poor guys hopping about in velour tracksuits and shelltop Adidas. What if their fellow b-boys knew they were performing for a bunch of fancy fashionistas who probably thought Afrika Bambaataa was an ethnic accessories boutique in Brooklyn?

She'd taken about two steps into the room when she was intercepted by Annabel Brixton, Clairene's gushing VP of marketing. Heavy of hip and wide of mouth, she was one of those pushy Southern women who repeated your name a lot as if to force intimacy. She relied heavily on scarves, brooches, and heavy clip-on earrings to look pulled-together.

"Billie *precious*!" Annabel bleated, kissing her on both cheeks.

"Annabel! How are you? You look divine, as usual," Billie lied, turning on her full-wattage grin and Big Important Event personality.

"Oh no, you!"

"Annabel, I am so, so, so sorry for being late. It's so tacky and not my style, you *know* that."

"Oh, Billie, I *know*!"

She began her speech, voice shaking ever so slightly. She'd practiced this on the train. "This morning was the worst. I had such a scare. I'd left my apartment door unlocked all night . . . I don't know what I was thinking, I've been working so hard, I don't know. And I woke up and my medicine cabinet had been ransacked!"

"No!"

"Yes!" Billie leaned in conspiratorially. "And, well, I have terrible migraines so I have some fairly potent painkillers."

Annabel's eyebrows raised and understanding flooded her face. "That devil is making a killing on the black market today," she announced, wisely.

"You're telling me."

"*Precious*, what a nightmare! You could've been . . . Oh, well, let's not even *go* there. Are you all right?"

"Of course, of course. Nothing else was stolen, and I had the locks changed." Billie exhaled dramatically. "But anyway, that's why I was late. You have to forgive me, I'm so flustered . . ."

"My Billie." Annabel beamed at her, and crushed her to her bosom in an enormous hug. "My darling, darling Billie. I'm surprised you came at all, after the horror you've been through. You know, you've always been my favorite."

Billie smiled bashfully at the VIP Clairene exec.

"So, come on in and I don't want you to worry about a thing." She took Billie by the arm and paraded her past the stations and the break-dancers toward the front of the room. A group of girls waved at her, and she smiled back sheepishly. Her mentor, Trina, from *Radiance* magazine, frowned disapprovingly and raised an eyebrow. As a black girl in a white industry, it's especially important always to be on point. Those are just the rules.

Then she did a double take. Why did three of those girls have cornrows in their hair? Had there been a press trip to Jamaica over the weekend?

"You missed the presentation and breakfast, but I'll catch you up. Do you like what we've done? Isn't it just *funky*, Billie? When I saw the space all decorated I just wanted to get on down, you know what I mean?"

"I do."

"Clairene, as you know, is a very classic haircare brand. Our tradition is soft hair, gleaming, touchable, silky-smooth hair. Christie Brinkley hair. But Billie, that's not really keeping up with the times, now is it?" It was a rhetorical question, and Annabel continued. "I'm sure you went to the collections, yes? The hair was edgy, it was textured, it was, well, Billie, it was *urban*. Did you see Kate Moss in those glorious cornrows? I tell you, a revolution has started, Billie, and Clairene is one step ahead of the bunch. That's why we decided to introduce Street Style. It can quite literally transform your hair into a gazillion different styles. And here's the most exciting news! We recruited none other than Christina Aguilera, princess of punky-pop, to be our spokesperson!"

Annabel seemed to be on the verge of hysteria. Billy reacted appropriately. "How thrilling! What a coup . . . Is she here?"

"Why, yes, she is, Billie, and so is the fascinating woman responsible for her signature look from her video . . . Oh, I've gone and forgot what it's called?"

" 'Make It Hurt.' "

"That's right. Catchy! Anyway, she's an extremely talented African-American woman named Pandora? You'll just adore her. Now, Billie, we've arranged a very special treat for you girls today. We've arranged for each of you to get a photo taken with Christina. And Pandora's actually giving some editors cornrows! Isn't that just *fun*!"

Aha! "So adorable."

"And, Billie, I have to tell you, I'm so pleased you really got into the spirit of the event. Especially after the traumatic morning you had!"

"What do you mean?"

"The spiked hair! Very Tina Turner!" Just then, they were interrupted by Christina's manager. She loudly whispered to Annabel that her client was due on TRL in twenty minutes, and could they wrap this up? Annabel excused herself with a jaw-breaking grin and bounded away.

Billie's hands flew up to her hair. It was everywhere. How could she have walked around like this? Should she borrow a Kangol hat from one of the dancers? Frantically, she looked around and saw a station that had been deserted by its model and National Hairstylist. Billie grabbed an abandoned jar of Gel-Wax, scooped out a huge dollop, and smoothed it down over her hair. Thankfully, it began to fall under the weight of the product. What was this stuff? It felt like something you used to polish your car.

"Sweetie, what are you doing?" said the National Hairstylist, appearing out of nowhere, clearly possessive of her materials. "Leave your hair alone! It looked so cute before, all spiky and crazy!"

"Yeah, but that wasn't the look I was going for," growled Billie, in no mood.

"Maybe it should be," she shot back, grabbing the jar from Billie and returning to her station.

Bitch, Billie thought, and sighed. Her game was slipping.

And in more ways than one. Pandora was here! Billie tried to tell herself that the hollow pit in her stomach was hunger, and not guilt for blowing off her interview with the hairstylist. Dammit. Pandora's presence was a sign from God to get back on the horse. She had to find her and schedule an interview—airtight, this time.

"Holy shit."

Billie spun around. It was her friend Monica, the aristocratic-looking, filthy-mouthed brunette from *Cosmo*. With a head full of braids and all kinds of scandal written all over her face.

"What? What's wrong?"

"My eyes are so deceiving me. Come here right now, missy." She dragged Billie into a corner.

"What?"

"Did you just, like, get back from *field hockey* practice, or what?"

"What are you talking about?"

"Billie Burke, in all my days I've never seen you in Abercrombie & Fitch."

Billie looked down. She was wearing the sleeveless knit mock-turtleneck she wore to do the laundry. She'd had it for a million years. Her boobs had stretched it out so far that it hung limply a good five inches away from her waist. And it was wrinkled to death. *And* it had "Abercrombie & Fitch" emblazoned across the chest in bold red letters.

"No, no, no, no . . ." Billie moaned, throwing her hands over her face.

"Now, technically there's nothing wrong with Abercrombie. Tenth-graders and dykes would be *lost* without them. But you work at fucking *Du Jour*, for chrissakes!" She stomped her foot for emphasis. "Woman, have you forgotten yourself?"

"I know, I know. You have no idea what I went through this morning . . ." Wait, she didn't have to lie with Monica. "Okay, I have no excuse. I was just in bed."

"Then, yeah, you have no excuse."

"I don't know what's wrong with me, Monica. I was so late today I shouldn't even have shown up. I'm a disgrace."

"No you're not. You're just fucking burned out. Grab something from the fashion closet as soon as you get to work. You'll be fine, sweetie."

"Okay, but look at my hair!"

"Look at *your* hair? Look at me! White girls in cornrows are the worst. I feel like Vanilla Ice in drag."

"Why'd you do it, then?"

"You know I can't turn down a freebie. But nobody else could, either. Look over there."

To the left, Pandora's fingers were flying over Randi Rimmerstein's long blond hair. *Mademoiselle*'s beauty director was freakishly tall and universally disliked for her grand sense of entitlement—she was rumored to have expensed her entire wedding *and* her honeymoon. At the moment, Randi was hunched down on a tiny stool, her bloodless face a portrait of mortal agony. Her lower lip trembled, her jaw was clenched, and her hands were knotted into tight fists. Through it all Pandora happily braided away, oblivious to the fact that Randi was near death.

"Karma's a bitch, right?"

Billie burst into a fit of giggles. "Somebody stop the bleeding."

"It did hurt though. Usually when my hair is being yanked that hard it's at least accompanied by a slap on my ass."

"You are such a slut."

"I know. I think it's catching." She winked at Billie. She'd heard rumors. "Okay, I'm leaving now. And listen, you just had an off day. You're the best-dressed bee-yatch I know. Byee!" She sauntered away singing LFO's "Summer Girls" . . . a little ditty about some guy named Rich and girls that wear Abercrombie & Fitch.

Billie made a face, decided to turn the bad shirt and the big hair over to the Lord, and headed over to Pandora.

The hairdresser had just finished up Randi's hair and was gathering up her supplies. The event was drawing to a close.

"Pandora, hi! Remember me? Billie Burke from *Du Jour*? We met backstage at Sam C. a couple weeks ago."

"Of course I remember you," Pandora said, delighted. She was massaging her fingers. "How are you, girl?"

"Good, good. Well, I had a crazy morning and I was horribly late, but I'm so glad I finally made it. Hi, Randi. You look *incredible*."

"Thank you." Trembling, she leaned in closer to Billie and said, "They should've handed out Vicodin before we did this."

"Such a thing to say, Randi, when you know Billie's meds were stolen this morning," hissed Annabel, who appeared out of nowhere.

"What?" Randi asked, puzzled.

"Nothing," Billie muttered.

"Now, Billie, even though the event is over, I'm so glad you had a chance to chat with Pandora," continued Annabel. "Let me know if you need any more information about Street Style Gel-Wax, okay? I'm just going to run and wrap some things up, but, Billie, let's stay in touch!"

Billie nodded and smiled, and Annabel scurried away.

Randi scowled. "This event is asinine. Annabel Brixton is a classless wretch, and I'm writing a letter to Clairene saying exactly that. See you soon, Billie. Lovely to meet you, Persephone."

"She's not very nice," said Pandora.

"Not really. But you did a beautiful job on her hair."

"Between us, this whole thing, I don't know, it's kinda cheesy."

"Well, yeah . . . but don't look at it that way. The most important magazines in the country were here. They'll think of you first when they're writing spring trend pieces. Of course, you have to talk to me before you talk to them . . ." Billie smiled at her.

Pandora smiled back. "No doubt."

"I'd love you to be the primary source for my article on beauty trends at the spring shows. When are you free?"

"Well, my book is at the salon. Do you want to call me later today?"

"Sure, I'll do that." She saw that Pandora was packing up, getting ready to leave. For some reason she wanted her to stay and talk. She felt comfortable with Pandora—she supposed it was the hairdresser thing. They always had a bit of therapist in them. "I wish we would've had more time today. It's my fault . . . I was so late, and I left my invite at work, so I forgot you were going to be here . . ."

Pandora put down her heavy duffel bag with her hair supplies. Billie supposed it was obvious she needed someone to talk to.

"What's going on? Is something wrong, girl?"

"No, no, nothing's wrong. I'm just a little worried. I've been sort of slacking off at work. I have this new boyfriend, and I've never really had one before, and I've kind of let everything go."

"Honey, you know that's such a mistake."

"I know. It's so not me. I hate what I'm turning into."

"Beyond it being wrong to pick a man over your career, don't you know that that's the kiss of death for them?"

"What do you mean?"

"As soon as a man sees you leaving everything behind for them, they lose interest. It ain't fun for him anymore. You have to make him work for it."

Billie raised an eyebrow. "You are very, very wise."

"Who is this guy? What does he do?"

She smiled. "He's a writer. A writer with a tortured past."

"Oh no."

"Oh no what?"

"He sounds difficult."

"He so isn't."

"Maybe not yet. I have one of those."

"Really? Can I be your relationship intern?"

"But he's not my boyfriend. Not really. Just a mad close friend that I've known for a mad long time. And he's wearing me out. I never know where we stand; sometimes it's on, sometimes it's off. He can be so moody . . . it's the worst."

"He sounds like a nightmare. Why do you keep him around?"

Pandora paused. "Because when he's good, nobody can touch him."

Billie nodded.

"Anyway, all I'm saying is be very careful with those tortured-writer types. They suck you in and it's impossible to get out. Like the mafia. Make sure you keep your own thing going, or else you'll disappear. Okay?"

"Okay." Billie smiled. "Thanks for listening to me whine. I'll call you today. Take care, girl."

"All right." Pandora watched Billie leave.

Later that evening, Billie and Jay sat on Billie's floor watching *The Real World* and eating Hot Pockets. The rest of her day had followed much like it started. She was late to an editorial meeting, passed off a cocktails event to Sandy, and put off calling Pandora until tomorrow. She did, however, borrow an amazing, one-shouldered Calvin Klein jersey top from fashion. She wondered how many comped spa appointments she'd have to book at Bliss for the fashion girls to let her keep it.

Except for the top, her day bombed.

"How was your day?" asked Jay.

"Fabulous!" answered Billie.

"That good, huh?"

"Yeah. I met the best girl. Did I tell you about her? She's the hot new hairstylist on the scene, and she's black."

"Word?" She knew he wasn't really listening, caught up in the antics of the Hawaii cast. He thought Ruthie was *bananas*. Was someone going to send her to AA, or what?

"Yeah. She's getting all this publicity. Her name's Pandora, which helps."

Jay looked at her. "What's her name?"

"Pandora. Do you know her?"

"No. No. Uh, no."

"Anyway, we really hit it off. My industry's so whitewashed, you know? It makes me so proud to see another one of us out there, you know, making it happen. But then I got sad."

"Why?"

"She was telling me about this sort-of-boyfriend she has? And she was like, he's moody and hard to read. And it just sucks. Here's a woman that's so successful and she's strung out on some loser that's playing her." She grinned at Jay. "I'm a lucky motherfucker."

Jay tried to smile back, but it came out more like a queasy grimace. "That you are."

"It's such a shame, though."

"Billie, I mean, there's always two sides to a story."

"I know, but still."

"Maybe it ain't even like that. Maybe she's making their thing out to be more than it is."

"I doubt it. She's sort of no-nonsense. She doesn't strike me as the head-in-the-clouds type." She paused. "What is this? Why are you defending him in absentia?"

"I ain't defending him," he said. "I'm just presenting another side. Let's watch Ruthie."

Billie ended up getting immersed in the show, and soon forgot all about the conversation.

* * *

The next night, Jay didn't stay over. He explained that meeting the Cinemax producer so soon after getting offered a book deal was like a sign from God for him. He had to buckle down and really focus, for the first time in his life. So that night, Jay stayed home to work on writing his manuscript. Billie was understanding.

The second night he stayed home she was sad. The third night, she was destroyed. And when he didn't show up for their date to see the *Mahogany* revival at the BAM theater, she was inconsolable. She waited for him outside the Brooklyn Acadamy of Music for half an hour, and then finally went in, alone. During her favorite scene, when dashing Billy Dee says to Diana Ross, "Success means nothing without having someone to share it with," she openly wept into her popcorn. *Life* meant nothing without having someone to share it with.

Back at home, she tried to call Jay a million times, but he wasn't picking up. It was so unlike him. Even if they didn't spend the night together, he always called to say good night. Torturous thoughts ran through her head. He's with another woman. He doesn't love me anymore. Maybe I shouldn't have put out on the first date—it's true, no man wants to settle down with a slut. Finally, at 1 A.M., he picked up.

"Hello?" He sounded groggy.

"Jay? Where have you been?"

"What?"

"Where the hell have you been? You totally stood me up at *Mahogany*. Don't tell me you forgot."

"Awww, *fuck*."

"I've been trying to call you all night. Where were you?"

"Baby, I'm so sorry. I forgot. I don't know what happened. I've been here, at home, writing and shit. I forgot. What time is it?"

"It's not about what time it is. Jay, how could you forget? We had a date. I waited outside for you for two hundred years. I really can't believe you just forgot." And now I sound like one of those shrill, demanding girlfriends.

"Baby, I'm so sorry. I was in the zone. I was flowin', and . . . I don't know," he said. He sounded like he felt horrible.

"In the zone? What zone, the Twilight Zone? You could've at least called, or answered the phone."

"I know, I know. I turned it off, though."

"You turned it off? You weren't going to say good night or anything?"

"No, I . . . no, it's . . ."

"I can't believe this. I feel so stupid." Billie's voice was shaking. She couldn't believe he could just shut her out like that, when all she thought about all day was Jay.

"Billie, I'm really sorry. I know I fucked up. All I can say is that I've been really focused, and I fucked up. I love you?" He obviously tried to sound cute, but it didn't come off. "Look, Billie, I was wrong. I know that. I mean, I got so much going on—the manuscript, the papers, the magazines, Cinemax . . . it's crazy. This shit is not a game. You feel me?"

"I do. You're telling me the line forms to the left."

"Oh, girl, stop trippin'. You know you're my heart. But it's weird cuz, like, I met you right when things are getting going in my career." Jay felt awkward saying "career." "It's almost like bad timing, or something. You know?"

"Bad timing?" Billie's stomach hit the floor, and she started shaking. "What are you saying? Just say it, Jay."

"I didn't mean bad timing, like we shouldn't be together. I just mean, in a perfect world, we would've met later. Like a year from now. Or something."

"Do you want to do this or not?"

"Of course I do. You know I love you. You don't gotta see me twenty-four/seven to know that, do you? Shit, you have a demanding job. You know what it's like to be busy. I mean, you used to be busy."

"Jay, I'm getting off the phone."

"Billie . . ."

"You've managed to be perfectly awful in the space of just five minutes," she said.

"Don't talk to me like my name is Edward."

"I'm getting off the phone."

"I'm coming over."

"No, don't do me any favors. I don't have to see you to know you love me, remember? I have an idea. Let's have a long-distance relationship. We can even pretend we don't live in the same city." Billie hung up, destroyed.

Billie was miserable the next morning. She'd cried all night long, which gave her a massive migraine. She sat at her desk, rubbing her temples and sighing. Attached to her forehead was one of those Mentholatum headache pads that cool your forehead. Mary and Sandy were used to Billie's episodes and left her alone.

Billie dry-swallowed a Percocet and called Renee.

"Crawford & Collier, this is Renee speaking."

"I think Jay and I broke up, and it's all your fault."

"What are you talking about? You and Jay didn't break up." Her tone was slightly patronizing.

"We did, we did. At least I think we did."

"Why is this my fault?"

"Because you gave him that goddamned book deal. And now he's busy writing all the time and don't want me no mo'." Billie was barely audible.

"You don't sound so hot. How's your head?"

"I think I need a newer model. Renee, are you listening to me? My life is over."

"Your life is over. Stop being so dramatic and tell me what happened."

She did, and Renee shook her head the whole time. "Billie, Jay is an artist. He's a creative being. You have to give him space to breathe, to produce. Granted, the not calling and standing you up thing is ugly—very ugly and he should be punished—but the reasons behind it are totally valid. I'll never forgive you if you prevent this man from working on my book. I mean, his book."

"I'm not trying to prevent him from anything! I just want him so badly. I want him to only think about me. Am I crazy?"

"Yes. He's working hard. And my question becomes this: Why aren't you doing the same?"

"What do you mean?" Billie knew what she meant.

"You do have a job, Billie."

"You know what he said? He said I should know what it's like to be busy because I am, too. And then he corrected himself and said that I *used* to be busy. I felt like such a loser."

"As well you should. You better get on top of your shit, girl."

"I can't think about work. I'm in hell."

"That's the lamest thing I've ever heard."

"It's true. Wasn't it Dorothy Parker who said, 'Hell's afloat in lover's tears'?"

"The second lamest thing I've ever heard. Billie, what I'm understanding here is that you need group. Badly. I'm calling Vida, and we're taking you to dinner tonight. What do you feel like eating?"

"My young."

"Okay, I can't talk to you when you get like this. We'll meet somewhere after work. I'll call you later."

Billie hung up, only to hear Paige's voice floating out of her office in her direction.

"Billie Putty, can you come into my office, please? We need to have a 'come to Jesus.'"

Billie groaned, and Mary and Sandy shot her sympathetic glances. A "come to Jesus" meeting involved Paige explaining to you that you sucked. Billie peeled the patch off her forehead, applied some Stila lip glaze in praline (the gloss said "confident, but non-confrontational"), and entered Paige's lair.

She was perched behind her enormous glass desk, smirking with barely contained glee. Paige enjoyed criticizing her staff—it clearly helped make the few days a month she was in the office more bearable for her.

"Have a seat." Paige leisurely picked at the half-eaten foie gras on her breakfast tray, and fixed Billie with her Sophia Loren–kohled eyes. "That Jill Stuart mini kilt is sweeter than sweet, Chicken, but it's a hundred seasons old. What's going on with you?" Paige squinted at her, crossed her arms, and took a deep breath. "I'm going to be honest. I think perhaps you're ill."

"Ill?" repeated Billie, confused. "What do you mean?"

"You can be honest with me if you're having a, well . . . a *problem*. And I'm convinced you do. You come in here late, leave early, and when you're here your head's in another place. It's like you're being broadcast via satellite."

"Paige, I'm not sick. Really."

"I don't think you're *sick* sick. I think you're addicted to pain-killers." Paige punctuated her remark by sticking the arm of her tortoiseshell Gucci glasses in her coral-lacquered mouth.

"What?" Billie whispered, mortified. Instinctively, she began to rub her pounding head.

"You heard me. You pop Percocets like I used to do with quaaludes, back in the gold lamé days. The thing is, Putt-Putt, it can be fixed. It's a delicate problem, and to be honest, it's not totally unsexy. It's very mod, you know, very *Valley of the Dolls*."

"Paige . . ."

"Pony, it can be fixed. I know a discreet, civilized little clinic that some of my very best—"

"No, no! Paige, no. I don't have a drug problem. Come on! I've had the same bottle for, like, six months, and I only take one when I'm in pain. I don't need a clinic."

Despite her protests, Billie suspected that Paige knew full well she didn't have a drug problem. She just wanted to fuck with her.

"Well then, what's wrong with you? You're not being yourself. And frankly, I'm shocked that right when I offer you this huge opportunity, you completely flake out on me. Did you think I wouldn't find out that you skipped the Estée Lauder cocktail party Monday night?"

"I know, I know. You're right; I haven't been myself lately. I think I'm just really burned out. But I'll get going again. I will." Billie looked curiously at Paige, who seemed to be ignoring her, preoccupied with pinching her waistline under the desk. "What are you doing?"

"I'm sorry, all that talk about clinics reminded me that I'm due for my monthly colonic. I'm feeling heavy." She pushed a button and screeched at Mary. "Mare Bare, didn't I ask you to book my colonic, like, two days ago? Work with me here!" She looked back at Billie, who was grimacing slightly. "Please, it's not as bad as it sounds. It's like anal sex, without having to pretend to like it. Now where were we?"

"We were exploring what my problem is." Ironic, thought Billie.

"Right. Now, because you're you, and you've never behaved like this, I'm going to let your lackluster moment slide. Besides, I've been waiting for years for you to get properly laid."

"Paige!"

"Come on, Chicken. I know everything. As Mommie Dearest said, 'I'll always win because I'm bigger and faster than you.' But listen. I've been down this road many, many times, and I know where it can go. Don't compromise your job for a man. I don't care how large his bankroll or his dick is. You are not a trailer park princess looking to be rescued by some guy in a mullet and a Budweiser tank. You're Billie Burke. You're fucking fabulous. And it's a *profoundly* stupid move to throw it all away for some guy." She paused, pleased with her speech.

"Thank you, Paige. I really appreciate the advice."

"Follow it. And I better see some changes around here. 'Kay, Pony?"

She was dismissed. "Okay. I promise."

"Oh, and, Billie Putty?"

"Yes?"

"The skirt's vintage. Donate it."

Billie looked down, gave Paige a sheepish look, and shrugged. "Pay me more and I could afford a new wardrobe."

Paige grinned and waved her away. Billie knew she respected her for being one of the only two women in the world who took her bitchery with a grain of salt. The other was her vicious mother, who Paige had once said liked to introduce her as "the best son a mother could ask for."

Billie returned to her desk, where an e-mail had popped up from Deeznuts1973. The subject was "Begging for Billie." She clicked on it, and a smile slowly crept across her face as she read.

Had deep thoughts watching
Lauryn Hill on MTV
Wyclef was a fool

Please please please baby please please please forgive me. I forgot to tell you something about myself: I'm stupid. But the sleepless night without my brainy, bosomy Billie cured me. I love you. I need you. I'm sorry. —Jay

All was forgiven.

* * *

That evening, Billie met the girls at Florent, an all-night diner in the West Village worshiped by Billie and drag queens everywhere. The waitresses looked like a cross between Bettie Page and Flo from "Alice," and were the types of girls who taught bondage classes on the side. Billie, happy to be reconciled with Jay, had found her appetite and was digging into her usual crabcake-and-English-muffin sandwich with gusto. Renee and Vida were worried about her and weren't holding back.

"... and you can't let his moods, his life, dictate yours," said Renee, whose remarks Vida punctuated with a strident nod. "It's dangerous to be that dependent on someone else for happiness."

"So dangerous," cosigned Vida.

"And when are you gonna tell him about London?"

"I can't tell him yet, I just can't. I want to be happy for as long as I can before I have to face that. And it's all so up in the air."

"What is?" asked Vida.

"The London thing. I mean, everyone at work thinks I'm on board, but I still haven't decided if I even want to go."

Renee looked at Vida despairingly. "Billie, you really need to think about what you're doing," she said. "I mean, this will *make* your career."

"And look, all you have to do is give it a year," said Vida. "You can always come back. Or, you never know, he could go there."

"More importantly, if it was the other way around, do you honestly think he'd stay home for you?" asked Renee.

"Okay, what is this?" Billie looked up from her sandwich, mildly annoyed. "I'm madly in love. This is a new emotion for me, which you both know. I just want to indulge myself."

They both looked at her like she was crazy.

"I know what I sound like. I'm setting back the women's movement a thousand years. It's tacky to admit to putting love first. And it's a played-out argument, the whole 'will she choose her career or her man?' thing. But, shit. I'm scared I'll lose him if I move to London. Is that so wrong?"

"No, of course not," said Vida. "But at least try introducing him into your life, you know? You've been to his shows, his old neighborhood. You've met his people. He's brought you into his world. What about bringing him into yours?"

"What world? I play with makeup all day and talk to you guys. I grew up in the strip mall hell that's northern Virginia. I've never suffered any real tragedy. I have no glamorous drug past. I tried eating shrooms once, and that thing with my back happened."

Vida suppressed a giggle at the memory of an eighteen-year-old Billie, weeping, convinced her back had floated away.

"You wouldn't believe what he's been through. After we went to Walt Whitman, I stayed up crying all night long. I just felt so bad for him. All I want to do is make sure he's okay from now on." Billie sighed, knowing she sounded starry-eyed but unable to be any other way. "He's such a vivid person. I feel so boring and blah next to him."

"What the hell are you talking about!" Renee's fist pounded the table. She'd had enough. "Look at yourself. Look at your life. People would murder to be in your Manolos."

Billie sighed. Her giddy mood was shot to hell. "I hated the way I felt last night. Like I didn't even matter, and all his other stuff was more important than me. He's always preoccupied. He has so much work to do, you know?"

"So do you," said Renee. "You're just not doing it."

"Exactly." Vida nodded, pausing to spark a Marlboro Light. "I think the perfect solution is for you to invite him to a beauty cocktail party. You'll be killing two birds with one stone—Paige will be happy you're there, and Jay can observe your natural habitat."

Billie raised her eyebrows. "Honestly, that never even crossed my mind. What if he hates it and thinks I'm a disgusting fashionista?"

"Well, you are a disgusting fashionista," Vida said sweetly. "But you have many other sides to you, and he should see them all. You are more than just his love slave. This isn't *9½ Weeks*."

"God, whatever happened to Mickey Rourke?" mused Renee. "That was a sexy white man."

"Heroin," answered their waitress, refilling the water glasses.

"See, Billie? Drugs are not glamorous." Vida punctuated her remark with a perfectly executed smoke ring.

"My thing is this," started Renee. "Why are you worried about him feeling out of place at one of your events, when you had to suffer through that night o' poetry?"

"Oh, it was the worst. I couldn't *believe* that LaLa bitch." Billie momentarily forgot that she was currently the subject of an intervention. "She tried to kick it to Jay—in my face!—and then had the *nerve* to challenge my blackness. Please."

"You're not allowed to be too fly," said Vida. "Apparently, nowadays black is draping yourself in muslin and mudcloth."

"Which was why it was so rich when that magazine outed Erykah Badu's fake dreads," Renee said, smirking. "She was so embarrassed! Next thing you know, she shaves her head for 'spiritual' reasons. How are you gonna talk all that shit about happy to be nappy and then get caught out there with a dreadlock weave?"

"Remember when I went with one of those one hundred percent

Asiatic Black Males?" asked Vida, laughing. "Remember? Noire? Worst sex I've ever had. We fucked to a Gil Scott-Heron CD. Can you imagine giving head with 'the revolution will not be televised' blaring in your ear? And he kept going on and on about how submerging into the ripe gourd of my womb is so uplifting it's like we're stretching over time and continents to grasp hands with our tortured ancestors and all this madness. I was like, nigga, go 'head! Why can't black people just fuck like everybody else?"

"Yikes. Is it even possible to have sex and think about our tortured ancestors at the same time?" wondered Billie.

"I mean, don't get me wrong," continued Vida, now serious. "If you ignore or dismiss your history, you're living a lie. But I sincerely believe that our grandmothers and great-grandmothers went through all they did so we wouldn't have to wake up in the morning with plight and torture and insurmountable odds on our shoulders. So all I'd have to think about are things like outfits, clients, parties, rocking my industry, and taking over the entire goddamned world."

Renee was incredulous. "That's what you think about?"

"Well, that, and what Lisa Lisa's up to these days."

"Ohhh," sighed Billie. "A moment of silence, please, for the phenomenon that was Lisa Lisa."

"I kissed my first boy during a slow dance to 'All Cried Out,'" reminisced Renee. "It's been downhill since then."

"Renee, you never give Go Down Moses any respect," said Billie. "You know you love him."

"Moses is like homemade lasagna. It can be really good, but perfecting the recipe takes years." She shrugged. "Most of the time I'd rather order takeout."

Billie nodded slowly, totally confused. "I never thought of it that way."

Vida rolled her eyes and changed the subject. "So, Billie, how much are you loving that gangsta sex?"

"Why do you think I'm so obsessed?"

"Girl, I hear that. Jay is so fine. *So* fine."

Billie smiled. "And sexy and charismatic and mmmmm. You know what? He just got approached from some guy at Cinemax to headline a special on the spoken-word scene. Isn't that incredible?"

"Why didn't he tell me that? I'm his editor!" Renee was talking very fast. "That's like built-in publicity for the book. Oh shit, he's about to blow up!"

Vida looked thoughtful. "You know, Billie, Jay might need a publicist. Someone to manage his exposure beyond the book. Look at how successful he's been on his own—getting write-ups in the hottest magazines, building a cult following. With my help, he can be huge."

"She's not wrong." Renee nodded. "Our publicist only deals with book reviews, Barnes & Noble readings, stuff like that. Vida can make him a superstar outside the literary world."

"Oh, I don't know," Billie said, making a face. "Jay's not really like that. He doesn't want to be a star, he just wants to be a writer. He's too real for a publicist."

Vida sniffed. "Baby, this is Manhattan. Ain't nobody too real for a publicist."

"Just run it by him," said Renee.

"And while you're at it, invite him out." Vida's whole face brightened. "Invite him to the Sam C. fragrance launch on Thursday."

Billie thought about it. "You know what? I will. If he walks away thinking I'm a total crème puff, then so be it. I have to learn to embrace the puff."

"Worked for Jennifer Lopez," Vida replied with a wicked smile.

• • •

Later, at 1 A.M., Billie and Jay were sprawled across her futon eating Doritos and watching an inexplicably themed movie marathon on TBS. It started with *Pretty Woman* and was followed by *Boomerang*.

"Did you ever notice that, like, everybody in this movie's plagued by tragedy?" asked Jay.

"What do you mean?"

"Bad things happened to them. Car-related things."

"This is sounding very urban legend-ish."

"No, it's for real. Okay, look. Eddie Murphy gets caught with a transvestite hooker in his ride. And Martin Lawrence almost gets run over stumbling into oncoming traffic while he's cracked out. Ha!" Jay looked triumphant and Billie began giggling.

"That's hardly everybody . . . Halle Berry never had a car-related tragedy."

"You wait."

"Jay, I think you have a problem," Billie said somberly.

"Whatever, man. My genius will be appreciated after I'm dead."

Boomerang had ended two hours before, and now the two were knee-deep in *Goodfellas*. Billie's favorite scene was on, the one where Lorraine Bracco has had it up to here with Ray Liotta's cheating and puts a gun to his face while he's sleeping.

"I love this part, I love this part!" Billie screeched. Ray Liotta wakes up and wrestles the gun away from her. He pushes her to the floor, climbs on top of her, and points the gun in her face, asking her how it feels. She's crying and screaming, but her shapely legs are wrapped around him and her filmy negligee has risen to her waist.

"This scene just speaks *volumes* about her character," she whispered, engrossed. "Even though she hates him and he's treated her so badly, she still wants him. The gun is turning her on. She's scared but she likes it. That's some deep shit."

Jay looked at her.

"No matter what he does, she'll always come back." Her eyes were fixed on the screen. Then she thought a minute.

"Jay, I don't want you to take me for granted."

"I don't. You think I don't know what I got? Look, I fucked up, and if I do it again you can burn my manuscript."

She was quiet. "Tell me something nice."

"I love you." He paused for effect, then gave her a very slow, very delicious kiss.

"More, please."

"I love you all day, I love you when I'm sleeping. I'll love you when I'm an old man sitting on a rickety porch, running outta stories to tell." He kissed her again, and she forgot what she was getting upset about.

"Speaking of stories, did I tell you about Mrs. Jones?"

"No, what?"

"This is gonna kill you. You know how Spike Lee lives over here? She ran into him at the Duane Reed on Myrtle, and he got a huge crush on her and asked her to play somebody's mother in the movie he's making. Some *West Side Story*-type movie about a Puerto Rican guy and a black girl falling in love."

"No!"

"I'm dead ass."

"Well, I believe it. She's so pretty."

"But the best part is, she told him she'd only do it if he hired her makeup artist."

"She has a makeup artist?"

"Yep. You."

"But I'm not a makeup artist."

"Try telling her that."

"What?" Billie was amused. "That's so crazy! Did you clear it up?"

"I tried, but like you said, it's hard for civilians to understand what you do for a living."

A perfect segue, thought Billie. "Jay? I was wondering if you wanted to go out with me on Thursday."

"Word? Where?"

"Well, it's this launch party for a new perfume. From Sam C. the designer. Have you heard of him?"

"I'm from the projects, not Venus."

"Oh, well yeah. So he's having a party. Actually, it's Vida's party—she's the publicist for the club. It's sort of a big deal. I mean, it'll be a fashion crowd, really silly and vapid. But I thought you'd . . ."

"I was wondering if you were ever gonna ask me to go out with you. My feelings were starting to get hurt." Jay's eyes twinkled.

"Why? It's not about you. I thought you'd think I was really shallow if you saw me, you know, doing that whole thing."

"Because what I do is so deep and complicated? Billie, that show ain't nothing for me to do. All I do is tell stories for two hours."

"Please, Jay. You change people's lives."

"So do you. You, uh, you . . . teach them how to keep their nail polish from chipping, and shit."

She giggled. "So do you want to be my date?" she asked. "I won't be able to spend that much time with you because I have to network, but I'd love you to come."

"Shit, I'm there. And don't worry about me. I can take care of myself."

8.
the glamorous life

illie and Jay made it to Heaven at ten, an hour after the party began. Spring Street was turned upside down for the night. A red carpet wound its way through the crowd loitering outside the club's fashionably minimalist, blink-and-you'll-miss-it entrance. Paparazzi cameras flashed as partygoers headed down the carpet. Nervous interns from Below 14, Vida's public relations firm, fiddled with their clipboards and directed revelers to either the press or the invite-only check-in desks. A Cro-Magnon–looking bouncer bellowed, "Yo, if ya not on the list, *go home*." Ignoring him, throngs of bridge and tunnel people crowded around the Darwinist velvet ropes, hoping that visible lip liner and crunchy curls would win them acceptance. Clutching Jay's arm, Billie expertly beat a path to the invite-only desk, where Vida's two assistants greeted her with squeals.

"Billie! Ohmygod you look *fierce*!"

"Yeah—you go, girl!"

Billie thanked Bonnie and Jodi with a festive smile. She no

longer tried to understand the particular brand of white girl who felt compelled to use late-eighties "homegirl" slang in her presence. As if she might feel disoriented and at a cultural loss without a "you go, girl" in every exchange.

"I don't know if I'm on the list or not . . ." started Billie.

"Oh please, girl," Jodi said as she hoisted up the front of her sparkly tube top. "You're VIP!"

"So when do we get an introduction to the new boyfriend?" Bonnie asked with a sneaky look. She flipped her glassily blown-out hair over her shoulder and held out her hand to Jay. "Hiiiii, we've heard a lot about you!"

Billie was embarrassed. "Jay, this is Bonnie and Jodi, Vida's assistants."

Jay grinned and shook their hands. He was looking relatively dressy in baggy khakis, a striped Phat Farm polo shirt, and Timberland boots. "Nice to meet you. Y'all look very official with those headphones."

"Oh, these are just so we can hear Vida if she needs us," replied Jodi.

"Like you need headphones for that," Jay muttered naughtily, and the two girls burst out in flirtatious laughter. Billie had had enough of Bonnie and Jodi, so she said goodbye and swept Jay down the carpet and through the door.

Inside, the infectious beats of Jay-Z's "Hard Knock Life" contrasted interestingly with Heaven's floaty, celestial-themed decor. Naked angels engaged in Kama Sutra–esque positions decorated the gilded ceilings, and yards of tulle snaked up the Greek-inspired columns positioned throughout the huge room. The stunning waitresses, decked out in halos and white tank tops emblazoned with "heaven-sent" in sequins, glided between the tables on the raised area overlooking the packed, writhing dance floor. The huge space was teeming with everyone who was anyone in the fall of '99 — supermodels, rap queens, pop stars, socialites, A-list actors, and Monica Lewinsky. All Sam C.'s famous devotees were thrilled to toast Thrust, his first perfume.

Jay turned to Billie and said, "Whoa."

"I know, it's a little intense."

"No, I mean whoa, you look beautiful."

"Really?" Billie had gone all out, wanting to impress Jay. After a bit of indecision, she had decided to wear a strapless, coral-colored Roberto Cavalli minidress and gold strappy stilettos. Her hair was in its natural state, a mass of messy curls. She knew she looked sexy. "This old thing?"

"That's how you refer to me behind my back?" exclaimed Paige, who'd materialized out of nowhere, as she was known to do. She gave Billie an air kiss. After exchanging compliments, Billie introduced Paige to Jay. Paige's body language seemed to change instantly. She flipped her platinum hair behind her shoulder, licked her lips, stuck her chest out, and posed with one knee cocked, so that the slit in her Versace wrap dress rose to her hip. No stranger to fucking black men, Paige gazed at Jay as if she knew what was going on in his khakis. Billie would've been livid if this was anyone else. But her boss's reaction to attractive men was totally involuntary and harmless.

Billie's only concern was that she'd call him Pony.

"Well, hellooo. So it's you who's making my Putt-Putt act all loopy. I can see why. In fact, if I were her I'd probably never come to work."

You never do, thought Billie.

Jay looked bashful. "I'm a Billie junkie."

"Anything worth doing is worth doing well." She surveyed Billie's new hair. "I love this wild, wanton thing you're doing."

"Thanks! Courtesy of Redken Fresh Curls Conditioner."

"Mmm. Remember that for our Editor's Picks Page." Paige noticed Jay's eyes glazing over. "So how do you like being a beauty boyfriend?"

"It's incredible, you know? My horizons are expanded. Billie taught me how to enjoy exfoliating without compromising my masculinity."

"Our Billie." Paige looked at her protégée with mock pride.

"So, where's Mario tonight?" asked Billie.

Paige snorted. "He was behaving so abominably I had to leave him home with a baby-sitter."

Billie didn't pry. Paige's love life was too tumultuous to keep up with. "Oh. Well . . ."

"Wait a minute. I know you. I recognize you from somewhere." Paige was studying Jay. "Were do I know you from?"

"I don't know. Spend much time on Myrtle Avenue?"

"Is that in Vail?" Paige was lost. "No, I know. You were in *New York* magazine last month. And the *Times* Style section, right? You have that show downtown?"

"Yeah, that's me." He looked very aw-shucks.

"As I live and breathe. You're famous. Billie didn't tell me she was dating an almost-VIP! Aren't you two just the glamorous young 'It' couple. You should sell your genes on the black market."

"Oh, Paige, stop it," Billie said, mortified. "We were on our way to the bar; do you want to come with?" She wanted to move away from the bustling entrance. Leonardo DiCaprio and his tabloid-christened "Pussy Posse" had just come in, and as the five guys shoved past her one of them grabbed her ass.

"Actually, I'm on my way out," Paige answered. Billie was mildly surprised to notice that her boss seemed sad. She wondered why.

"Didn't have a good time?" asked Jay.

"What I had was too many Cosmos," Paige said, flipping her hair. "No, this was just a drive-by. I've been to this party so many times I've memorized the lines. Besides, nowadays when I stay up past midnight I wake up looking like Keith Richards." She gave them both a kiss, and left in a cloud of Chanel No. 5.

"She seemed weird," said Billie. "Didn't she? Like she was upset, or hiding something."

"Most drag queens are," replied Jay.

"Better get used to it," she joked. "That's gonna be me one day."

"Naw, you're too real. She's totally fiction. Like one a those social x-rays in *Bonfire of the Vanities*."

"Those characters were based on real people, you know," said Billie. "And half of them are here tonight."

She scanned the club, wondering how they were going to make it across the room. In the middle of the sunken dance floor's writhing crowd, long-stemmed supermodels Gisele, Naomi Campbell, and Shalom Harlow grinded together to Missy Elliott's "The Rain," creating eye candy and numerous hard-ons. Gossip columnists and publicists mingled ferociously on the outskirts of the dance floor. Puff Daddy, Jennifer Lopez, and their joint entourage spilled over onto three tables. Nearby, Jay-Z and the Rockafella crew were downing Cristal, enveloped in a thick cloud of fragrant smoke. Holding court on the outskirts of the dance floor was the impenetrable Fashion Mafia crowd, who could hardly mask their horror as Lil' Kim strutted across the dance floor in a fringed thong, pasties, and a smile. Cameron Diaz and Drew Barrymore sat sipping cocktails at their own table, while gossip columnists strained to overhear their conversation. The two were rumored to be starring in a *Charlie's Angels* movie, but the third Angel was unknown . . . maybe they'd drop a hint tonight? Madonna, Gwyneth Paltrow, and Jade Jagger chatted up a storm with Sam C. while pretending to ignore the surrounding crush of paparazzi. Monica Lewinsky tried hard as hell to look glam and unperturbed as she patronized a nosy scandal sheet reporter. She was there to gain publicity for her new handbag line, dammit, and all anyone cared about was That Dress. Occupying prime real estate at the bar on the opposite side of the room was Vida, who was waving frantically at Billie. She waved back, and began beating a path across the room.

They hadn't walked two steps before coming across a babbling herd of beauty editors. The beauty girls usually stuck together at parties of this caliber, as they only knew each other. They certainly weren't celebrities, and weren't there to up the A-list quotient, but Sam C. depended on them to cover his perfume in their magazines. He had a built-in audience with all his celebrity friends, but he needed the women's magazines to reach the regular ladies in the heartland. If homemakers in Iowa didn't buy Thrust, it would tank. Beneath the various layers of celebrity, the beauty editors were probably the most important people there.

When they saw Billie with Jay, the girls abruptly ceased their tipsy, arms-in-the-air dancing and silly lip-synching to Big Pun's "Don't Wanna Be a Player." Billie with a boy was a sight to behold. Between press trips, weekly industry events, and working together, the beauty bunch saw more of each other than they did their best friends, boyfriends, and families—and nothing was sacred. Everyone knew Billie was perpetually single, and misguided attempts to be helpful often inspired the girls to try to set her up on blind dates. It was so annoying—it was always with the only black guy they knew. Billie wanted to tell them that (a) if the guy hangs out with you and all your white friends, chances are he's not into black girls; and (b) this means he's wack; and (c) just because the guy's black doesn't automatically mean he's my soul mate. If the only black man you knew was Steve Urkel, then what?

But the beauty bunch had heard rumors about Billie's new boyfriend, and was delighted to finally feast their eyes on Jay. She gave kisses, compliments, and introductions all around, and stopped to chat with Kim and Monica.

"It's Billie I'm-dropping-off-the-face-of-the-earth-to-have-sex Burke! And who the fuck is this vision of loveliness?" cried Monica.

"Monica's thoooo drunk," said Kim, who was also slaughtered. She turned to Jay. "Ignore her, really. But hiii! Welcome to the family. What'th your name?"

"Oh, Kim, don't pretend not to know his name," Billie said, giving her a kiss and introducing Jay. "I know you people have already Googled him within an inch of his life. Oh, Monica, I *live* for those shoes."

"Thanks, sweetie! And your dress is the *cutest*."

"Ugh. I was running late, and this was the only thing I didn't have to iron. You don't think it's too much?"

"No, no, no," cried Kim. "You look like a Tholid Gold dancer!"

"Huh. Well, then I've managed to meet at least one of my childhood goals."

Monica examined Jay. "Did anyone ever tell you you look just like Allen Iverson?"

"You think so?" asked Billie. She didn't see it.

"Yeah, I get that a lot," said Jay. "He's my brother."

"Shut*up*!"

"Well, I mean, we got different fathers . . ." Jay was thrown off.

He hadn't anticipated that the girls would believe him. It was a little cocktail joke.

"Are you therious? Can I meet him?"

"No," Billie replied quickly.

"You know what? I propose a toast," said Monica. "To Billie's fancy new boyfriend. And no, not your average, bean-counting, Wall Street motherfucker, but an edgy, downtown writer with favorable reviews from the *New York Times*."

"You did Google him!" Billie was incredulous.

"No, I didn't," Monica said, looking insulted. "Hello? I do read. Anyway, how about a toast?"

"They don't have drinkth, you idiot."

"Oh. Well, forget it. Billie, that reminds me. Did you see Beige?"

"Yeah, on her way out. Why?"

"Oh. My. God. She was so fucked up."

"Oh no," Billie moaned. "What happened?"

"She came in with this, like, twenty-year-old Enrique Iglesias lookalike, and she was rubbing those skinny tits all over him . . ."

"I told you, I think he *is* an Iglethiath," Kim said, frustrated. "Just not the famouth one."

"Anyway. She looked so desperate. And he was totally ignoring her. It was like in *Sixteen Candles* when Molly Ringwald just turns around and leaves Anthony Michael Hall on the dance floor looking like a fucking tool. *And he left with one of the Hilton sisters*."

Billie gasped in horror. She couldn't imagine that happening to Paige. She seemed like such a mankiller, with all the fancy husbands, and the jewels, and everything.

"I thought she was with that rich Italian guy," said Monica. "What's the deal?"

"I really don't know. I'm sort of shocked, to tell you the truth."

"So am I," said Monica, leaning in conspiratorially. "But you wouldn't know it, would you? I just got BOTOX! My forehead's totally frozen. Look, I'm trying to look shocked." She stared at Billie and Jay, her face registering no emotion.

"Sweetie, that's really creepy," said Billie. She shot Jay a sympathetic look.

"God, she's been doing that all night," said Kim.

"Monica, why did you get BOTOX? You're twenty-eight years old and have zero wrinkles."

She shrugged. "It was free. Go ahead, Jay. Touch my forehead. I'll try to frown."

"That's okay. I believe you."

"No, really. It's fucking wild. Just try it."

Jay gingerly touched Monica's forehead, his expression reading "How did I *get* here?"

Billie was instantly over this moment. "Well, ladies, we're heading to the bar. See you later?"

"Okay, doll," said Kim. "And, Jay, you're a very lucky man, you know that?"

"I tell myself that every day," he said, flashing the grin that made Billie's thighs tremble.

As they were walking away, Monica shouted her name. Billie turned around, and Monica mouthed, *"So. Fucking. Hot."*

Billie giggled and waved the girls away.

The music then switched to "Back That Ass Up," the current smash by southern fried rapper Juvenile. The crowd went wild, and watching the super-sleek celebrities and fashion people "back their asses up" was a sight to see.

Even more interesting was that the guest celebrity DJ spinning the track was the famed department store heiress Tuffy van Arsdale, a twenty-year-old zillionaire who, a mere two years before, had been named "Deb of the Year" (a title for which Jackie O had only been a runner-up). She had been such a vision of pristine femininity in a taffeta Oscar de la Renta ballgown. At the moment, Heiress Tuffy was behind the DJ booth clad in a distressed leather micro-mini dancing quite provocatively with Bijou Phillips, a cigarette hanging from her pouty, highly glossed mouth. The next day, Page Six would label her "*Bare*-ess Tuffy" because at around 3 A.M. she began showcasing her early gymnastics training by doing back handsprings along the bar, all the while flashing her raunchy pearl G-string.

Billie and Jay squeezed past throngs of dancers and made their way to the landing on the other side of the room. Billie heard her name being called, and she turned around to see who it was.

"Billieeeee!" Sam C. was full of cheer. He'd loved Billie ever since she'd been responsible for the only positive review of his fall 1995 collection. So what if it had been a beauty, not a fashion, piece? "Howareyouohmygod! You look so sexy, you slut, though I could smack you for wearing Cavalli!"

She threw herself into a breast-first hug. "SweetieIwasinsucharush! This was the first thing I grabbed. And you, look at you! Very sleek in your all-black ensemble."

"Well, we're all black on the outside."

Billie burst out laughing. Jay chuckled, too, but was momentarily distracted by the stunningly beautiful Tyra Banks and Kimora Lee Simmons shimmying past him to get to the bar.

"Even though it's not mine, I have to say, this little minidress is darling. It's so, like, cheap 1980s slut, I love it. Very Jodie Foster in *The Accused*."

"Excuse me for a moment while I go set myself on fire." Billie was outraged. "Who gets compared to a Solid Gold dancer and a trashy rape victim in one night?"

"Honey, calm down. Those are such clever references! In fact, I think I'll base my entire fall collection around them both."

"Hmph."

Sam changed the subject. "So, Billie, I am deeply interested in your professional opinion. Above all others. No, I'm *serious*. What do you think of Thrust?" Sam looked like the Wicked Witch gazing into a crystal ball. "Be *brutal*."

"Oh, I love it! It's just *delicious*, you know? It's quite crisp at first, but the drydown is so sensual and whisper-soft. Oh, it's to die. *To die!*"

Earlier, she'd told Jay she thought it smelled like Glade. She hoped he wasn't too disgusted by her.

Sam was nodding ferociously. "Oh, yes. Oh, yes. It's all about the drydown. That's exactly the effect I wanted. Like a lingering kiss." He looked at Jay, who seemed to be trying to figure out what "drydown" meant. "I like your look."

"I'm sorry. Sam, this is my boyfriend, Jay."

"I really like your look, Jay. Very, like, preppy meets gangsta-homeboy-chic. What do you do?"

"I'm a writer."

Sam looked shocked. "Really? You look like a rapper! I actually thought you were Method Man. You know, from Wu-Tang Clan? Did anyone ever tell you you're the spitting image of him?"

Jay shook his head no, visibly through with him.

The designer jabbered away. "I just love Meth. He looks so delicious in my clothes. I'm sure he looks even better out of them. You have an incredible look . . . it's very tough. Grrr. I love it."

Billie wanted to die. "Wow. Well, darling, we were just heading over to the bar, so . . ."

"You know what I'd love, Jay?" Sam continued, enchanted with the handsome homeboy. "I'd love to see you in an Oxford and fitted chinos. Something with a fitted leg."

"I don't know, man, that just don't make it for me."

"No, really. It would be thrilling to see someone like you in a very lean, tailored look. Sort of a JFK Jr.–at–Hyannisport vibe."

Jay's expression darkened. "Someone like me?"

"I didn't mean to offend you, I simply wanted—"

"Why don't I forget the chinos and audition for the cast of *Oz*?"

"*Oz!* What? *No!* Oh, heavens, I've created a *situation* . . . "

"Sam, Sam, please, just stop talking, okay? No, it's fine. Just let it go. Really." Billie was talking very quickly in an attempt to smooth things over, while Jay glowered with anger. She knew the only reason he didn't knock Sam C. out was because it surely would've confirmed what he thought about him. Luckily enough, at that very moment a Patrick McMullan, party photographer extraordinaire, demanded a photo of Sam with the sexy black couple. "Wait!" shouted Sam, as he thrust a bottle of Thrust in Billie's hand. Then, a lightning-bright flash was met with two nervous smiles and a withering, don't-fuck-with-me glare that would later be immortalized in *Paper* magazine.

After much pomp and circumstance, Billie and Jay managed to extract themselves from the designer. They gave each other "we'll talk about it later" looks and made their way over to the bar. There were cries of "Billie!" and "Look, there's Billie and Jay!" from a crowd that included Vida, Git TaSteppin, Renee, and Moses.

"Wassup! Where you been, Miss Stop and Chat?" Vida looked like a rock star in Dolce & Gabbana beaded hip-huggers and a plunging white tank top. With her sky-high stilettos, she clocked in at about six-foot-three. Billie felt like her backup singer.

"I know, right?" Renee said, indicating to Moses that she needed a refill. "I could've died and risen in the amount of time it took you to get here."

"There's my cheery Renee," said Billie, giving her a kiss. "Look, I can't help it! This isn't just a party for me, you know. It's work, too." Renee was wearing Prada's signature fall piece, the leaf-embroidered skirt. "Girl, I *see* you!"

"Isn't she pretty?" Moses was starry-eyed. Git appeared to be resisting the urge to bitch-slap him.

"And I'll be eating with food stamps for the rest of my life," said Renee.

"Oh, you don't eat much anyway," said Billie.

"How's my writer doing?" Renee had talked to Jay the day before, but couldn't resist bugging him a bit. "I need an update."

"Two more chapters, love, two more chapters."

Renee beamed, clasping her hands together under her chin. "You're such a star!"

Jay was utterly relieved to see Git, his old friend. They gave each other pounds. " 'Sup, baby?"

"Chillin', chillin'," said Git, nodding as usual to the beat in his head. "What the deal, baby?"

"A nigga needs to get quite drunk."

"True, true." Git signaled the bartender, and Jay ordered a gin and tonic for himself and a Cosmopolitan for Billie.

"How long you been here?"

"Man, too long. This party ain't shit."

"Git!" Vida was furious. "I don't want to hear it. For real, I've had it up to here with you tonight. I try to hook you up and this is the thanks I get."

"I ain't asked you to pimp me out. I ain't asked you for shit."

"Billie, you will never believe what just happened. I got Gracie Cullen over here. *Gracie Cullen*, the head of artist development at Artistry Records. And I introduced Git to her. Do you know what struggling singers would do just to get her *secretary* on the phone? I get her over here, totally big Git up, and then this motherfucker refuses to flow in front of her."

"I ain't no motherfucking puppet."

"You flowed on the spot at Jay's show."

"That's different, he's my nigga."

"That's bullshit, Git. How do you expect to get anywhere if you don't seize opportunities like this? You have to put yourself out there. You can't get bought without selling."

"That ain't me. I'm keepin' it real."

"Keepin' it real? Nobody ever makes it keeping it real. I'm so sick of black people and 'keepin' it real.' That's just laziness. It's an excuse to accept whatever wack situation you're in and not be ambitious. If Biggie kept it real he'd still be selling crack in Clinton Hill. If Renee kept it real she'd be somewhere in North Carolina right now, trying to control her five screaming kids at the Waffle House."

Moses smiled wistfully at this warm-and-fuzzy domestic image, but Renee fumed. "Why'd you have to pull me into this?"

Git interrupted, "It just ain't me. I'm about blowin' up from the streets, on some grassroots shit."

"You know what?" said Vida. "I just hit the wall. It's a wrap. I'm tired of trying to put you on."

"Good. Leave me the fuck alone and worry about your own shit."

"Look around, Git. Check this party. Clearly my shit is on point." Proving her point, she waved back at Courtney Love, whose new cheekbones were lovely.

Moses looked very uncomfortable. "Git, maybe I can help if you have problems with public speaking. I've taken some courses . . . maybe I can give you some pointers? First of all, try imagining yourself in a safe place . . ."

A vein popped out on Git's forehead. "You know what, nigga? I got your safe place—"

"Whoa, whoa, whoa," Jay interrupted. "This ain't the time, son. It ain't the time. Come on. We'll be back." He threw his arm around Git's neck and dragged him away from the group. Moses excused himself to go to the men's room.

"I've told him not to be so damned chipper," Renee said gravely.

"Oh, Renee."

"I am so fucking tired of carrying that man, y'all," said Vida, as TLC's "No Scrubs" started playing in the background. "Hah! Tuffy has good timing." She began fiddling with her earpiece as her assistant's high-pitched voice came squeaking through. "What's up . . . Whitney and Bobby? No, they're not on the list, but let them in. No, I know he's a fugitive; we'll just deal with the cops later. Can you imagine the press?"

"There goes the neighborhood," muttered Renee.

Vida clicked off her assistant and sighed. "My cup runneth over."

"Sweetie, maybe you should go a little easier on Git," suggested Billie.

"Why? I'm just trying to help him further his career."

"But you're his girlfriend, not his publicist."

Struck silent, Vida lit a Marlboro.

"I mean, it's so the classic black male thing," philosophized Renee. "Too proud to accept any help, but so afraid of failure and insecure about his place in society that he subconsciously keeps himself down."

"Wow, Renee, that's too deep for a party."

"But it's true," agreed Vida. "And I'm tired of being the stereotypical black woman that believes in him, and carries him, and keeps getting let down. It's just not a good look." She exhaled wearily and untangled her dangly earrings out of her headphone wires. "I mean, I can't be responsible for uplifting an entire generation of young black males."

"Oh, girl, don't kid yourself," said Billie, downing her Cosmo. "You wouldn't give a man who had all his shit together the time of day."

"The fuck I wouldn't. Moses is looking cuter to me every second." Just then, Vida broke out in a victorious grin. "Look, Moby's here! God, I'm so glad he showed."

Renee squinted at the bald, pasty techno-pop star. "He looks like a suppository."

"Yeah, but he's so hot right now. He's filling my alterna-quotient." Vida winced as Bonnie screeched through her earpiece again. Apparently, Australian singer Kylie Minogue was trying to get in. "Kylie Minogue? The chick who sang 'Locomotion' like ten years ago? Where'd she come from? She's such an eighties One Hit Wonder . . . what, does she have Toni Basil with her? I don't care if she's huge in Europe, so's David Hasselhoff. No, our stock will plummet. Tell her we're filled to capacity."

"Did you ever think," said Billie, "growing up in Bermuda, that one day you'd have the power to turn away the 'Locomotion' girl from your party?"

"Just a simple girl with a dream," Renee said in amusement.

"Go ahead, you bitches, make fun of me. It takes very careful editing to pull off the kind of party Sam C. wants. Did you talk to him, by the way?"

"Yeah," said Billie. "He told Jay he looked like a rapper."

"No!" cried Renee.

"Hmm. Jay and Git are *so* not coming back," surmised Vida.

A t that moment, the two of them were at the bar across the room doing tequila shots.

"That girl's on some real different shit, yo," mumbled Git, slamming his shot glass on the bar.

"I ain't *never* seen no shit like that." Jay was adamant. "She made you look like a thundering idiot, son. I don't care what the pussy's like."

"The pussy's *nice*, son."

"Still." He motioned to the bartender for another round of shots.

"It's like this. I want my shit to be organic. You can't force your art. Like you. You ain't runnin' around pimpin' yourself. You got discovered on the word-of-mouth tip, nahmean? That's whassup."

"True."

"Vida's talking about she wants to be your publicist."

"The fuck outta here. When'd she say that?"

"The other day. I told her she was trippin'. We ain't products to be packaged and sold, nahmean? I ain't . . . I ain't . . . *Will* mother-fucking *Smith*. I ain't gonna rock some shiny suit and coon around in a Hype Williams video. A nigga got integrity, nahmean?"

A nigga also has no job, thought Jay. "True. But lemme get at you for a minute."

" 'Sup?"

"Are you putting yourself out there to be discovered? I mean, what's your plan?"

"I mean, I . . . it ain't about a *plan*, per se. I'm just busy writin' and shit. I'm honin' my craft."

"Yeah, but what about open-mike nights? You got a demo tape? I mean, who's really heard you? It ain't a game, son. Don't sleep."

The bartender brought them their shots. They clicked the glasses together and downed the tequila. "Uh, I'ma just lay in the cut for a minute, ya heard? I . . . uh . . . I don't want nobody to really hear my shit till it's mad tight."

Jay looked at him like he was crazy.

"I mean, I ain't tryin' to be no *baller* and shit. It ain't about the paper, son, it's about the art. I'm on my own time. Nahmean?"

"Whatever man. Just don't fuck around and end up talking about you coulda been a contender."

"Jay, you my man, but I ain't come here for no heart-to-heart."

"Right, you came here to get publicly shat on by your shorty."

"Awww, fuck you," chuckled Git.

"Look, I'm out." He missed Billie. "You leavin'?"

"Naw, I'ma chill for a minute. I'll holla at you later, man. Keep it gutter."

"All right, playa. Hold your head."

Jay headed back across the floor, thinking about Git's situation. Vida really did have a point, but goddamn if she wasn't out of line.

It was so humiliating. Billie would never drag personal business out in the open like that. She had class. She was . . .

"Tammy!" Suddenly, she was standing right in front of him. Where had she come from?

* * *

They stood awkwardly in front of each other, not knowing whether to hug, or shake hands, or what.

"Hi." Her voice was controlled. She looked gorgeous. Her fiery, dyed-red pixie-cut hair was extra flippy, and she wore a short, emerald-green slipdress that clung to her petite figure.

"What are you doing here?"

"What are *you* doing here?"

"I'm . . . uh . . . here with my editor."

"Hmm. She must be fancy."

"Yeah, well . . ." He trailed off. "What about you? Is Pete here?"

"No, we broke up. I'm here with Mariah Carey." She tried to sound nonchalant.

"Word? I guess I didn't see you behind all her hair."

"Yeah, I'm working with her on her new video. She just asked me to go on tour with her."

"That's hot, Tammy. I'm proud of you."

"Yeah. Let's cut the bullshit."

"What, already? *What.* Why did it take you three weeks to return my calls?"

"You really don't know?"

"I have no fuckin' idea."

"I can't believe you, Jay."

"What did I do?" He was pleading with her.

"You treated me like you didn't even know me. Like I'm not your family. You got all vague and secretive with me about this girl, and then insulted me by telling me to go get my own piece of ass. I don't deserve that. First of all, when have you ever not been able to talk to me about a girl? About anything? It hurts to think that you can't tell me that." She couldn't believe the lies she was telling.

"Look, Tammy, I'm sorry. You know you're my family."

"I know you better than anyone else, Jay."

"I know this."

"Why won't you talk about her? Is she here? I want to meet her."

"I . . . uh . . . no."

"Why are you stuttering?"

"She ain't here."

"Are you ashamed of me?"

"Jesus."

"Does she know that you like to fuck your ex-hooker best friend when you can't sleep?"

Jay felt like he'd been punched in the stomach.

"Hurts, doesn't it?" Tammy walked away, leaving him standing alone.

* * *

Jay found the girls as the old school classic "The Glamorous Life" banged through the club. He wanted to go.

"I was feeling abandoned," Billie said, smiling up at him. "What were you guys doing?"

"Deconstructing the power struggle between the sexes."

"He hates me," Vida anounced to no one in particular, suddenly worried that Git really was mad at her. He hadn't returned with Jay.

"Naw, he's chillin'. Just give him a minute."

"I think I really got in his craw," Moses said sadly. Renee, who was happily drunk, gently patted his arm. She was in a good mood. A full night of oral sex awaited her.

"Naw, you're good," Jay said, dismissing him. "Yo, I'm tired. What time is it?"

"It's almost two," said Billie. Her feet were killing her. "I'm tired, too, actually. Are you ready?"

He was so relieved she didn't want to stay. The couple said their goodbyes, assured Vida that this was the best party ever thrown, and made their exit. Jay held his breath, hoping they wouldn't run into Tammy on their way out. They didn't.

He felt sick anyway.

So did Git. He was still at the bar, on his fifth tequila shot, when a pretty, petite girl with fiery-hued hair elbowed her way up to the counter next to him.

"Can I get a gin and tonic, please? With lime."

Git stared at her. She was an elfin, delicate little thing, but there was a sexy toughness about her. He stared until she shot him a look that said, "What the fuck do you want?"

"What's that for, ma?"

"You're staring at me, and that's rude. You're throwing my energy all off."

"Your energy's already off."

"How do you know?"

"You seem mad sad."

"You seem wack, Jack."

"I'm a rapper. The rhymes come natural."

"Hmph." Tammy got her drink, threw the straw on the counter, and took a hearty gulp.

"What's wrong, ma?"

She looked at Git for a long moment, and decided he had kind eyes. And she liked the soft way he called her "Ma." What the hell? "I think my heart is broken."

"Maybe I got the tools to fix it."

Any positive thoughts she had about him disappeared at that moment. He'd just revealed himself to be The Jackass at the Bar. She began to walk away, and Git stopped her.

"Wait, wait, wait. I'm sorry. My game's all fucked up tonight. The thing is, I think my heart's broken, too."

"Is that right."

"Yeah. My girl, yo, she really played me tonight. I ain't fuckin' with her no more."

"That's too bad."

"Yeah. Maybe they don't deserve us."

"Maybe." Tammy sipped her drink. She wished she could believe that.

"What's your name?"

"Pandora."

"Awww, girl, that's your club name. What's your real name?"

She glared daggers at him. "That *is* my real name."

"Oh. That's . . . uh . . . exotic. My name's Git."

"*Git?* Git what?"

"TaSteppin."

Tammy spit out a mouthful of her drink all over his Knicks jersey. She was laughing so hard she couldn't catch her breath. I'm gonna die, she thought to herself. I'm gonna die in a club with a stranger named "get to stepping."

"I know, it's clever, right?" Git looked pleased. Tears streaming down her face, Tammy tried to wipe off his jersey with tiny cocktail napkins. "Chill, it's all good, I don't care. I'm happy I made you smile."

After she regained her composure, she looked at Git and thanked him. "I needed that."

He smiled and nodded at her, struck by her sad eyes. Then, he did the inexplicable and kissed her hand.

"Why did you do that? You don't know me!" She was shocked but wondered why she wasn't more incensed. She usually got very loud and belligerent when guys took liberties with her. She supposed she was too forlorn to work up the energy.

"I want to, though. Can I . . . uh . . . can I get your number? Or can I give you mine? I just wanna call you sometime." He paused to note her attitudinal expression. "Would you pick up the phone?"

She decided she must be drunk because this flew out of her mouth: "Fine, gimme your number. But hurry up because I'm leaving."

He scribbled his cell number on the back of Gracie Cullen's card, and Tammy stuffed it in her clutch.

* * *

Traffic was a mess of limos and paparazzi and security, and there wasn't a cab in sight. Hoping that they'd find one farther east, Billie and Jay walked down Spring Street toward Broadway. It was 2 A.M., but outside it could easily have been 2 P.M. It was a clear seventy degrees, the sidewalks were full of hipsters and Soho nightcrawlers, and the cobblestoned streets were illuminated by the strobe lights flashing outside Heaven.

For the moment, Jay felt incredibly lucky. He'd been saved from a potentially disastrous situation, and he was with the woman he loved. Walking with Billie on his arm (leaning heavily as a result of her four-inch stilettos), the night's close call seemed far away.

"So, what did you think?" Billie asked with a hopeful smile. "You had a terrible time."

"I had a great time."

"You lie."

"I was with you." He kissed the top of her head. "I like your hair like this. Why you always wear it straight?"

"Come on, Jay. Be honest. The thing with Sam was horrible."

"Yeah. I absolutely did not appreciate that shit."

"That's all you're going to say?"

"What can I say? You work with that person. You two have a professional relationship and I have to respect that. I couldn't say what I really wanted to say."

"There was more than the *Oz* comment?"

"Was that out of line?"

Billie grinned. "No, I was glad you said it. His expression was priceless." She walked in silence for a while. "I'm really sorry. I guess I'm just used to how offensive they can be, you know? It's almost like I don't even let myself hear it anymore."

"I ain't trippin'." Jay shrugged it off.

"So what else did you think?"

"About what?"

"Okay, there's something you don't understand. After a party of that magnitude, we're supposed to break the whole thing down. You know, dissect the entire night. That's half of what makes it fun."

"This is mandatory?"

"Yes."

"Hold on, lemme think. I thought Naomi Campbell and Tyra and Jennifer Lopez were sexy as hell. . . . Ow!"

Billie punched his arm. "That's not the kind of dissecting I'm talking about. What did you think of the beauty girls?"

"They were cool, I guess. They were regular white girls. There was a lot of squealing and kissing and excessive complimenting. I don't know, it seemed kinda fake."

"Well, duh."

"The whole night woulda made a brilliant sociological study."

"The fake thing is just part of the game. Like, I really did like Monica's shoes, but I wouldn't *die* for them. Everything is magnified to the nth degree. It's how you get on the inside, you know? You can't get ahead without speaking their language." She paused. "You thought it was gross, huh?"

"No, I just can't believe you do all that shit. That would wear me out."

"What would?"

"All the acting and speaking the speak and all that. The drama. I guess I don't get the whole game thing."

"Oh please, Jay, *everybody* has to play some game to get ahead. Especially us. What black person doesn't wear some kind of mask? Finance people do, doctors do, we all do. Mine just happens to talk like Isaac Mizrahi."

"I hear you, but I don't wear masks. Never have. What you see is what you get."

"How can you say that? Look at your life, Jay. How did you get through four years at Eardale Academy? How did you get into UVA? How'd you end up at the Playhouse?"

He shrugged. "Hustlin'. Hustlin' and hookups."

"Same thing. Hustling is seeking out people who have something you want, and getting it by giving them what *they* want."

"But I never change my personality."

"What, so you talk the same around Git as you do around people at Crawford & Collier? No."

"Clearly not, but that's just being black in America, ma."

"Exactly." Billie paused, stuck on his earlier comment. "Hustling and hookups. You're so funny. Did you ever notice how many of your so-called hookups were through women? Who booked your first reading? LaLa. Come on. You dropped that vocabulary, and those dimples, and your whole poetic-thug thing, and the world was yours. That's playing the game."

"Hold up. I do have vocabulary and dimples, and I'm from around the way. That's me, shit. What anybody else does with that is on them. At the bottom of everything is what you do and how well you do it. If it's hot, it speaks for itself."

"That's awfully naïve, sweetie. This is New York. There are a lot of very talented people walking around who can't get a job to save their lives. You have talent, but you're also a hustler and you know how to get what you want. And so do I. That's where the squealing and air-kissing comes in."

Jay looked down at Billie. Softly, he ran his palm along the back of her neck, drew her face up to his, and kissed her. And kissed and kissed her.

"Point taken," he said when he finally stopped.

Billie felt dizzy. "We're more alike than you think."

"Maybe so." What he didn't tell Billie was how naïve she sounded, telling him what hustling was about. In the fifth grade, he had more game in his size-five Adidas kicks than anyone at that party could ever hope to have. He hustled to *survive*. It was either get out there and sell the shit out of some crack, or eat grape jelly for dinner and hope the rat that bit you in your sleep wasn't carrying anything lethal. When Billie talked about hustling and playing the game, what she really meant was that she was ambitious. She was a go-getter. She set high goals for herself and met them, exceeded them. But the bottom line was that she had been born into a supportive, loving, comfortably middle-class family that took care of her and nurtured her and provided a security blanket. Jay came from nothing. Worse than nothing. He could take or leave all this New York industry bullshit. To Jay, he'd made it when he saved enough money to stop dealing drugs.

But he kept this to himself. He didn't love to talk about his former life, and besides, he didn't want to make her feel silly.

"Hey, I just got an idea." She looked around and noticed that they'd walked to Chinatown. "You wanna go to Double Happiness and get a drink? I just got a second wind."

"What about your feet?"

"I'm one Cosmo from not feeling them." She wrapped her arms around his waist and looked into his eyes. "I love you."

"I love you, too. You hustler, you." He kissed her and squeezed her and wished that moment could last forever, that they could be transported to a place where there was no controversial past, no Sam C., and no Tammy.

That last, unnecessarily evil thought would fuck with him for days.

9.

nobody puts billie
in the corner

The night had held so much promise. Paige had asked Billie and Jay to dinner with herself and her fiancé, Mario. This was totally unprecedented. Paige hinted that she had something to tell her, some breaking news that she wanted Billie to know before anyone else, but she wouldn't give any more details. Billie'd been antsy the whole workday, wondering what exactly the dinner was about.

Instead of the fascinating evening she'd imagined, she got this: At 6:45 Jay called to tell her he couldn't make it.

"What?" Billie was aghast. "I hear the words, but I'm not understanding you."

"I just really can't go. I'm sorry, I know I shoulda called sooner—"

"Jay, what are you talking about? This night is so important to me, don't flake out. Please."

"I have to turn in my first draft by the end of the week. I can't come out," Jay said. He sounded weird—guilty, even. "Baby, I love you. But my draft can't wait." And this really was true. He did have to work, and he couldn't concentrate around Billie. "I gotta do this, ma."

Billie's lower lip trembled. "And I gotta do this." She hung up on him and stormed out the door.

Now, the threesome was dining at the outrageously hot restaurant Nobu. But she hardly appreciated the gourmet Japanese menu. Her mood was a mixture of humiliation, confusion, hurt, and blind rage, and her teeth were clenched so tight she could barely speak. Her head was exploding. Her social skills weren't happening. She couldn't understand why Jay would do this to her. Maintaining a close relationship with an industry icon like Paige was wonderful for her career. Jay knew this. How could he be so selfish? So inconsiderate? All he had to do was come out for, like, two hours. That wouldn't have killed him.

But based on the past week, his behavior wasn't so out of the ordinary. An unfortunate pattern was forming. It seemed that when things were going really well between them, he freaked out and pulled away. He was so inconsistent. After the Sam C. party, Jay became distant again. He stayed home almost every night to write, and the one night he did spend with her, he was sullen and far away. Billie was patient. She realized how important the writing was to him, and she wanted to give him space. The last thing she wanted to be was one of those obsessive, needy girlfriends . . . not a good look. And she understood that he probably had all kinds of commitment fears as a result of his traumatic childhood.

But, dammit, where did she fit in? She couldn't take one week of ravenous love, one week of nothing, and back and forth again.

So there she was, having green tea ice cream with Paige and her ridiculous Eurotrash man.

". . . so, cut to me telling him that he must be snorting again to think we're running that vile fragrance."

"It smells like Glade," Billie said automatically, her lips barely moving.

"At some point, we have to retain some semblance of integrity. Plus, we've done enough for Sam. I'm through with him." Paige was ruthless. "That party was a disaster. Too many celebrities, too much hoopla. That kind of thing doesn't work anymore. It's so eighties. Now, it's all about a lounge, a Cosmo, popping a Vicodin. The social scene is much more civilized than it used to be."

"I'm not sorry I missed it," Mario said in gruff, Italian-accented English.

"Like you had a choice, Mars bar." She gave him an arsenic-laced smile. Billie had learned that she hadn't invited him to Sam's party. He was on probation for taking too long to finalize his divorce from the mother of his three teenaged children. The only reason he was allowed to come out tonight was to keep up appearances. It was okay to go to a party alone, but dinner was another story.

He ignored her and fixed his piercing emerald-green eyes on Billie. "Beelie, you are quite a stunning specimen. Why do you waste-a your time on a man who is not-a there for you? I know many handsome, extremely wealthy men who would die for the love of a young, café au lait–skinned goddess like-a yourself."

Billie smiled through the pain. European men get right to the point, she thought to herself. At least he's stopped staring at my breasts. "Thanks, Mario. Jay's sorry he couldn't make it. He's finishing up a manuscript, so—"

"That's-a no excuse. If you were mine, I'd never let you out of my sight. I'd bathe you in so many kisses there'd be no question of-a my love. Paige, we must-a have her out to Tuscany, some-a-time."

"For God's sake, Mario, stop verbally molesting her."

"No, it's fine. It's fine." Billie wanted to go home. She wanted this nightmare dinner to be over. "You know, I'm not feeling very well. My head . . ."

"I know." Paige got the point. "Mario? Would you be a darling? I seem to have run out of cigarettes. Can you go to the bar and buy me some?"

"Anything for-a you." He kissed her hand and slithered away.

Eyes following him, Paige commented to Billie, "The problem with Mario is that he's the greasy Guido in a bad script. Everything he says, it's like the first season of a sitcom when all the actors are trying too hard. You know, when they haven't settled into their characters yet?" She downed her third glass of merlot. "I want to tell him, 'Once more, with less feeling!'"

"Oh, I think Mario's sweet," Billie managed.

"Anyway, I made him go away because I could tell you needed a moment, Chicken," Paige said softly, using her sympathetic voice. "You look like you're nursing an ulcer."

"I'm sorry for being such depressing company. I think I should go."

"I met him, Billie. He's very handsome and smart and he looks like he's hung like a horse. I totally get it. But this is very lax on his part."

"I know."

"I've dated those creative types before. I know how exciting they can be. Did you know I used to go with Sting?"

"No!"

"Uh-huh. During the Early Mullet years. Oh, we were fabulous. I couldn't get enough of him. And this was before all this tantric drama. I can't imagine what he's like now."

"How glamorous. What happened?"

"Well, it was a great ride until I realized that both of us thought he was God." She eyed Billie pointedly.

"I hear you," Billie said with a sigh.

"I'm loath to say it, but Mario's right. You could have anybody. You could have Mario. You want him?"

"Thanks for the offer, but he's too old for me. And besides, you love him, right?"

Paige looked alarmed. "Love him? Are you mad? I grew out of that years ago."

"Grew out of loving him?"

"No. Love, in general. I'm too old for that. It's all messy."

"Paige, forgive me for sounding naïve, but why are you marrying him then?"

"Why not? He's a billionaire, and we like a lot of the same things, and he has a great big yacht. He's really sweet when he's sober. It's a good match. But don't compare yourself to me. I've been in love so many times, I've built up an immunity. Now I'm just looking for somebody who won't yell at me for shopping too much or for fucking underwear models."

"You can't be serious."

"Why the hell not?" She seemed very matter-of-fact, but she looked weary. And she was wearing a lot of eyeshadow. Billie wished she didn't know that Paige had gotten rejected by the mysterious Iglesias at the Sam C. party. What had she been through that made her this hard? She shuddered. She didn't want to end up like Paige, whatever that was.

"Listen to me, Billie. I'm only going to say this once. Don't let this man take advantage of you. He's just a man. There are many more to be had. Understand?"

Billie nodded sadly, just as Mario returned to the table with a pack of Marlboro Ultra-Lights. Paige announced that Billie was leaving to sleep off her migraine, and Mario feigned a heart attack.

As Paige kissed her goodbye she said, "Nobody puts Billie in the corner."

At midnight, Billie was lying in her bed with her rosebud-embroidered duvet pulled up to her chin. She vaguely wondered what Paige had wanted to tell her over dinner; it was as if she'd changed her mind when she saw how brave Billie was trying to be about Jay blowing her off. What a hideous night. She had an ice pack balanced on her forehead, and her cheeks were damp with tears. A Percocet had numbed the pain in her head, but not her aching heart.

She didn't want to call Jay. Actually, she was hoping he'd call her and apologize profusely. But that didn't happen, and now she was lying there, morose, listening to Mary J. Blige's classic my-man-done-me-wrong-but-you-know-I'll-never-dump-his-sorry-ass CD, *My Life*.

After a lengthy discussion with herself, she finally reached for the phone to call him. At that very moment, it rang.

"Hello?"

"Billie?"

"I'm the only one who lives here."

"Hi, baby."

"Don't 'baby' me. I can't believe you did this again. You stood me up again." Her voice was shaking.

"I didn't stand you up. I called first."

"When you call fifteen minutes before you're supposed to show, it's a stand-up."

He was silent for a second. "You know where my head's at, Billie. I got caught up in the manuscript. I know it's not an excuse, but it is a reason."

What? "What kind of bullshit is that? Which talk show did you pick that up from?"

"Billie . . ."

"You know, I'm so stupid. I'm totally ignoring the signs here. I invite you out, you don't come. And this happens over and over. Clearly you don't care about me or my life. Clearly you don't care about anybody but yourself."

"Listen to yourself. You know that ain't true."

"Why isn't it? You may feel like you care, but you don't show it. This was so important to me, Jay. In all the years we've worked together, Paige's never invited me to dinner. You always insist that I understand your writing time. And I do. But you don't care about my career." She paused to take a breath. "You know what the problem is? The most important person to both of us is you. We both think you're God!"

"Whoa. I walked into the wrong conversation. How'd we get to God?"

"It's true! And where does that leave me? With no date at a double date, dodging advances from Eurotrash."

"I know that motherfucker didn't try anything . . ."

"Oh, shut up, Jay," Billie said, really incensed. "You're so hot and cold. I can't read you. One minute you're so in love with me, and I can *really* feel that you are. The next minute, you couldn't care less. God, now I know how Pandora feels!"

Jay dropped his beer bottle on the floor.

"I feel crazy, Jay, I really do. I'm starting to wonder if I'm making our whole thing up. Like you're not even real."

"Who am I, Keyser Söze? Listen, Billie, I don't want to lose you. Please. I know I ain't doing this right."

"But we keep having the same conversation over and over!"

"I know, I know." Jay was beginning to panic. "Look, I feel like I'm always apologizing to you. The only thing I can say is that I've never been in this kind of relationship. This is all new to me."

"Come on," she said, sniffing. "I deserve better than that."

"It's true. I mean, I ain't tryin' to sound like psych one-oh-one . . . but it's a new thing having someone else to care about and think about and really consider. I gotta get used to it. I ain't never been this deep with anyone before."

"What you're saying is you're totally self-absorbed." She tried to sound tough, but Jay always got her with references to his rough past. Her heart melted for the little boy he didn't get to be.

"Basically."

"At least you admit it. So what were you really doing while I was choking down chicken yakitori?"

"So now you think I got other bitches in here? I was *working*, Billie."

"But so what? Everybody works. We all manage to have lives, too."

"It's *different*, ma. I've been waiting my whole life for this. Book deals do not happen to people like me. I know I seem sometimey, but I have to figure out how to be with you and work at the same time."

"People do it every day. Why are you so special?"

"Cuz I just am."

"*What?*"

"Look, I ain't grown up with shit. I ain't had the opportunities you had. Your life is unreal to me, nahmean? We come from two different worlds. I can't take this for granted. I can't sleep on it. I came from nothing . . . and if I don't focus, I'll end up right back there."

He always had a way of making her feel ridiculous. Like a silly bougie girl with no problems. Suddenly, the dinner began to seem not so important. Why was she really upset? Because Jay had embarrassed her in front of a snotty, middle-aged socialite and a playboy with a million hands? She was ashamed. Jay had risen from the depths of ghetto hell to land a book deal with the biggest publishing house in the world, and she was whining about superficial nonsense.

"I know," she whispered.

"It's gonna be like this for a minute. This is me. I gotta get this done. I wanna be with you, I do, but . . ." He stopped, realizing that he was going down the wrong road. "But beyond all that. I shoulda gone anyway. I was wrong. I just get so caught up, it's like I'm possessed. I'm sorry I hurt you."

"I know you are," Billie managed. She forgave him. What could she do? She loved him desperately. "But I don't ever want to have this conversation again. And if you stand me up again, it's a wrap."

"I won't do it again. I was a selfish bastard." Jay breathed a tiny sigh of relief. He'd really fucked up this time, and he knew it.

"I guess there's something to be said for your dedication."

"Not for nothing, I've always had an outstanding work ethic. I was the most upwardly mobile kid on my block."

"Yeah. Lucky for you your block never got into that whole 'just say no' thing," said Billie.

"I want to see you."

"No. My head hurts. I'm going to sleep now."

"Why can't I come over?"

"Because it shouldn't take me kicking and screaming to get you over here."

"But I thought we were growing."

"And also because then we'll have sex, and I still want to be a little mad at you."

"You can't do both?"

"Nope. Good night, Jay."

"Good night, Billie. I love you."

She wondered if that was enough.

* * *

Dew of the Alps was having a breakfast event at the Bryant Park Hotel. The event was divided between two huge suites, each devoted to one of their new lotions. The first room celebrated the Skin Silkening Intensely Hydrating Moisture Surge Lotion for Dehydrated, Parched Skin, while the second room was all about the Skin Cooling Pore Clearing Astringent Activating Lotion for Oily, Pimple-Prone Skin. To keep things lively, the beauty editors were divided into two groups, each assigned a "tour guide" from Dew of the Alps public relations.

Billie's group was first led by their guide to the Skin Cooling Lotion room, which was decorated to look like a Polynesian island. It certainly *felt* like a Polynesian island. Between the heat, which was cranked up to ninety degrees, and the industrial-strength humidifier hiding behind a huge potted palm tree, it was outrageously steamy. The tour guide was draped in a sari and some sort of complicated, flowered headdress. The editors were handed terrycloth flip-flops as they entered the room and, to their horror, were asked to dump their Manolos into a Pier 1 straw basket. The floor had been covered in sand, and baskets of pineapples and hibiscus were strewn all over the room. The waitresses, who offered tropical juice drinks to the sweating editors, wore nothing more than bikini tops and grass skirts. Everyone was miserable.

The tour guide was explaining to the editors, who were trying to keep their balance while perched on unsteady hammocks, that in hot, humid climates you sweat. And the Skin Cooling Lotion, with its astringent properties and tingly texture, makes you feel better.

"Ohhh, okay," whispered Monica. "See, now it all makes sense. Now I don't feel so horrible about them fucking up my perfect blowout."

"I know, right?"

"Does my hair look like Gene Wilder's?"

"Well, yeah. But look around. Everyone's does."

"Fucking *shit*. I knew I should've listened to my mother and become a real journalist."

Just then, a hearty "thunk" interrupted the tour guide's speech. One of the poor waitresses had passed out, knocking over a tiki torch on her way down. She was immediately whisked away by a couple of assistants, never to be seen again.

"Whew!" exhaled the tour guide. "I'm sure glad that torch wasn't lit!"

With that unfortunate mishap, the Skin Cooling presentation was over. The editors all but sprinted out of the room. Passing the other group in the hallway, they exchanged desperate glances.

As Billie and her group were ushered into the Skin Silkening room, they were greeted with an icy burst of air. At first it was refreshing after the sweltering hell of the Skin Cooling experience, but it soon became clear that the freezing room was a different kind of awful. The air conditioner was on thirty-five degrees, and a mighty fan was producing an authentic, Arctic-type wind. The room was decorated to resemble the slopes of Aspen, down to the last detail. There was polyurethane snow everywhere. Male models in ski outfits ushered the editors to their seats, stationary ski lifts plunked in the center of the room. The tour guide here was dressed like a ski bunny, in a fuzzy pink parka and big fuzzy boots. Someone had erected a mural depicting snowy mountaintops and a distant ski lodge

"Is this Auschwitz?" asked Monica, her teeth chattering.

"Just pretend it isn't happening," said Billie. A skier lumbered by, offering each of the editors a cashmere wrap and a mug of hot chocolate. Billie took them both and held herself back from pouring the hot cocoa down his snowsuit.

This was the most monstrous event in history.

Fifteen minutes later, the ski bunny was droning on through a slide show presentation.

"... and in arid, cold temperatures your skin tends to feel parched and dry. Dew of the Alps recently ran a groundbreaking test on women with dry skin, and we found that they develop what we've termed 'compensatory behavior.' In layman's terms, this means they, er, have the urge to apply lotion ..."

On the heels of this stunning revelation, Billie decided to take her own advice and tune out. She burrowed further into the wrap, and reflected on her love life. Could she really handle such a topsy-turvy relationship? The one good thing that came out of Jay's disappearing acts was her realization that she needed to get a life. Her love for Jay was bordering on obsession, and it wasn't healthy. She had taken on an unflattering manic personality. Her mood would crash if he wasn't attentive enough, and it would soar if he was. It was how she used to be about good and bad days at work.

Billie stiffened, feeling a revelation coming on. In her adult life, she'd never dated, never had a man. There was no love in her life, so she was obsessed with working. Now, it was the other way around. She was obsessed with love, and let her job fall by the wayside. And neither way worked for her. What she needed was balance, dammit, *balance*. She wondered if she also needed therapy.

Now, she understood what the girls had tried to tell her at Florent. It's okay to surrender to love, but it's not okay if you forget who you are. She could handle Jay's crazy moods so much better if her own life was more fulfilling.

It was a ridiculously simple concept; why was it so hard to put into practice?

She smiled, her heart racing. What was she thinking, not being thrilled at the chance to become a beauty director—and at such a young age. In London, no less! She'd be making history. Billie took a sip of the hot chocolate and decided she had to gain some perspective. If she and Jay were meant to be, it would work out, London or no London. They could figure out a long-distance relationship, right? Other couples do it every day.

Billie managed to tough out the rest of the event. (A week later, all the beauty departments in the city would be stricken with identical bouts of the flu.) Feeling renewed and inspired, she ran the two blocks back to her building. Once in her office, she flung her goody bag at Sandy, who was thrilled at the rabbit-fur earmuffs and a gift certificate for a Polynesian body wrap at Om spa. Billie immediately dialed the editor in chief's assistant.

"*Du Jour*, Tiffany speaking?"

"Hi, sweetie, it's Billie. Does Fannie have any time to meet today?"

"What is this regarding?" Poor, shell-shocked Tiffany was all business. Fannie had beaten all the emotion out of her.

"Um, I wanted to talk to her about . . . well, it's private."

"Private? Billie, Fannie's schedule is quite packed . . ."

"Okay, tell her it's about London."

"Very well. Hold, please."

Billie chewed at a hangnail and wondered if she'd let too much time pass. She should've met with Fannie when she first found out she was being considered, like Paige had suggested.

"Billie? Please come in now. Fannie has a few moments before her lunch appointment."

Breathlessly, Billie thanked her and checked herself out in the mirror. She smoothed out her Anna Sui peasant top, and silently thanked herself for wearing her red Gucci slingbacks with the skinny wooden heel. It was well documented that Fannie did not suffer editors in sensible shoes.

Billie entered Fannie's office with great trepidation. She could count on her hands the number of times she'd spoken to the industry legend in the five years she'd worked at *Du Jour*. Fannie Merrick was a total enigma. A tall, chic woman with short, flaming red hair, she was most likely in her early sixties, but one couldn't be too sure. Her exact age was unknown, as was her place of birth—she had one of those accents that changed depending on whom she was speaking to. What was known was that Fannie had been around the block. She was mostly famous for being, well, famous. She'd been a top fashion model in the fifties and had had numerous top-shelf affairs. She was rumored to have slept with Elvis, Frank Sinatra, and, by many accounts, Marlene Dietrich. The girls in the office referred to her as a "hasbian," a lesbian only when it's fashionable. In the sixties, she moved to London and ran around with a jet-setting mod crowd that included famed fashion photographer David Bailey, Mary Quant, the Rolling Stones, and Marianne Faithfull. In the seventies, she became BFF with Halston, and along with Liza Minnelli, put the doomed designer on the map. During a drug-fueled night at Studio 54 in 1978, Warhol photographed her with her still-luscious breasts exposed, French-kissing the supermodel Gia. This candid shot would go on to be an iconic symbol of the freewheeling pre-AIDS era. And in 1983, after recovering from a decade-long hangover, she somehow became editor in chief of *Du Jour*, with no more editorial experience than Colonel Sanders. It didn't matter. Fannie had extraordinary style, great connections, and most important, a knack for reinvention. When she decided to be a magazine editor, everyone just somehow bought it.

These days, however, she was more of a figurehead than anything else. She'd lost interest. She rarely knew what was going on, editorially. She masked her lack of knowledge by never answering a question directly, and running off on lengthy tangents. Many people found her eccentricities charming, but her staff and her enemies (who were, most of the time, one and the same) found her insufferable.

Fannie sat on the other side of her desk, waiting as Billie took in her exquisitely decorated office. The room was done in tawny earth tones, with minimalist Philippe Starck furniture and antique wood-framed photographs of her fabulous friends adorning the walls. Everything was very, very sleek. When Fannie began to yawn, Billie got the hint and started talking.

"Fannie, thank you so much for fitting me into your schedule. I know how busy you are . . ."

"No, you don't. But go on." She gave Billie an encouraging look.

"Well . . . I just want you to know I'm so thrilled at the opportunity to go to British *Du Jour*! I mean, it's such a dream of mine, Fannie. Thank you for considering me, really."

"Don't thank me. It isn't personal. I'm not doing you a favor, I just know you can handle the job."

"Oh, I know, I meant—"

"I'm going to be frank, Billie. This is based solely on your performance. I don't know you from a hole in the wall." Fannie paused, and looked wistful. "That makes me sad. I'd like to know all my staff, but my life is incredibly chaotic. I've always stood in the eye of the storm, Billie, and the fact is, most people aren't comfortable there. I have to pick and choose my friends very wisely. Do you understand what I'm saying, Billie?"

Billie nodded. She had no idea what she was saying.

"Let me back up a bit. You're very young. How old are you?"

"Twenty-six," Billie replied dutifully.

"Twenty-six. Ahh, twenty-six. When I was your age, I was gracing the pages of this very magazine in an advertisement for Revlon 'Cherries in the Snow' lipstick. My waist was cinched beyond recognition. I was quite beautiful, but I was a jackass. You, Billie, are not. Are you?"

"Um, no. I don't think so."

"No, I can tell you're not. You're very smart. Your writing is very strong. I know that you lead that department. You're ready to be a director, age be damned! That's why I agreed to it when Paige suggested you. Which says a lot, because I'd rather pass a kidney stone than indulge the whims of that peroxided gargoyle."

"I'm glad I have your support." Billie was unsure that this was the proper response, but she went with it.

"You know, you're a very attractive girl."

"Thank you, Fannie."

"You're pretty and you're African-American."

"Um, yes."

"That will get you far, dear."

"I'm not sure I . . ."

"You have a look. It's all about a look in this industry. Many girls can write, lots can turn a phrase, a few can string an outfit together correctly. Pairing a Gucci stiletto and a peasant shirt, mixing high and low, that's style. But most importantly, you're a pretty African-American girl. That's your punctuation." Fannie was standing behind her desk, staring at Billie with her arms folded.

"Really? Well . . ."

"Don't look so shocked, I'm just telling it like it is. I'm going to tell you a secret. White women love to be around exotic women. It makes us feel like we're privy to a secret. Use that, Billie. *Use that.*"

Billie was at a loss for words. "I'll . . . um . . . I'll remember that, Fannie."

Fannie looked at her for a moment, in silence. She'd recovered from her rousing speech, and as far as she was concerned the meeting was adjourned. "So. Is there anything else you wanted? I have After Eight mints."

"No, no, no. No thank you. I just wanted to tell you that I'm working very hard on my Fashion Week report. I think you'll be very pleased." Fannie's craziness was throwing her all off. She felt like she'd been transported into a scene from a David Lynch film. Now, she wasn't sure what she was even doing there.

"Brilliant. Are you sure you don't want an After Eight?"

"No thank you," she said, then, thinking better of it, "Well, okay." Billie accepted the mint from Fannie and scurried out of her office.

Back at her desk, she immediately tried calling Renee to tell her about her insane conversation. She wasn't there, so she tried Vida's cell.

"Hello?"

"Vida? *Girl.* You would never *believe* what Fannie Merrick just said to me."

"Oh, thank God it's you, Billie. I've been wanting to cry all fucking day." And she burst into hearty, indulgent tears.

"Sweetie? Honey? What's wrong? Where are you?"

"I'm j-just l-leaving a meeting with my new c-c-cell phone client," Vida barely stuttered. "Billie, Git b-b-broke up with me!"

"Oh, Vida. Are you sure you didn't just have a bad fight?"

"No, no, it really happened," Vida said, pulling herself together. "He told me I humiliated him and offended his manhood and all kinds of other shit, and that he wanted to be with a girl who was more on his level."

"What?" Billie whispered loudly into the receiver, outraged. "What the hell does that mean, on his level? In other words, you totally intimidate him and he wants a girl who won't present a challenge."

"You know? These niggas. I can't even. And it's all because of the thing with the record company chick. I was trying to help a brother out, right? If he's not man enough to accept help, than he can kiss my ass. *Taxi!*"

"Sweetie, if it's like that, he doesn't deserve you."

"Ugh. I hate this conversation," groaned Vida. "I sound like one of those chicks from *Waiting to Exhale.* 'My triflin' man done me wrong . . . '"

"Vida," Billie started, cautiously. She knew Vida hated looking vulnerable. "You sound like that because you're forever trying to save the black man. What about dating somebody who takes *you* out for once. Who wines and dines you, who pays for things. You need to be Thomas Crown-ed."

"That gold-digging thing is so not cute."

"I'm not saying be a gold digger, I'm just saying let somebody wow you for a change."

"I don't know, girl," sighed Vida. It was apparent she wasn't really listening to Billie. "Maybe this is a sign from God to slow down."

"No, Vida. Git just wasn't the one."

"Whatever. I don't want to talk about it anymore. Thanks for listening, baby."

"Anytime, honey. I'm sorry this happened."

"Don't worry about it. The other day, I peeped this FedEx guy that came to our office. Girl, he's hot to death. He looks exactly like Tupac, but taller? Wait, here's a cab. I'll holla at you later."

Billie hung up, speechless.

But she didn't have time to muse over Vida's attention-deficit love life. Today was Tuesday, and her final "Culture Club" copy was due on Friday.

She knew right where to start. After what seemed like hours thumbing through her gargantuan Rolodex, she came across Pandora's card. "Call me anytime," it said. She should've done this a long time ago.

Pandora answered the phone on the fourth ring. "Hello, Fresh Hair."

"Hi, this is Billie . . . Billie Burke?"

"Oh, hey! What's up, girl?"

"I'm good, and you?"

"Can't complain. I thought you'd forgotten about me."

"No! Of course not. I . . . it's just been so busy here at the magazine. This is the first chance I've had to call."

"Cool. That's okay, I'm kidding."

"Well, Pandora, I finally have a sec to interview you for my runway trend piece."

"Great. So what's it all about?"

"Well, there seemed to be so much ethnic borrowing going on. I was hoping we could explore that somewhat."

"Ethnic borrowing. That's a cute way to put it."

"Girl, I'm trying to be PC here." They both giggled.

"I'd be honored to be in your story. Really."

"Perfect. And I wanted to congratulate you. In just the short amount of time since I've met you, you've gotten so much publicity."

"I know . . . I sometimes can't believe it. And now Britney Spears wants me to add colored extensions to her hair for her next tour."

"No!"

"Can you believe it?"

"That's really incredible. And after this article, you'll be unstoppable." She paused. "I didn't say that to big myself up, it's just that *Du Jour* is the most widely read fashion magazine in the world."

Tammy grinned. "No, believe me, I knew what you meant."

"So, when do you want to talk? Are you available now?"

"I actually have to finish up a client. Why don't you come out to the salon? It's in New Jersey, but it's right off NJ Transit. You can really get a feel for what it's like here. You can come out anytime; we close at nine."

"Sounds good. I just have some stuff to finish here, and then I'll come out."

"Your job will let you leave?"

"Girl, this is my job!"

"Okay, then. I'll see you in, like, three hours?"

"Oh, and, Pandora?"

"Yeah?"

"How's the man?"

"Shady as ever. How's yours."

"As crazy as you said he'd be. But as good, too."

"Girl, what'd I tell you! See you soon. Peace."

"Okay, bye."

Billie hung up, exhilarated. She was back.

10.

one big, happy family

t Fresh Hair, Tammy hung up with Billie and grinned at her right-hand man, Sabina.

"Who was that?" she asked, blowing out her client's hair.

"Oh, just Billie Burke, the beauty editor at *Du Jour* magazine."

"Get outta here! *Du Jour?* My, my, my, that's quite white."

"I know. But she's black."

"Go 'head! What does she want, to interview you or something?"

"Yep. She's coming here today."

"I can't believe it! Girl, we're blowin' up. You hear that, Monica?" She gently tapped the top of her client's head with the blow-dryer. Monica muttered a disinterested "Mmm-hmm" and went back to her magazine.

"It's all so surreal," Tammy said flatly, her fingers robotically working on her client's waist-long braids. "It's like it's happening to another person."

Sabina exhaled loudly. "Girl, what is *wrong* with you? If I was you, I'd be bouncing off the walls. I'm so tired of you moping around here all sad and serious. Are you depressed or something? Do you need Prozac?"

"You think I'd tarnish my temple with that stuff? I do take St.-John's-wort, though."

"Don't change the subject. You worse than that sad donkey in *Winnie-the-Pooh*."

"You really wanna know?"

"What am I going on about? Damn."

"Fine. Whatever. Fine. I'll tell you." Tammy took a deep breath. She didn't worry about her client overhearing her conversation because she'd been asleep for the past three hours (it took six hours to complete her hairdo). And Monica was too uppity to care. "I've been in love with Jay my whole life and I've never told him. And it's eating me up inside. It's killing me."

"Is that all?"

"What?"

"Girl, I *been* knowin' that."

"I just poured my soul out to you, and this is what I get?"

"Baby, anyone with two eyes coulda seen that's what's been going on."

"Why can't he see it, Sabina?"

" 'Cause he's a man. Men don't know anything."

"What am I supposed to do? I'm miserable."

"Tell him."

"Hell no. No."

"Pandora! Get it off your chest, girl! You can't live like this!"

"Ow," yelped Monica. "My scalp!"

"Sorry, baby."

"*Gah*-aahd-duh," Monica whined, highly irritated. "Can you please just concentrate on blowing?"

"If I had a nickel for every time I've heard that . . ."

"*Sabina.*" Tammy didn't allow off-color jokes in front of clients.

"Okay, so why can't you tell him?"

"Because I think he's in love with somebody else."

"How do you know this?"

" 'Cause she's the first girl he won't talk to me about."

"Oh." Sabina didn't have much to say to this. "Well, forget her. You've known him longer. You won't know how he feels about you till you ask. Please, girl. For your peace of mind, please call this man."

Tammy braided in silence, letting their conversation sink in. Maybe Sabina was right. What did she have to lose if she came clean with Jay? Certainly not him . . . he wasn't hers to lose. In fact, she could only gain. Either she'd find out that he loved her back, or at the very least, she'd be relieved of a tremendous emotional weight.

Tammy would be a grown-up about this. She would be Zen and confront her fears with serenity and calmness.

Twenty minutes later, after rousing her gorgeously braided client, Tammy banished Sabina from the back office. She couldn't be Zen in front of an audience. Then she slowly approached the phone. She had a good three hours before Billie would arrive . . . that was enough time to talk. She took a deep breath, and dialed.

. . . .

Jay Lane stood in the center of his loft, cell phone in hand. He was disturbed. Tammy had just called him and said she needed to talk to him right away. Her voice was eerily . . . *even*. This made him nervous. He was well acquainted with her volatile temper, but didn't know how to react to the calm, cool, and collected Tammy. Goddamn, he thought to himself. Feng shui is a motherfucker.

Well, here it was. He was actually relieved to finally be coming clean. They were going to get down to the bottom of things. What was she going to say to him? Jay frowned and rubbed his temples, subconsciously mimicking Billie's stressed-out-with-a-migraine move. Things were so bad between him and Tammy, he didn't even know anymore how they'd gotten that way. This was ridiculous. Tammy was the closest thing to family he'd ever had . . . he'd be crazy to let her slip out of his life because of some mysterious, vague misunderstanding.

He was determined to make it up to her. He'd tell her all about Billie, and then he'd tell Billie all about her. And then they'd all go to Friday's, or something. They'd be one big happy family. Like on *Friends*.

Jay frantically searched his pockets and found that he had enough change for the NJ Transit. Maybe he should even bring her flowers or candy, as sort of an olive branch. What did she like? He looked around and on the kitchen counter saw Billie's fancy, beribboned tea. Briefly, he felt a flash of guilt for giving away her present to him, but it wasn't really a real gift, was it? Plus, he never drank tea. Tammy would *love* this, though. He grabbed the gift and raced out the door, with newfound hope in his heart.

* * *

When Jay showed up at Fresh Hair, he was shocked to find that his presence elicited even the smallest smile from Tammy. She motioned for him to join her in the back office, and he followed her, closing the door behind him.

He stood in front of her for a moment, not knowing if he was allowed to hug her. Instead, he awkwardly half-offered, half-shoved the tea in Tammy's direction, in a move reminiscent of Billie's the night she gave it to him.

"What is this?"

"It's a gift. For you—I want you to have it. You like tea, so . . ."

"Oh. Thanks," she said, examining the package. "It's chamomile and lavender, the relaxing blend. That's my favorite."

"You know how I do." Jay grinned at her, proudly.

Tammy looked at the cocky, clueless man before her, took a deep breath, and expelled all the negative energy from her body. "Okay, let's get right to the point. I wanted you to come here today because I have something very important to tell you."

"I'm listening."

"I love you."

"Me too, Tammy. That's why—"

"No, Jay. Stop talking and listen to me. I love you. I'm *in love* with you. I have been my entire life."

"What?"

"Don't tell me you didn't know, Jay."

The color seemed to drain from his face with understanding. He felt like he just got shot in the stomach. This couldn't be what all of this was about. No, no, no! How could he have been so stupid not to see it? Tammy was in love with him? He thought they had an explicit understanding. That they were best friends, brothers. That sometimes they slept together but it was purely . . . well, *familial*, somehow. And she had a man, for Christ's sake.

"But you had a man . . ."

"Pete was just a front."

"A front? You were together for two years!"

"It doesn't matter. He was a good guy, but he wasn't . . . you." She looked Jay directly in the eyes. "How do you feel about this girl? Do you really love her?"

So this was it. She was jealous of Billie. She was mad at him for falling in love. All the girls before didn't matter because she knew they didn't matter to him. But Billie was different. And he'd made things worse by being so opaque and secretive.

"Well, are you going to say something, or are you catatonic?"

"I'm catatonic."

"Look, this is your chance to come clean. Don't punk out."

Jay rubbed his temples and sighed. "Yeah. Yeah, I do. I love her, Tammy. I don't know. I feel like she's supposed to be mine."

Tammy nodded somberly. "I know exactly how that feels."

"This is a terrible moment."

"No it's not," she said firmly. "I wanted the truth. But I don't understand why you kept her from me. I don't know who this girl is, if she's like, rich or bougie or white or what, but if you plan on keeping her you can't hide your past. I'm your family, Jay. You can't hide me forever."

"It ain't that. I already told her all about when I was a kid and everything. It's just that, you know, in the beginning, it's like . . . it can maybe be hard for her to understand me being so close to another woman and shit. You know?"

Tammy just looked at him and shook her head. "You're a goddamn coward. Tell her, Jay. Does she know how we met? Our relationship?"

"Not everything. No."

She paused a beat. "What are you so afraid of?"

"I just want her to stay, that's all."

"You don't want her to know we used to sleep together."

"Well, shit . . . yeah."

"I can't believe I let you use me."

"Use you? I never used anybody. Who are you all of a sudden? Where is this coming from? What we did was out of love, just a different kind."

"A different kind." Tammy wanted to knock him out. "When you were lonely, you'd come knocking at my door at like 4 A.M. and we'd fuck. Then you'd disappear for weeks. I was always there when it was convenient for you. Yeah, that kinda love is *mad* different, Jay."

He was stunned. That was so not how he saw their relationship. "Naw, man, naw. . . that ain't how it was. We had an understanding, right? I mean, I was with other girls, you was with Pete. I thought we knew you and me were a . . . comfort thing. That's the way I saw it."

"Because you can't see past yourself." Tammy struggled to keep her voice from cracking. She would not let him see her cry.

"You never said anything . . . how was I supposed to know? I ain't a mind reader."

"God help your girl. You got a lot of work to do on yourself before you can ever really be available to another human being."

"The fuck is that supposed to mean?"

"Nothing. Nothing. Just . . . forget it."

"No, I want things to be right between us. I'm sick of this shit. You're my girl, Tammy. I want us to be family again."

"It's always about what you want!"

"You know what? Fuck it." Jay threw up his hands. "I'm just a callous, brutish motherfucker. But look. If I used you all these years, you let me do it. So what's that mean?"

Tammy glared at him, silent.

"You got your crystals and aromatherapy and all that other Mr. Miyagi shit, but maybe *you* the one that's got a lot of work to do." With that, Jay stormed out the door. He'd had it.

Tammy stood tapping her foot with her hand on her hips, thinking. After about two seconds, she decided that she didn't want to lose her best friend, even if he wasn't in love with her.

And after all, he did have a point. Sort of.

She ran after him through the salon and stopped him outside, in front of the entrance. She threw her arms around him and burst into long-pent-up tears.

"Jay, Jay, please don't leave. Let's just forget everything. I wanted the truth. I asked for it."

"Shhh, shhh, I know," Jay said, hugging her tight and soothing her. "I'm sorry for everything, Tammy. I'm sorry for so much I don't even know what I'm sorry for. I just want us to be tight again."

"Me too." She pulled his face in front of hers. "I love you, goddammit."

Jay smiled, wiped her tear-streaked cheeks, and kissed her forehead. "I love you, too."

"*Excuse* me?"

Jay and Tammy's heads spun around. Standing on the sidewalk with eyes as wide as saucers, was Billie.

"Billie!" they both exclaimed simultaneously, followed by Tammy's baffled, "You're early! Wait . . . how do *you* know her?"

"She's my girlfriend," he said with a nervous grin. His life flashed before his eyes. "I was just about to tell you . . ."

"*No!*" Tammy couldn't believe it. What a fucking soap opera!

"She's right. I am not your girlfriend. I am not your anything." Billie's voice was shaking. She was shaking. Just as she was about to turn on her heel for the train, she noticed the tea in Tammy's hand. *Her* tea that she'd given him the night they met. "Jay, tell me you didn't."

"Billie, I can explain . . ." He started toward her.

"Don't come near me," she spat at him. She turned on a very cold, professional voice to speak to Tammy. "Pandora, we'll have to reschedule."

"Of course. But, Billie, please . . ."

"Just stop," she said sharply, squeezing her eyes shut. "Jay, I'm leaving. I don't want to hear from you unless it's to tell me I had some bad sushi and this was a nightmare. And don't even *think* of following me. This isn't the movies."

She ran off into the night, leaving Tammy incredulous and Jay crushed.

Later, at 3:30 A.M., Billie was sprawled on her sofa blankly watching *Golden Girls* reruns on Lifetime. It was raining, which was a fitting backdrop for her mood. She was beyond tears. Her eyes were swollen and her throat was scratchy. She felt like she'd been smushed by a waffle iron.

Jay called practically every fifteen minutes, but Billie refused to answer the phone. She even turned down her answering machine so she wouldn't have to hear his voice. When she first got back from New Jersey, she made only one call—a two-way to Vida and Renee. Horrified, they wanted to come over, but she pretended she was going to sleep. The last thing Billie felt like doing was revisiting tonight's horror over and over. For now, all she wanted to do was watch Rose tell another bad St. Olaf story.

Buzz! Buzz!

Her doorbell. Billie remained still, but raised an eyebrow. No fucking way. That couldn't be Jay.

Buzz! Buzz! Buzzzzzz!

It rang and rang until Billie had no choice but to get up and answer it. She padded over to the door in her "I'm miserable" uniform (the *Purple Rain* concert T-shirt she'd had since she was eight and grandma panties) and pressed the talk button.

"What."

"It's Jay. You gotta let me up."

"I don't have to do anything. Go away."

"Let me up, Billie. Please. I gotta explain. It's not what you think."

"You don't know what I think. I'm going back to sleep."

"I swear to God I'll ring your buzzer all night long."

"And you'll die in the rain like the goddamn dog you are."

"True, I deserve that. Please. Just for a minute."

Billie rested her forehead on the door, torn. Even though she thought better of it, she buzzed him up. She unlocked the door and returned to the sofa, telling herself to remain calm. She folded her arms and waited.

Jay came bursting in, soaking wet. He stood by the door, clearly assuming it wasn't safe to walk in any farther.

"So."

"So. The reason why you need so much 'space' and you've been standing me up and being so distant is that you're in love with someone else. And you're here to convince me that this isn't the case. Am I right?"

"You're so wrong." He knew he had to start talking quick, before she threw him out. "There's something I haven't told you about my past."

"Oh Jesus, what is this? The 'Thriller' video? You're not like other guys? *What.*"

"Listen. I've known Tammy . . . er, Pandora, since I was thirteen. But it's not what you think." And then he told her everything.

The night he met her, the blood, how she saved him. The three days they spent getting her off crack. He told her that he'd bought her salon and her apartment, and that they were like brother and sister. And he told her that they used to sleep together, on and off, but that they were never in love. It was just an extension of their friendship. Jay completely opened up to Billie . . . he told her she had nothing to be threatened by, nothing to worry about. He had not told her about Tammy because he didn't think she'd understand him having a relationship that deep with another woman. But he wanted Billie to know Tammy—she was a sweet, loving woman, and he was convinced they'd be fast friends.

When he finished his speech, Jay looked at Billie expectantly. There was a huge, pregnant pause. Finally, Billie smiled.

Jay breathed a tremendous sigh of relief. "I knew you'd get it."

Billie nodded pleasantly, but remained silent.

"So, I was thinking maybe we could get up for dinner or something . . ."

"Oh really?"

"Yeah, yeah. What do you think?"

"That would be cute. I have an even better idea." Billie leaped from the sofa and got in his face. "Take your fucked-up girl and your fucked-up baggage and get the HELL OUT OF MY LIFE."

"Come again?"

"How *dare* you come in here with this hooker-with-a-heart-of-gold shit? Who the fuck do you think I am?"

"Whoa. Chill, chill. You know my story, Billie. Don't act surprised."

"Surprised? I'm *floored*. Pandora, the humble hairdresser to the stars, was a crackhead whore named Tammy? My boyfriend is her sugar daddy? I'm going to *kill* myself."

"Here we go with the drama . . ."

"How could you lie to me?"

"I was gonna tell you, it's just . . . a complicated situation."

"Jay, what were you thinking? You had every chance in the world to come clean, and you didn't. When I think of all the times I mentioned her . . . oh my God! And she was talking about you! To me! You were the shady on-and-off sort-of-boyfriend."

"But I was never her boyfriend. It was this whole, fucked-up, unrequited thing. This is what I'm trying to explain."

"I feel like such an idiot. How could you let me go on about her, and not *say* anything? How could you put me in this position? What if we figured it out at an event or something? You knew you were going to get found out, sooner or later."

"Billie . . ."

"How could you lie to me?"

"On the off chance that you'd react like this? I shoulda known."

"Should've known what? Oh forgive me, Jay. Forgive me for not being from the hood, for not being from such tragic beginnings. For not being as bonded in the struggle as you and Pandora. Poor me. I'll never get it. I'll never know how it feels to have to fuck to have some tenderness in my life."

"That's very ill, Billie. That's very ill."

"Oh, look at this. Now *you're* mad? Let me ask you something, Jay. How could you give her my tea? It was my first gift to you, how could you?"

"Why you trippin' off that? That wasn't no real gift . . . you just gave it to me to be doing something."

"That doesn't matter! It's what it symbolizes! It was a special moment!"

"Symbolizes? Oh God, Billie. You didn't want it and I ain't

never gonna use it and she will. That's all. I ain't the sentimental type. Can't afford to be."

"Oh, okay. Good to know. And I have one for you: I'm not this girl. I'm not supposed to be this girl."

"This girl. What girl?"

"The girl wrapped up in a ghetto love triangle."

"Guess what, Billie. If you're here, you're that girl."

"The hell I am."

"Besides, it ain't a love triangle! I don't know what I got to tell you, damn!"

"I don't care what you call it. Where I come from, Pandora would be your girlfriend. After all these years and everything you've been through, you'd probably be married. Why aren't you with her? It doesn't make sense! This is some ghetto shit that I don't understand. Don't pull me into it."

"Look, I ain't pulling you into shit. You ain't here under threat of death."

"I guess you expect me to just be some ride-or-die bitch, right?" Billie was on a roll. "To just stick through all your bullshit? To just accept that you have a whole other life with this woman? To take you however I can get you? I'm not one of those girls in the hood that has no choice but to cling to her trifling man and deal with baby's mama drama and hide the drugs in her weave because he keeps her laced in the latest Chinatown Gucci ensembles or whatever. Hello? News flash? I don't need it."

Jay stared at her like she was from a different planet. "Yo, you really need to stop watching all that *Rap City*."

"I'm serious, Jay. I've had it."

"Look, this is my life. I've been in ugly situations, but I made it out. And Tammy was there. End of story. It ain't neat, it ain't pretty, and it might be 'ghetto' to you, but there it is." He paused. "I am who I am. Either you with it or you not."

"Maybe I'm not with it."

"No?"

"No! *I'm not!*" screamed Billie, pushing Jay back against the door with all her strength. "I'm tired of worrying about your life all the time. I worry to death about what you had to go through as a kid. I stay up at night, crying about it. I excuse you from so much because you've had such a fucked-up life." Billie launched into a faux-Jay voice. " 'Oh, I came from nothin', book deals don't happen to people like me. I have to write, so I'm gonna stand you up at the movies, and dinner with your boss . . . ' "

"That ain't fair, Billie. I never wanted you to feel sorry for me. Ever!"

"It doesn't matter, I do anyway! I worry, worry, worry and *I'm sick of it*! I'm sick of your life, I'm sick of the streets, I'm sick of your story, I'm done." She paused, catching her breath. "We're from two different worlds. Maybe we can't work."

"You serious?"

"I can't believe you gave Andre money to buy drugs."

Jay just looked at her, disbelieving. "That's been killin' you, huh?"

"How could you fuck her if she's like your sister? And then give her money, too? It's like you're her pimp." She eyed him with utter disgust. "It's . . . it's *uncivilized*."

He flinched, then chuckled. "You're a bitch."

Billie slapped him as hard as she could. Instinctively, his right hand balled into a fist, but after a beat he dropped it. Billie saw this and glared at him archly, a triumphant look in her eyes. He wanted to kill her. Instead, he grabbed the front of her T-shirt and slammed her hard against the wall, her feet barely touching the ground. And then seared her mouth with a kiss so devastating she didn't know what hit her. For a couple of seconds. Then, she realized what was happening and turned her head away. She tried to wrench free, but Jay grabbed her arms and pinned them to her sides. She was literally trapped between a rock and a hard place.

"Let go." Billie's tone was harsh, but she was quivering from head to toe. "You're hurting me."

"Don't kid yourself."

"What's that supposed to mean?"

"You love it."

"Bullshit."

He kissed her harder this time, sucking her tongue into his mouth. Her thighs turned liquid. She moaned, despite herself.

Jay put his mouth to her ear, talking low. "What do you think you're in it for? I know what you want. I made you want it."

"I don't know what you're—"

"The ghetto shit," he said, his mouth open on her neck. He sucked, then lightly bit the soft skin there, and she whimpered. "The *uncivilized* shit. Don't pretend it don't get you off."

He kissed her again until he knew he had her, until the last of her resistance melted away, then let go of her arms. He ran his hands over her body, shoving her T-shirt over her breasts and kneaded them, fingering her puckered nipples. Wanting him, Billie tried to unbutton his jeans, but he roughly pushed her back against the wall. He twisted his hand in her hair, holding her still. With his other hand, he tore down her underwear and inserted three fingers deep inside her. She gasped, arching her back.

"Tell me it gets you off," he whispered, gruffly, into her ear.

Speechless, she just shook her head.

Over and over, he moved his fingers completely out and plunged them back in. Again, he covered her mouth with his, locking her in a kiss so deep, so delicious, it felt like a tongue in her cunt. He had her where he wanted her—soaking wet, wide open, and desperate. Right now, Billie belonged to him.

"Please," Billie breathed, out of her mind.

"Please what?"

"S-stop. Don't do this."

Jay yanked Billie's hair even harder, and she groaned. Plunging his fingers in to the hilt, he pressed his thumb over her clit, gingerly stroking. Billie sobbed, on the brink.

"Tell me you love it."

"N-no."

"Tell me." He took his hand away.

"Jay . . ."

"Say you love it," he murmured in her ear, "and I'll let you come."

"I love it, I love it, love it," she moaned deliriously, arching toward him.

In an instant, Jay had picked Billie up so she was straddling him. He unhooked his jeans and sank his cock deep inside her, filling her up so completely she knew nothing else but him. Grasping her waist, he brought her up and down, fucking her with a controlled, steady rhythm. Jay felt all her muscles tighten as she came in a series of violent shudders, totally losing it, chanting his name like a prayer, coming as if she'd never stop. Only then, with Billie completely shattered in his arms, did Jay finally explode inside her.

Afterward, they slid down the wall and landed on the floor in a tangle of sweaty limbs and half-on, half-off clothes. Too physically drained for words, they lay together, staring off into space, each lost in their own world.

Jay was relieved. She'd been so furious, ready to leave him.

Billie was stone-faced. She'd been so furious, ready to leave him, but he knew how to break her down. She had zero resistance to him. And she hated it. Okay, sometimes it was thrilling, but on the other hand, it was dangerous to be so vulnerable. What was she getting herself into? This man, in some capacity, was involved with another woman. Despite what she let Jay think, Billie believed it was platonic, but on many levels it was threatening, nonetheless. Beyond that, he hardly ever made himself available, but still had the power to make her *beg*? No. She didn't like feeling this out of control. She didn't like it one bit.

Jay turned to Billie, who was curled into the crook of his arm. She looked like an angel, all messy and satiated. She looked back at him, memorizing his beautiful face. Closing her eyes, she squeezed him as hard as she could. Then she let go.

"I'm moving to London," she announced.

Jay looked at her blankly.

"For work. It was just offered to me, and I'm going."

"Wait, wait, wait. I ain't got a say in this?"

"No." Billie untangled herself from him, pulling up her underwear and smoothing down her T-shirt. "Please don't say anything. Don't try to call or write, it'll be easier this way."

Leaving him on the floor, she walked back to her bedroom and closed the door. She set the alarm for 7:30 A.M., crawled into bed, and pulled the covers over her head. An hour later, she heard her front door slam.

11.
the good witch

or the next two days and nights Billie stayed up writing the hell out of her "Culture Club" article. She didn't eat or sleep, just wrote. And she turned it in on Friday, meeting her deadline.

It was good, and everybody knew it. Paige thought it deserved a bold-faced coverline, and the editorial director agreed. The article was FedEx-ed to the editor in chief of British *Du Jour*, who responded by sending Fannie an e-mail saying "Ms. Burke has the exact eye, sensibility, and tone we so desperately need to fill the position. What a clever girl! I'd like to issue a trade agreement with you ASAP."

Unfortunately, the e-mail wasn't opened until a week later, because Fannie's assistant was out with a urinary tract infection, and the temp wasn't aware of her boss's inability to operate e-mail. Or computers, in general. When a new message popped up, Fannie actually pressed the "open" icon on her screen, with her finger. Then, she tried pressing "new message" and "send," but nothing happened. Frustrated with technology, she had the temp book her a ticket to Palm Beach, where she visited Lilly Pulitzer for five days.

When Fannie and her assistant returned, Billie found out she was wanted in London. She was beside herself. She couldn't believe she had this opportunity before her . . . and that she'd let it sit on the back burner for so long! Every day after work, she and Vida ran around buying things they felt would be absolutely essential for her trip: Lulu Guinness makeup bags, a travel flat iron, Liz Tilberis's autobiography, lots of Burberry. At Barneys, Vida persuaded her to buy an obscenely overpriced Chloé handbag stamped with a Union Jack flag. She'd be broke the entire time she was in London, but the bag was *fabulous*. She even reread *Bridget Jones's Diary* (which she vastly preferred to the scores of knockoff novels starring single girls who work in publishing). One night, she invited Renee, Moses, Vida, and her new boyfriend, James the FedEx Guy, over for a traditional English dinner: shepherd's pie and baked beans. Everyone got diarrhea, but it was an interesting cultural moment. Billie was just happy that London had McDonald's and Pizza Hut.

And then she went to Kate's Paperie in Soho and bought a journal. For the first time ever, Billie felt like her own life was worthy of documentation. She had a sneaking suspicion that she would soon be living the life of the divas she worshiped and whose biographies she'd always read—the ballsy ladies who did what they wanted to do, on their own terms, and in fuck-me heels, no less. She was going international! No inexperienced, insecure naïf was she! Billie had never felt so empowered.

But the nights were brutal. If she kept herself busy during the day, she could forget. It was at night that she'd stare into space, clutching her stomach, wondering how she'd make it without him.

• • •

Jay was wondering a very similar thing. He was at Renee's Crawford & Collier office, reviewing some of her final edits. Much to her chagrin, he was having trouble concentrating. He was jittery and antsy and seriously preoccupied.

"Okay, Jay, what is it? What? You're not listening. Would you like some Ritalin?"

"You got some?"

"It's Billie, isn't it?"

"Billie Jean is not my lover."

"And what are you gonna do about it?"

Jay sighed, and pulled the rim of his baseball cap way down over his bleary eyes. He hadn't slept in days. "I don't know, man. I can't let her go to London."

"Really."

"What's she gonna do out there? I mean, she don't know nobody out there. What if she gets lonely? Or sick? What about her migraines?"

"It's nice to see you so concerned about her health."

"I'm wondering if she really thought this through. It seems so, so . . . impulsive."

"Sometimes that's the best way to make decisions, don't you think? You just go with your gut."

"Yeah. I guess so."

"Sometimes thinking too hard about things screws you all up. You just have to go for what feels right to you, you know?" Renee looked at him pointedly.

"Mm-hmm." Jay fidgeted around in his seat. "So, uh, Billie told you what happened with us, right?"

"Of course she did. I'm her best friend. But I'm also your editor. We're supposed to be keeping all that separate."

"No, I got you, I got you. I just wanna ask you something, off the record."

"Go ahead. But you know where my loyalties lie."

"Do you think what I did was unforgivable?"

Renee squinted her almond-shaped brown eyes. There were some things she had to know before letting him off the hook. "Are you sleeping with that hairdresser?"

"I swear to God, no. I used to, a long time ago, before I met Billie. But no. The girl is not even like my sister, she's like my *brother*, you feel me?"

"Will you ever lie to Billie again?"

"No!"

"Why did you do it, Jay? Why, why, why?" Rene pounded her fist on the desk.

"'Cause I thought she'd bug out. Which she did. But that's beside the point. I don't know. I was so confused that I was, I guess . . . plagued by indecision."

"Impotent, you might say."

"I'd never say that."

"Jay, Billie is very important to me. I cannot approve you stepping to her again until I know you're no longer plagued by indecision."

"I'm not! I learned my lesson, Renee. I'm a changed man. No more lies. From now on I'm an open book."

"Then, yeah. I think what you did is forgivable."

Jay suddenly leaned forward onto Renee's desk. "You gotta help me. I'm all fucked up. I love her so much, man. I need her back. I'm shook. And I ain't the one to admit shit like that, neither."

Renee smiled. "Well, then I appreciate your candor."

"What should I do?"

"If I were you, I'd tell her. You've got nothing to lose, right?"

"When does she leave?"

"I can't tell you. I promised."

"What? No, man, nooo . . . I thought we were having a moment . . ."

"'Having a moment'? You've been hanging out with Billie for too long!" She was enjoying torturing him.

"Please tell me. Look, I'll do anything."

"Anything?" She raised an eyebrow.

"Yeah. Yeah, fine, I'll take my shirt off for the publicity photo. Okay? I'll do it. When does she leave? Don't fuck with me."

"Her flight leaves on October thirtieth."

Jay thought about this. "Whoa! That's a week from today . . . next Friday!"

"Then you better get to work."

Jay froze for two seconds, then jumped out of his chair and headed for the door.

"Hello? Where are you going? We're so not done, here."

"You want me to do that photo, right?"

"Yeah."

"Then I'm out. I'll holla at you later, Renee. Thanks, baby . . ."

Renee was furious, but realized that she'd left that door wide open. How in the world did Billie deal with that manipulative child?

.   .   .

Billie spent the weekend in Virginia saying goodbye to her family. Her parents were fiercely proud of her in a vague way. The thing was, they were always proud. They never really worried about the details. For example, her mother had never met Jay, had no clue what went down between them, but managed to produce this gem: "Bey, look like to me you doin' the right thing, liberatin' yourself like this. I don't care how good-lookin' your Jay is, if he's pressurin' you to marry him and you ain't ready, then, sugah, go 'head and exfoliate that dead skin! Bein' tied down is only sexy if *you* providin' the ties. So go to London and kick up them heels, Bey, and remembah—*use protection.*"

And her father was just as high-spirited and complimentary as ever. He almost—but not quite—got it. "I can't believe a genius sprang from my loins," he gushed. "To think, that British magazine recruited you to be their editor in chief . . . and you're just a baby! High five!"

Back from her dizzying trip home, she now had to deal with leaving her dear, dear friends. It was the last Sunday before Billie was to leave, and the three of them were having brunch at Chez Oskar.

"So, how are you feeling at this very second?" Renee asked, sipping her white wine spritzer. "Are you nervous, excited, what?"

"You know, I'm so busy packing and making sure everything's taken care of at work, it's like, I'm just overwhelmed," Billie said, chomping on a french fry. "I'm excited. I just wanna *get there*, you know?"

"I know, right?" said Vida. "Sometimes it's easier to just up and go, instead of having loads of time to think about it. Then you get scared and shit."

"Yeah," Billie said, nodding overenthusiastically. "I don't want to think, I just want to go."

Renee took the plunge. "I know we're not supposed to bring this up . . ."

"Oh, please don't," sighed Billie.

"Look, I just spent my entire Friday talking to this man. We barely even talk about his book . . . all he talks about is you. I need an outlet."

"Well, since it's about you . . ."

"Sweetie, he's not doing so well. He really, really misses you."

Billie just looked at her. "I don't know what to do with that."

"Nothing, if you don't want," Renee said gently. "I just thought you should know. It didn't affect his finishing the book, so on a professional level, things could be worse."

Billie tried to mask her delight but failed. "He finished the book? How is it?"

"Brilliant!" gushed Renee. "I can't even lie, it's so good, y'all. It's funny, it's deep, it's just tight. We're crashing it for a spring release. Not only that, but the little guy from Cinemax you guys met?"

Billie nodded sadly. That had been a good day.

"Anyway, he booked him as a headliner for the premiere episode of the new *Wordstock* show. He's blowing the fuck up, y'all."

Eyeing the expression on Billie's face, Vida deftly changed the focus of the conversation from Jay to Renee. "I'm so proud of you, girl. You'll be running that place soon."

"You know? Anyway, like I was saying," Renee started, never easily swayed. "I totally support your decision to break it off with Jay, Billie. I think it's incredibly strong of you to put yourself first."

"Now maybe he'll learn his lesson," said Vida.

"It's not about him learning a lesson," Billie said, suddenly losing her appetite. All the talk about Jay and his success—without her—was making her nauseous. "I did it for me. I felt like I was getting lost. Whatever epiphany he comes to as a result is totally on him."

Vida was visibly impressed. "That's so . . . healthy, Billie."

"But how are you *doing*, honey?" asked Renee.

"I'm fine." Billie sighed. "Okay, I'm not fine. I'm miserable. I'm *destroyed*."

"Let it out, baby, let it out," said Vida.

"I miss him, you know? I love him. But what can I do? It was the right thing."

Vida and Renee nodded.

"Maybe it was just good sex?" said Billie.

"Sweetie, if that was all it was you'd still be fucking him," reasoned Vida.

"Billie," started Renee, "what if he tries to stop you from going?"

"He hasn't," said Billie, not without a trace of bitterness. "The bastard."

"Well, you did tell him not to," Renee pointed out.

"I know! But still." She paused. "I just wonder if he cares as much as I do. It does help to know he's actually suffering. I know it shouldn't, but it does."

"Would you come back if he asked?" asked Vida.

"No," she said firmly.

"Billie, have you really thought this thing through?" Renee asked, cautiously. "You are going to London for the right reasons? You're not running away, right?"

"I can't believe this," Billie said, slamming her fork down with a loud "clank." "You tell me I'm insane for not wanting to go, and now that I am, it's because I'm running away. I'm not an idiot, Renee."

"Look, I'm just making sure—"

"I know you guys are trying to protect me, like you always have.

Poor Billie, she's so clueless, she doesn't know dick about shit, make sure she unplugs her curling iron before she leaves so she doesn't burn the dorm down."

Vida and Renee eyed each other, eyebrows raised.

"I'm sick of it. Give me some credit. I know what I'm doing, here. This isn't about running away from him. It's about running toward something. It's about *me*. I have to do this for myself, for my career. I want to see where it takes me—and I can't let my fear of losing him hold me back. And besides, what kind of real relationship can I ever hope to have if I'm not a full person, if I'm always putting myself and what I want last? That's not a girlfriend, that's a groupie."

Billie's friends just stared at her for a moment, blown away. Then Vida broke the silence.

"'Sistuuhs are doin' it for themselves!'" she sang, a huge grin spreading over her face.

"Billie, I've got to say, you've just matured in a thousand ways before my very eyes," said Renee. Beaming proudly, she raised her mimosa. "I propose a toast."

"To the new Billie," continued Vida, raising her glass. "A girl who now, given a chance to go back, wouldn't even have *considered* the bangs that called for that goddamned curling iron."

The three girls happily clinked together their champagne flutes. And then Billie's mood darkened.

"The thing is," she started, "what if he's the one?"

Renee looked at her searchingly. "Is he?"

Billie said nothing, then put her face in her hands and groaned. "Can we change the subject, please? I feel like I'm on Barbara Walters."

"Okay," said Vida, her turquoise-mascara'd eyes twinkling. "I have an entertaining bit of gossip."

"Oh good! What is it?" Billie was relieved.

"It's sort of related, but it's funny, not traumatic. Guess who Git's going out with?"

"Foxy Brown?" asked Billie.

"Keshia Knight Pulliam?" asked Renee.

"No and no. *Pandora!*"

"Shutup!" yelled Billie. "When . . . how . . . when did they even meet each other?"

"Not a clue. But I saw them together at Lotus last night, and it was very 'get a room.' "

"That girl!" exclaimed Renee, awestruck. "Forget Kevin Bacon, it's really all about 'Six Degrees of Pandora.' "

"Did they look happy?" asked Billie. Her feelings toward Tammy had gone through many stages over the past month. First, she had hated her. The cheap tramp. Then, she had been wildly jealous of her. How could she compete with the history she and Jay had shared? What could she possibly offer Jay that Tammy couldn't? Here was a girl who knew exactly where he came from — a girl he never had to explain himself to. And then she had felt threatened. Like she'd never stood a chance with him. Like he had hoodwinked her into a false sense of security . . . when all along he had had another soul mate waiting in the wings. But in the past couple of weeks, Billie had softened toward Tammy a bit. She thought a lot about her past, and actually started to feel for her. She even quoted her in the Culture Club article, though she couldn't bring herself to actually speak to her—she'd had Sandy call and conduct the interview.

"They looked thrilled," admitted Vida. "I think they're a better match than we were."

"Were you mad?"

"Hell no! You think I'm trippin' off him when I got James? Whose dick I can barely fit in my mouth?"

"Ouch," grimaced Renee.

"How did you do it, Vida?" asked Billie. "You guys broke up, and you moved on in, like, five minutes."

"It's different. I was feeling Git, but he was never in my blood, in my bones. It wasn't like you two."

Billie didn't have anything to say to that. She didn't have much to say for the rest of the brunch, either.

* * *

The next day at work, Billie was swamped. Not only was she putting through her executive editor's final edits on Culture Club, she was also trying to clear out her office and make sure her work visa would be completed on time. Today was the first day of her last week.

That morning, Billie had walked into what she thought was a production schedule meeting, and was heartily surprised by a little breakfast in her honor. The whole staff had turned out to nibble on chocolate-covered strawberries and toast her with mimosas. Billie was mortified. Being put in the spotlight like that always made her nervous. The worst part was when she was forced to make a speech about her years at *Du Jour*, while Mary and Sandy cried hysterically. She knew they were crying less out of sadness than out of fear—Billie would no longer be there to act as a buffer between them and evil Paige. And Paige eyed her suspiciously, seeing right through her line about how "the most valuable thing she picked up working with Paige was her work ethic."

Now back in the office, Billie was frantically typing away at her edits, trying to get most of them done before lunch. Of course, her phone wouldn't stop ringing, but the caller ID allowed her to screen her calls. When "Lobby Reception" popped up, she heaved a distracted sigh and decided to pick it up. It could be an important delivery, like her visa.

"*Du Jour*, this is Billie."

"Hi, Billie, I have a Mr. Jay Lane to see you?"

She froze, her heart stopping. She almost dropped the receiver. Should she let him up, or send him away? Oh God.

Buying time, she said, "Jay Lane? Hmm . . . where's he from?"

The receptionist put her on hold, then said, "Um . . . he says the bowels of misery, ma'am."

Billie was torn. She was dying to see him, but she knew she had made the right decision and wanted to stand her ground. God, why was he making this hard?

"Hello? Billie, are you there?"

"Yes, yes, I'm here. Uh . . . uh . . . okay. Okay. You can send him up. Thanks."

"*Shit!*" she said out loud, not knowing what to do. What was he here for? What would he say? And most important, how did she look? She pulled out her compact and hurriedly dabbed on some blush and lip gloss. She pursed her lips together and decided she was ready for anything. War, famine, confrontations with ex-boyfriends . . .

"Just stay strong, Billie," she told herself. "Stay strong." She tried to think fast. . . . Where would they talk? Certainly not in her cubicle—both Mary and Sandy were right over the partition, and Paige was across the hall in her office. They'd all hear everything. Billie wanted to burst into tears. Why'd he have to come to her office? She felt so trapped. . . .

It didn't matter. Because there he was, knocking on the wall at the entrance to her cubicle. Jay. With an enormous gift bag.

"How did you know where my office was?" Billie asked when she found her voice.

"Your friend Mary showed me," he said. Mare Bear popped out from behind him, grinning mischievously.

"I was on my way from the bathroom," she confessed with a shrug, and scurried back to her desk.

"She's cute," said Jay.

She nodded, feeling incredibly uncomfortable. They couldn't look each other in the eye. "So, what's up?"

"I, um, found out that this was your last week at work, so I wanted to come say goodbye. You know, in person."

"How thoughtful."

"I try."

"I guess Renee told you, huh?"

"I forced it out of her. She didn't want to tell me."

"Oh. No, I guess she wouldn't want to."

"Renee's a good friend. To you, I mean."

"Yeah, she is."

"So are you ready? Are you packed and everything?"

"Yep, all packed." Billie was incredibly sad. She never thought she'd ever be having this kind of stilted, generic conversation with Jay. Of all people. All of a sudden, she wanted him to leave.

"So this is your office. I can't believe I've never been here."

Billie nodded and smiled, but it didn't reach her eyes. "Me either."

"Can I come in?"

"Oh, of course."

He came in and sat on the edge of her desk, in front of her. Taking a breath, he handed her the gift bag.

"I brought you something, a sort of farewell gift."

"Jay, you shouldn't have," she said, taking the bag from him. It was outrageously heavy. "Jesus, what's in here?"

"It's no big deal. Just some reading material for London. If you get bored. Whatever."

Billie opened the bag and found a stack of books. Used biographies, all stamped with the logo from the Biography Bookshop. Their first date. She looked at him, and something passed between them.

"Pull them out," he said softly.

She unloaded the bag, gasping with delight. They were biographies of her all-time favorite ladies: Elizabeth Taylor, Dorothy Dandridge, Bette Davis, Ava Gardner, Lana Turner, Billie Holiday, Josephine Baker, Joan Crawford, Diana Ross, and on and on. At the bottom of the bag was a tiny, plain card, on which Jay had handwritten: "To my Billie, whose luscious Southern charm, jazz baby wit, and doe-eyed beauty make these 'divas' seem like little boys. From Fort Greene to London to wherever, forever, I love you. Jay."

Billie felt like her heart would leap out of her chest. She looked at him with absolute wonder, wanting to jump in his arms, to forget everything. But then she thought about her journal—how much longer was she going to obsess about other people's larger-than-life stories? It was time for her to create her own. She had to stay strong.

"I . . . I don't know what to say. This is the best gift anyone's ever given me."

"Say you won't go."

"I have to."

"Please stay with me," he said, his black eyes gazing intensely into hers. "Please. I'll do anything you want."

"This isn't fair. Don't do this now."

"Why?"

"Shhh!"

Jay lowered his voice to a movie-theater whisper. "Why?"

"It's too late, Jay. I've made my decision, and I'm leaving. Why are you making this harder for me than it already is?"

"Because I can't let you go. I can't. You're necessary to my existence. You're *necessary*. I don't know when or how or why it happened but it did, and it's like I ain't even got a choice. I love you, Billie, more than I have any right to. And I think you know that. But it's true, I didn't do it right. I know now that I didn't.

"Listen, excuses are played out, and I ain't trying to waste your time. All I can tell you is this. I spent my whole life learning how to just get through it, you know, how to be numb to all the drama and turmoil and bullshit it brings. And then you fucked up my whole worldview. I realized how . . . *good* it could be. How bright it could be. It's like, you . . . ever since I met you . . ." He paused, visibly struggling for a fitting metaphor. "This month with you, it's been like living in the colorized part of *The Wizard of Oz*. No, listen. Everything was so dreary, so black and white, and then you came along—outta nowhere—and you brought yellow brick roads and the Lollipop Guild and jolly, dancing midgets with you. You're my Glinda the Good Witch.

"And I know that I hurt you. I was a selfish motherfucker.

Believe me, I know this now. I'm choking on it. But, Billie, I've only been sure about one thing in this world, and it's that people leave. They fucking up and disappear. So I learned to play my cards close. But here you are, and all that don't mean shit. Because whether it's safe or not, you're mine. That's all there is to it. I don't want you to go, but if you have to, I'll wait for you. Just tell me you feel the same way. Tell me you'll take me back."

Jay stopped talking and stared at Billie expectantly. He'd never said anything like that to anyone. Later, he'd suffer mild embarrassment for pouring out his soul like that—and for the *Wizard of Oz* thing—but for now, he was beyond feeling self-conscious. He needed her back.

Billie's eyes welled up with tears. She couldn't speak for a while, or even look at him. More than anything, she wanted to go to him, kiss him, hold him, tell him how much she loved him and how it was killing her. She didn't. Finally, she got up the courage to say what she knew she had to say.

"Jay, I can't be with you," she whispered, barely audible. Tears streamed down her face. "I'm going to London. I'm sorry, but it's just something I have to do. It's just . . . We can't happen."

He caught Billie's gaze, and wouldn't let it waver. He saw a different truth there. But he couldn't force her to change her mind. With a sigh, he stood up to leave. He leaned forward, kissed her cheek, and said, "I love you anyway." And then he was gone.

And Billie collapsed onto her chair in a paroxysm of tears.

Immediately, Paige burst into her cubicle. "Have you lost your fucking mind?"

"What?" Billie said, wiping her cheeks. "What are you talking about? Paige, why are you crying?"

"Why is Sandy Pants crying? Why is Mare Bear crying? Why are *you* crying?" Billie peered over the partition and saw that, indeed, the girls were sobbing. Paige continued yelling at her. "I'm crying because I'm moved! How can you let that man walk out the door?"

"What do you mean? Because he's not right for me. You saw how miserable he made me. Hello? You were there at our hideous dinner! He's . . . he's inconsiderate, and selfish, and—"

"Oh, who the fuck cares?" Paige waived Billie away. "Everybody makes mistakes, Billie. You guys are like nine years old. You'll make mistakes, too. Listen to me, Pony. I was wrong. He's not like Sting. He loves you so much. You only get love like that once, maybe twice in your life."

"Paige, but what about London!" Billie was caught in the crossfire of a thousand conflicting emotions. "I mean, this is huge for my career. And I just got that great Union Jack bag. I can't turn my back on all that for a man."

"You would if you had some sense," Paige said, trying to regain her composure. She shook her head, clearly attempting to stop crying, but the tears kept coming. "I was in love only one time in my life. So in love. My story is different than yours, but the moral still holds. Long story short: I was about your age. His name was Tony, and my father wouldn't let me marry him because he didn't have any money. Well, he wasn't poor—he owned a nightclub—but his family had mob connections, and it just wasn't our scene. The point is, my father didn't approve. If I married him, I would've gotten cut off without a cent. So I married my first husband to forget about him. It seemed like the proper thing to do at the time. He worked with my father, he was a trust fund baby like me. It looked great on paper. But I was miserable. Secretly, I kept seeing Tony. And I got pregnant. Oh, it was dreadful. I decided to give up the baby. And the week after the operation . . . he died in a freak accident during that huge blackout in 'seventy-seven."

"A freak accident?"

"Well, one could call being stabbed fourteen times by a member of a rival family a freak accident. Anyway, my whole life I've wished I'd kept his baby. I've always wondered if he'd be alive now if we'd stayed together. Soon after, I divorced my first husband and kept marrying other men to forget Tony and the whole thing. Never worked.

"The point is, Chicken, you only live once. Take it from me, regrets are a bitch. To hell with what *seems* right. Go ahead, turn your life upside down for your man. Fight for him. You don't want to end up like me."

Billie stared at Paige, her hardened, jaded personality finally starting to make sense. "Paige, I had no idea."

"It's ancient history, whatever," she said. "Another thing, if your thong's in a knot about losing the director position, get over it. This is what I was going to tell you at Nobu, but then you were clearly so upset it just didn't seem appropriate. Mario and I have decided that, within the year, we're going to move to Tuscany and live in the villa, full-time."

Billie's eyes widened.

"And, it goes without saying, you'll be promoted to beauty director."

Billie's jaw dropped.

"So you can either go to London and come back when I call, or stay and wait it out. Either way, you'll end up beauty director. So go get your man, Billie Putty."

Without saying a word, Billie sprinted down the hall to the elevator bank, but he was gone. She pressed the down button, praying for it to hurry, then hopped on. Once on the main floor, she raced out into the huge lobby, searching frantically for him. "Please still be here, please still be here," she chanted under her breath, shimmying through the turnstile and out the door.

He was gone.

"Shit!" Billie wailed, and frantically looked up and down the street for signs of Jay. Nothing. She hung a right and ran up the sidewalk to the corner of Forty-second and Sixth Avenue. She stopped at a souvlaki stand and tapped the sweating operator.

"Excuse me, sir?" she asked breathlessly.

"What you need, pretty lady?"

"H-have you seen a guy . . . I'm looking for a guy . . ."

"Want souvlaki?"

"No, uh, no thank you. Did a tall guy, wearing a jersey, about six-one . . . did he walk by here?"

"Of what team player is the jersey?"

"What? Oh, I don't know, I don't know sports." Upset and distracted, she rubbed her temples and looked up and down Sixth Avenue. She couldn't let him get away. Maybe he went in the other direction, toward Times Square. Maybe the pretzel-and-hot-dog man would know. Then it hit her. Hot dogs. Nathan's. There was a Nathan's Hot Dogs in the middle of Times Square. It would be very Jay to be nursing his sorrows with a Nathan's hot dog. That is, if he was even feeling sorrowful. Maybe after he left, he'd decided he was over her. Oh my God!

Billie turned on her considerable heel and sprinted back down Forty-second Street and made a left on tourist-congested Broadway. There was Nathan's, on the other side of the street, shining like a neon North Star. Narrowly avoiding sending a kindergarten field trip sprawling, Billie managed to make it to the median strip halfway across the street before the light changed.

Just then, Jay walked out of the hot dog chain, looking defeated and stunned and sad.

"Jay!" she called out.

He looked up and smiled, like he knew she'd come after him the whole time. She smiled back. They stood there, hearts pounding, staring at each other for what felt like ages. Then the light changed, and she ran toward him, jumping into his arms, and he hugged her so tight she thought she would break. They kissed each other like it had been ages, desperately happy to be this close again.

"What changed your mind?" Jay asked, when they finally came up for air.

"I don't know. I guess . . . I can't think of anything I'd like to do more than be your Good Witch."

"Are you sure?"

"Surely."

Jay kissed her sweetly.

"More please."

He kissed her again, and it was all settled.

"You smell like hot dogs."

"Told you I can't get enough of a good thing."

"Jay?"

"Billie?"

"I'm still going to London."

"What?" Jay's face completely fell. "I don't get it."

"But I'll be back. I'll be back in, like, six months. They want to promote me here. Paige is moving to Italy."

At first he just looked sad. And then he smiled. "Congratulations. I mean it."

"Does this change things?"

"Never. We'll make it work, we'll make it work."

"Really?"

"Yeah. I never been to London, I could visit."

"Yeah! For, like, weeks. And we could write romantic love letters . . ."

"Renee was talking about me getting exposure in London and Amsterdam. We could travel, stay at hostels and shit . . ."

"Or we could stay at fancy hotels and get *Du Jour* to pay for it."

Jay's eyes twinkled. "Hustlin' and hookups."

"It'll be perfect."

"Yeah." Jay paused and nodded, taking it all in. "Yeah. It'll be perfect. We'll be perfect."

"That German tourist seems to think so." Billie nodded toward an older gentleman in lederhosen who'd been filming the whole thing. His wife waved a tiny American flag and gave them the thumbs-up sign.

"That's gotta be good luck," said Jay.

"Um, one more thing."

"What?"

"Pandora stays home, okay?"

He laughed and wrapped her up in his arms.

An hour later, Billie floated back up to her office on wings of love, humming "Reunited" the whole way. All was right with the world.

acknowledgments

Endless thanks to my agent, Mary Ann Naples, for believing in my manuscript enough to shop it around during her fifteenth month of pregnancy; and to my brilliant editor, Jennifer Hershey, "The Cherry Girl," for totally, totally getting it.

Thanks to my idols, my little sisters—Devon, the coolest girl in the room, and Lauren, the sassiest. I'm beyond blessed to have such supportive, loving, brilliant, and snuggly girls in my corner.

Miles of gratitude to my parents, Andi and Aldred. When I was fifteen, I confessed to my "Christ, I'm depressed" journal that I was an incurable nerd—I didn't want to party with kids my age because I always had more fun at home, watching *The Thin Man* and *What's Up, Doc?* with my parents. Thanks to Mommy, the man of the house, and Daddy, the man in the mirror, for making my world so special and rich and magical. Never mind that, as a result, I became a total social misfit.

And finally, thanks to my best friend and best inspiration, Lola Oguinnake. If it wasn't for her shut-up-and-do-its over the past ten years, I'd have never written a word. For a thousand reasons, this is as much hers as it is mine.

about the author

Tia Williams is the beauty director of *TeenPeople* magazine and has
been a beauty writer and editor at *YM, Elle, Glamour*, and *Lucky*. A
native of Virginia, she lives in Fort Greene, Brooklyn.